Other books
by Charles L. Ross

Inside

Out of the Shadows:
A Gay American Timeline
from Police Raids to Stonewall Riots
1903-1969

Stella: A Dog's Thoughts

What Happened in Lake Erie

Charles L. Ross

a Novel

LETHE PRESS

TO CHUCKIE

Age eight

Lake Erie

DADDY SPREADS HIS LEGS.

"I'm a bridge," he says, "and you're a submarine."

I squeeze my nose, raise one arm, and sink into the murky water of Lake Erie. As I glide between the hairy legs, my hand grazes the bulge in Daddy's swimsuit. I am embarrassed, but he doesn't seem to notice.

"Should I go through again?"

He nods. "Don't forget to put up your periscope."

Daddy has freckles and Mercurochrome-red hair, which is why everyone calls him Rusty. He is not tall but has a firm torso with a hairy chest. He is thirty. I think he's beautiful.

I am eight and am round like my mother. My too shiny maroon swimsuit sags below my pudgy stomach.

Daddy wears trim white trunks decorated with black shells and starfish.

Swimming underwater, I lift my arm above my head. Daddy's bulge feels firmer and pushes against my palm.

Dogpaddling around in front of him, I glance up, but again he seems unaware of what happened, so I make another dive.

The next time I swim between Daddy's legs, I touch the soft flesh of his penis bobbing in the water.

Surfacing, I shiver even though the sun blazes in a clear sky.

I look toward Mommy, reading on a blanket in the sand. She waves.

Daddy had told me, before we went swimming, not to open my eyes underwater, that Lake Erie was polluted, and I could get an eye infection. Of course, I immediately took a peek. I expected the water to be blue or green. This is a dirty yellow, like day-old piss. After that. I kept my eyes shut tight.

But now I want to open them. I want to see what I touched. *Okay, Daddy,* I think as I go under. *Spread your legs.*

This time he takes my upraised hand and encircles it around his penis, which has swollen so much bigger.

Daddy pumps my hand up and down… up and down.

I am fascinated, but I am running out of air. As I start to surface, Daddy holds my head underwater.

My face is only inches away as a white stream flows out of Daddy's penis.

I rise out of the water, gasping for air. Mommy stands up with a worried look on her face.

Daddy sweeps me to his chest and shouts, "He's fine," then adds softly so only the two of us could hear, "My boy's just fine, isn't he?"

Age three

Up High

I JUMP ONTO my parents' bed. Mommy is already up, frying bacon. I snuggle next to warm Daddy. Closing my eyes, I hold my breath. I know what is going to happen.

Daddy grabs me and growls. "Who woke up Papa Bear?"

I cower with anticipation.

"There's only one thing to do with such a naughty boy. Tickle him!"

I laugh so hard I nearly pee in my pajamas.

"He's going to start wheezing if you don't stop," Mommy shouts from the kitchen.

Daddy kicks off the sheet that covers him. He's wearing only white boxer shorts.

"Airplane, Daddy! Airplane!"

Daddy positions me on the soles of his feet and lifts his legs toward the ceiling. As he swirls me in the air, I stretch my arms out as wings. I make a buzzing sound, and Daddy sways his knees from side to side.

"Tower to Anthony," Daddy says in a voice that sounds as if it's on the radio. "Come in for a landing on runway two."

I dip my head as Daddy bends his legs. I land on his chest. My nose twitches in the mass of red hair. I breathe in his Daddy smell, then turn my cheek and settle into the soft cushion. Daddy puts his arms around me.

"Breakfast is ready," Mommy calls.

But Daddy and I stay in bed a little longer.

MOMMY LIFTS ME out of the bathtub. Usually she dries me, but tonight she and Daddy are going out to dinner for their anniversary. Grandma Peruzzi is babysitting.

Mommy hands me a towel. "Dry yourself off while I tweeze my eyebrows." Her nose almost touches the mirror.

I rub the towel all over my body, inside my ears, between my toes, everywhere, just like Mommy says. "Look what happened." I point to my pee-pee, which sticks straight out. "I think I broke it."

"No, you didn't. Go and show your father."

I drop the towel and run into their bedroom. Daddy is getting dressed.

"Look, Daddy!"

Daddy yanks me by the arm and pulls me back into the bathroom.

"Isn't that cute, Rusty?"

Mommy turns around from the mirror, and Daddy slaps her face.

"I didn't do anything," Mommy says with tears in her eyes. "It just happened when he was drying himself off."

My pee-pee is not sticking out anymore.

Mommy bends down and puts on my pajamas. Then she goes into the kitchen and calls Grandma, telling her not to come over.

*

STANDING IN OUR backyard, I cannot see downtown Castleton; trees in the valley hide it, and I look toward the hills in the distance. Our hill is so steep that the roofs of the houses below us are level with our yard. There is no fence, just a few shrubs scattered at the edge of the property. Mommy has warned me many times not to get too close to the drop-off.

I got a red tricycle for my second birthday, but there aren't many places I am allowed to ride it. On the front sidewalk, Mommy lets me go only to the end of the block. I am not to turn the corner! The concrete walk from our front yard to the back is all broken up, so that isn't a smooth, easy ride, especially since my feet barely reach the pedals.

One Saturday after breakfast, Daddy tells me to go ride my trike because he and Mommy are going back to bed. I think this is silly, since they have just gotten up a half-hour ago, but Mommy just kisses my forehead and says, "Be a good boy, Anthony."

I am always a good boy.

I carefully ease my trike down the two steps of the back porch. A cloud of black smoke rises from somewhere down the hill. I want to see what's on fire and try to pedal across the grass, but it's too hard, so I get off the trike and push it in front of me. As I near the edge of our yard, I push too hard and the trike tips over and tumbles down to the yard below.

I stretch my neck, looking to see where my trike has landed. It is on its side, one back wheel spinning. It seems awfully far down, and I suddenly feel dizzy.

I want to cry, but instead I call out.

"Mommy! Mommy, my trike fell down the hill!"

I look over my shoulder, but the back door stays closed.

"Daddy! Come help me!"

No one comes.

They must be asleep.

I peek over the edge, but my stomach feels funny. I sit down. "Mommy! Daddy!"

I call softly. I know they are not coming.

Even in winter when the trees have no leaves, I can't see Mama Luisa's house on the cross street way at the bottom of the hill. Somewhere north is Grandma Peruzzi's house, and although I can see a part of the river that is along the road that twists up to her house, I can't make out her street. I am alone. No one is coming.

Of course, I know how to walk—I know how to ride a tricycle! —but the drop-off seems so terrifying that I am afraid that if I stand up, I will totter over and fall all the way down.

I crawl across our backyard. Even when I reach the porch, I do not stand up. I crawl up the steps. I lean against the screen door. I close my eyes and breathe out.

I think: "I have to take care of myself. No one's going to help me. I have to take care of myself."

Age six

Mommy and Daddy

DADDY DOESN'T WANT to go to "a stupid musical," but Mommy just has to see *Singin' in the Rain* because Debbie Reynolds is in it. Usually we go to the drive-in, where we can bring our own popcorn and Kool-Aid. Sometimes we go in Aunt Joan and Uncle Bob's station wagon, but I don't like that as much because my cousins Donny and Ronny tease me for wearing my pajamas. I like it best when it is just the three of us—Daddy, Mommy, and me. Sometimes in the back seat, after the newsreel, a cartoon, and previews, I fall asleep even before the movie starts.

Singin' in the Rain isn't at the drive-in. It is downtown at the Castleton Theater, which has the highest ceilings I've ever seen, even higher than Saint Michael's church. The usher says there aren't seven seats together, so Uncle Nick and Aunt Lily sit in the balcony, Mommy and Daddy sit downstairs in one row, and Nick Junior, his sister Rose, and I sit in the row in front of them. Mommy folds Daddy's jacket under me so that I am tall enough to see the screen.

There is a fat lady sitting on one side of me, and I don't like sitting next to a stranger, even though Mommy says it's okay, so I sit way over on one side of my seat, but if I get too close to Nick Junior, who is two years older than I am, he pinches my leg. Hard.

Before the movie begins, I keep turning around to see that Mommy and Daddy are still there. As the theater goes dark, Mommy whispers to me to stop fidgeting. During the newsreel, I discover that if I turn my head a tiny bit—not so much that Mommy will notice—and if I roll my eyes to the left, I can see Daddy's knee. Every minute or so, I make sure he is still there. But once the singing and dancing start, I stop looking back. I don't even push Nick Junior away when he falls asleep on my shoulder. I stay awake through the entire movie, and when it's over, I want to dance in the aisle.

USUALLY MOMMY GOES to Gernano's Grocery, which is just a few blocks along our street, when I'm at school, but some days she waits until I get home to go the A & P on Main Street, past Mama Luisa's house and The Sons of Italy hall where Daddy goes to play cards with his friends. At the store, Mommy checks the price of each item to make sure she has enough money.

We always sit together on the bus, but one day on our way home, it is too crowded.

"Sit here," Mommy says, indicating an empty seat with a jerk of her head, two brown grocery bags held tightly in front of her. I sit sideways in the seat, watching her walk to the back. More people board the bus, and the driver shouts, "Move your feet out of the aisle so that people can pass." I know he is talking to me.

People fill the aisle, mostly men with banged-up metal lunch pails going home from work. I turn my head around, but it is too crowded to see where Mommy is sitting. How will I know which stop is ours? What if Mommy leaves through the back door without me? Where will I end up?

More people get on at the corner of Hill Street. The bus is so crowded, I wonder if it will make it up the hill. And that's when I have my answer: We live at the top of the hill. If Mommy forgets about me, I know our stop.

People get off the bus as we climb Hill Street, and no more come aboard. Soon, Mommy is sitting across the aisle from me. She looks tired, her hair frizzing in the humidity, but she smiles at me and says, "Almost home."

TEDDY IS MY stuffed panda. Black and white: black ears, arms, shoulders, legs; white stomach; white face with black spots around his eyes. The fur is so long and thick that it hides most of his eyes, which is good because there are no whites in those eyes, just solid black buttons that are a little scary.

I sit talking to Teddy by the tall hedge that separates our backyard from the neighbor's, the Salvatores.

"What are you doing, Anthony?" Mommy calls from the kitchen window.

"Feeding Teddy berries."

"Well, don't talk to yourself. You're six years old. People will think you're crazy."

I sit on the porch step clutching Teddy, sucking one of his ears. I want to be a good boy.

Through the screen door, I can see Mommy washing the kitchen floor on her knees. She looks up. "What are you doing now?"

"Nothing."

"Well, don't just sit there. The neighbors will think I don't let you play. "

*

"RUSTY RARELY TALKS about his childhood," Mommy says, sipping lemonade on Aunt Lily's porch.

Rose sits on a stool pretending her pudgy doll is drinking. Nick Junior and I already drank our lemonade, so we play with Slinkies, seeing which one goes down the steps first..

"How old was Rusty when his mother died?" Aunt Lily asks.

"Just over a year. Thirteen months."

"Of course, he doesn't remember it, but it still must have had a tremendous effect on him," Aunt Lily says. "Nick said after Rosa died the three of them—Nick, Rusty and their dad—moved into Mama Luisa's front room. She was already a widow and owned that big house, and all she gives them is one room. Her own son and grandchildren."

"Why didn't she give them the upstairs?"

"It was rented. But she could have kicked her tenants out. They weren't family. But no, she squeezes all her living room furniture into the dining room and gives her family the front room. Nick said that room was so crowded with their three beds, even if Rusty was still in a crib, that they could hardly walk. Nick Junior, don't you shove Anthony! He might fall and crack his head on the concrete."

"Aw, Mom." Nick Junior sticks his tongue out at me.

"If you can't play nice, I'll send you up to your room."

"I'd rather play by myself than with that baby." Nick Junior throws his Slinky at me and stomps into the house.

I don't care. I don't like the old meanie anyway.

Mommy presses her lemonade glass to her forehead. "How long did they stay with Mama Luisa?"

"About four years, until their dad remarried. Only then did Mama Luisa offer to get rid of her tenants and give them the upper floor, but the new bride did not want to live that close to her mother-in-law. Who can blame her? Margaret wanted her own home—across town. At the time, she worked at the pottery factory painting gold trim on dishes. I still have a few pieces."

"Rusty said she was 'money conscious.'"

"He's just repeating what Mama Luisa told anyone who'd listen. I didn't know Margaret that well, but I thought she was a nice lady. Maybe she put on airs sometime, but she didn't mean any harm."

Aunt Lily fans herself with a magazine. "Mama Luisa was always strict with the boys, so Nick, who was ten at the time, was only too glad to get out from under her wing when his dad married Margaret, but Rusty refused. Nick said Rusty was a skinny runt but faced them all down. He said Rusty stood there, tugging at Mama Luisa's black dress, shouting, 'She's my mother!'"

"That must have taken a lot of courage to stand up to his father like that. He was only six."

"Dad Dimora sure hasn't been lucky with wives," Aunt Lily says. "Twice a widower. Usually, it's the wife who's left behind."

Mommy stands up. "Anthony, what do you have on your arms?"

"The Slinkies." I jiggle my arms. "They're my bracelets."

"Boys don't wear bracelets." She picks up her purse. "Come on, we have to go. We don't want to miss our bus."

"RUSTY ALWAYS KNEW I wasn't his real mother," Mama Luisa tells Mommy. "He knew I was really his grandmother. We told him his mother had died of pneumonia. Every morning, he stopped in front of the living room mantel to look at her photograph. It was taken on her wedding day, with Rosa clutching a small bouquet of lilies of the valley. I grow lilies of the valley in the backyard, beside the porch. Of course, Rusty's always had a special fondness for them. And he always mentioned his mother at night in his prayers. I made sure of that."

Mama Luisa's hands move so fast that she makes twice as many rosaries as Mommy. I sort the glass beads by color and size. The large black ones are for the *Our Fathers*, the smaller gray ones for the *Hail Marys*, and the tiny silver ones for the *Glory Bes*.

Mommy twists the wire with tiny pliers so each bead stays in place. "How did Rusty's mother really die?"

"You know, he asked me that same question when he was six, the same age as Anthony." She smiles at me. "Are you hungry? There are cookies on the counter."

I know this means she wants to get rid of me while she talks to Mommy. Grown-ups have lots of secrets. I go to the kitchen and take an oatmeal cookie in each hand, then stand on the other side of the doorway so that they can't see I'm listening.

"I guess Rusty always sensed there was more to how his mother died," Mama Luisa says. "So one day I'm in the kitchen peeling potatoes at the sink, and he leans against the yellow cupboard and twists the chrome knob round and round, and I know it's coming. *That* question."

"Did you tell him the truth?"

"I told him she died in childbirth. And he asked me what happened to the baby. I said it was stillborn. And then he wanted to know if it was stillborn, how come he didn't have a younger brother or sister. So, I told him 'stillborn' means the baby was born dead. Rusty didn't have any more questions that day. But there was more to it than that."

I don't really understand what Mama Luisa's talking about, and I don't want to think about dead babies, so I go to the refrigerator to get some milk. The pitcher is heavy, but I carefully take it out and put it on the counter. I drag a chair across the floor so I can climb up and reach the cupboard, then I pour milk into a glass without spilling a drop. I drag the chair back, take two more cookies and my glass of milk to go sit at the kitchen table.

Mommy suddenly appears in the doorway. "What's going on in here?"

I jump; the glass slips out of my hand, and milk splatters all over the floor.

"You frightened me!" I cry. "It wasn't my fault."

"It doesn't matter, Mary," Mama Luisa says. "I'll clean it up."

"Anthony will do it."

Mommy hands me a dishtowel, and while I soak up the milk, she fills a bucket with soapy water and hands me a sponge.

"You might as well scrub the whole floor while you're at it."

She and Mama Luisa go back to the card table in the living room to make more rosaries.

"DADDY," I ASK as he tests the water to make sure it's not too hot before he rinses the shampoo out of my hair, "how come you're the only one in your family with red hair?"

"I wasn't the only one, Anthony. My mother had red hair."

"I wish I had red hair."

"No, you don't. Be happy you have dark brown hair." Daddy dries my hair with a soft towel. "People with red hair usually have pale skin, like me. Redheads sunburn easily, which can be painful. I know. And redheads have freckles. Some people think

freckles are cute, and maybe a few of them across the nose"—
Daddy rubs my nose—"are cute, but if you have freckles all over
and bright red hair as a kid, you get teased a lot by the other
kids."

Kids tease me. They pinch my round cheeks and call me
"Meatballs." I can't imagine Daddy being teased. He combs my
hair, making a sharp part on the left side. Mommy parts my
hair on the right.

Daddy squeezes toothpaste on my brush and hands it to me.
"Two minutes." He leaves the bathroom, and I have to brush
my teeth until he comes back. Finally, he returns, and I rinse
out my mouth.

"What did the kids say to you?"

"When?"

"When they teased you about your red hair?"

"*Redhead, piss the bed. Blame it on the cabbage head.* I don't
know why they said that because I never wet my bed—ever.
They also called me 'Freakles.' Of course, that was because I
have a lot of freckles, but I also think it's because of my light
eyes. Most Italians have dark eyes, like yours."

"Mommy says your eyes are amber."

"Yeah, I guess they are. Okay, come on, I'll tell you a story
after I tuck you in."

I sleep on the green-and-brown-striped sofa in the living
room. It folds out into a bed. I get under the covers, and Daddy
sits next to me. He pushes my bangs across my forehead.

"So, like I said, the other boys teased me about my hair and
my eyes and my freckles, but I had one thing over them. I could
run. *Fast.*

"We all liked to play baseball, but none of us could afford
mitts. We didn't even have a baseball. We used crumpled newspaper

wrapped with rubber bands. We found a bat with a little crack in a trash can, and we used that.

"One day, your uncle Nick said he and a bunch of guys were going to watch a game at Shenango Field, and he asked me to tag along. I was excited, because you know Nick's a few years older than me, and usually he didn't want me hanging around with him and his buddies. Anyway, we headed over to Shenango Field, but we didn't sit in the bleachers. We sat in an old boxcar in the railroad yard behind the right field fence.

"'Listen, Rusty,' Nick told me, 'I want you to do me a favor. The next time a batter hits a foul ball over the backstop, I want you to pick it up and run home. We'll never be any good until we get a real ball.'

"Every time a batter swung, I held my breath. Then, at the bottom of the fourth inning, a batter hit a foul ball over the backstop. I jumped down from the boxcar, scooped up the rolling ball, and started to run home. As I was running, I heard someone in the bleachers yell so everyone could hear: 'Hey! That's the Dimora kid with the red hair!'

"I kept running.

"Fifteen minutes later, the umpire knocked on Mama Luisa's door. I was hiding under my bed. Mama Luisa made me return the ball and apologize. We didn't get a real ball for another year."

"Can I count your freckles until I fall asleep?"

He lifts his shirt and turns his back to me.

"One, two, three, four, five, six...."

I get to forty-six before Mommy makes us stop.

AFTER SCHOOL, I walk home. It's only five blocks. I always do my homework right away, then I help Mommy bake bread or clean the house. I enjoy folding laundry and arranging cans in the cupboard so all the labels face straight out. After supper every evening, I dry the dishes that Mommy washes in the deep white sink

One night, as I wipe the silverware and carefully place each spoon and fork in its spot in a drawer, Mommy hands me a newspaper.

"Don't you hear your father calling?" she says. "He forgot the sports page."

I sigh, take the paper, and head to the bathroom. I crack open the door and stretch my arm inside. "Here's your paper."

"I can't reach it," Daddy says. "Bring it in."

Daddy's pants and shorts are down at his feet as he sits on the toilet. I stare at his pee-pee, pointing out of bright red hair. It's as pink as the tiles around the sink. A thick blue vein flows down the center of it. Will my pee-pee ever get that big?

Daddy reaches out his arm. "Anthony."

We stare at each other, then I hand him the paper.

Age seven

The Sons of Italy

MOMMY KNEADS DOUGH in a large yellow bowl while she watches me write the alphabet on a sheet of white, lined paper at the kitchen table.

"That's really good, Anthony. You're so neat and careful."

"I like to stay inside the lines."

"That's good."

She forms the dough into two loaves, places them into greased tin pans, and puts them on top of the stove to rise one last time.

Mommy smoothes my hair across my forehead while I draw perfect circles. "Put your homework away now," she says, taking thick white plates out of a cupboard, "and get out the silverware and napkins."

"Can we get a television set?" I carefully fold the white paper napkins in half, so they form triangles.

"I told you before. We can't afford one."

I put the silverware at each place. Mommy taught me that the fork goes on the left of the plate and the butter knife and spoon go on the right. "Uncle Nick's family has a television."

"Nick makes more money than your father." Mommy quickly covers her mouth. She knows she shouldn't have said that. "We'll get a television soon, Anthony. I promise. Maybe Santa will bring us one for Christmas." She pats my head. "Now, please go and get your father."

"Where is he?"

"Where he always is: gambling in the back room of Gernano's Grocery with all the other Italian men."

"What am I supposed to tell him?"

"What do you think?" Mommy is impatient. "Tell him I said to come home for dinner."

"I can't, Mommy. Rags Gernano will make fun of me."

"What does he say?"

"That I'm a 'mama's boy.'"

"Don't you want to be your mama's boy?"

I stare at her.

"If you don't get your father, he'll gamble away all our money. We won't be able to pay the rent," she says, "and we certainly won't be able to buy a television set."

"But what if Daddy's winning?"

"He'll keep playing until he loses all he won and more."

"One time he won."

"That's right, Anthony. *One* time. Now, please go get him."

I WANT TO believe in Santa Claus, but I know if we are ever going to get a television, Santa is not going to lug it all the way from the North Pole in a sleigh.

On Christmas morning, still in my flannel pajamas, I walk into the living room rubbing my eyes. And there it is. A television set. I jump up and down as if I am on a trampoline. Daddy turns it on and adjusts a knob called Vertical Hold. But there is nothing on at six o'clock except a test pattern.

Daddy says the black-and-white Zenith screen is nineteen inches. Mommy says the cabinet is blond veneer. I don't know what that means. I don't care what it means. All I want is to keep the television on all day, but Mommy says it uses too much electricity, and I can pick three programs. I browse the free issue of TV Guide that came with the television and select *The Howdy Doody Show* and *Kukla, Fran and Ollie*. Since it's Saturday and I don't have to go to bed early, I also plan to watch *Our Miss Brooks*, which airs at nine-thirty.

Each night for a week, we each get to pick a show to watch. Sometimes we only watch a few minutes before we all agree to change the channel. Daddy says there are "four networks—and that's a lot of programs!"

On New Year's Day, Mommy insists we take down the Christmas tree. Too many needles are falling off, and she is tired of sweeping them up. She carefully removes the delicate ornaments and places them in flimsy cardboard boxes divided into sections to hold each object. I lift off the long strands of silver tinsel and wrap them around thin cardboard so that we can reuse them next year. Then Daddy takes off the string of lights and carries the tree out to the backyard. As he saws the branches off the tree, I carry them in stacks down to the furnace in the basement. Mommy says we'll save money by not having to burn so much coal this week.

The next day, while Daddy is at work, Mommy stands in the middle of the living room and says, "Except for the new television set, not one piece of furniture in here is mine. The sofa originally belonged to Joan. The maroon club chair came from Mama Luisa, and my mother gave me the other chair. The end tables and lamps came from my other sisters. I *hate* all this stuff. I want my own things."

She sits staring for a long time.

"Can I have a peanut butter sandwich?"

"In a minute."

She looks around the room. Then she goes into the kitchen and slaps a glob of peanut butter on a slice of Wonder Bread, folds it in half, and hands it to me.

"As soon as you finish that, come and help me."

"What are we going to do?"

"Move the furniture. I need a change."

Our house was not built as a duplex, as Daddy calls it. Originally, it was one big home, but it's divided now so two families can live separately. We live downstairs, and an older couple without any children is upstairs.

Our front door opens into what was originally the living room but is now Mommy and Daddy's bedroom. Our living room—my "bedroom" when the sofa is folded out—is what was once the dining room. We eat in the kitchen at a chrome and Formica table. And of course, there's a bathroom.

I take a big bite of my sandwich. Mommy says, "We have to keep the television against this wall because of the antenna connection, but the wire's long enough to move it down a bit. Then we can move the sofa down too."

It's too heavy to push, so we take off all the pillows and cushions. Once it's where Mommy wants it, we move the maroon chair by the window that looks out on the Salvatores' driveway. We placed the other, smaller chair on the opposite wall. Before, the sofa and the two chairs faced each other. Now they all face the television set. Next, we position the end tables and rearrange the lamps and knick-knacks that they hold.

Mommy sweeps her arm just like the lady who sells refrigerators on television. "Well, it may not look any better than before, but at least it's different."

"Can I have another sandwich?"

"It's too close to dinner. We're having *pasta e fagioli*."

"I hate *pasta e fagioli*."

"Your dad likes it. You can have yours without the beans if you want." When she goes into the kitchen, I follow behind, hoping she will let me have at least a cracker with peanut butter. "Let's not tell Daddy that we rearranged the living room. I want to see how long it takes him to say something."

"Won't he notice as soon as he walks in?"

"He probably won't notice for a week. And even if he does, he may not say anything."

I love afternoons like this, being alone with Mommy. But when Daddy comes home, I love being with him even more.

Every night after dinner, our family of three welcomes new friends into our living room: On Tuesdays, we laugh at Milton Berle dressed as a woman. Wednesdays, we watch *I Married Joan* and *My Little Margie*. Thursdays, it's *You Bet Your Life* with Groucho; Friday, *The Adventures of Ozzie and Harriet*. Saturday, Jackie Gleason and Sid Caesar keep us laughing. On Sundays, we have trouble deciding between Jack Benny and *Mr. Peepers*. But Mondays are the best. At nine o'clock—

"You have school tomorrow," Mommy says.

"I'll get up without any trouble," I promise. "I've got to see *I Love Lucy*, Mommy. Everybody at school talks about it."

"It's only a half-hour," Daddy says. "Let him stay up."

That night, Ricky Ricardo tells Lucy she spent too much money and is to return the Handy Dandy kitchen helper she just bought. But instead, she buys a Handy Dandy vacuum cleaner. Ricky insists it, too, must be returned, but rather than face the salesman, Lucy tries to sell it herself and makes a mess. Ricky says he'll handle the salesman—and ends up buying a Handy Dandy refrigerator.

Also on Mondays, is my favorite program. It's only fifteen minutes, right after the news. Sitting between Daddy's legs in the maroon velvet chair, I lean against his chest as Perry Como, sitting on a stool, sings.

Just like the song says, Daddy made me love him.

I didn't want to do it.

I tilt my head back.

Daddy kisses my lips.

"WHY DON'T YOU go next door," Mommy says as she washes the kitchen window, "and see what Noreen is doing."

Sometimes Noreen Salvatore and I play house together, but I don't really like her. We are the same age, seven, but she is tiny, and everyone says she looks like an angel. She isn't. Sometimes she comes to our back door, her hands behind her back, her face tilted up with pleading eyes, and asks my mother in a sing-song voice, "Can Anthony come out and play?"

"Go on," Mommy says. "You'll have fun."

As soon as I am out the door, Noreen swings her hands in front of my face, revealing what she has kept hidden from my mother. "I have a Popsicle." She twists her mouth. "And you don't!"

Then she runs back to her yard, and I stand there on the porch, wondering if I should go inside and face my mother's questions about why I'm back so soon.

Once in a while, Noreen's sister Nadine, who is five years older, shares her colored chalks, and we draw a house on the sidewalk. One square is the living room, where I sketch a blue sofa, a red chair, and two tables; Noreen draws the kitchen in another concrete square, and Nadine creates a bedroom.

Noreen's mother lets us use a real table, with one wobbly leg, that we drag from the backyard into our chalk-outlined dining room. I always want to set the table, but Noreen insists that since it's her tea set, that's her right. It is white with pink scallops around the edges and a silhouette of a yellow daisy in the center of each piece. I beg Mommy for my own tea set, but Daddy won't let me have one.

The Salvatores are an Italian-American family, just like us, Daddy says. A lot of our neighbors are Italian—and Catholic. I see them at St. Michael's at Sunday Mass. Each family has three or four children. We are the only one with a single child. Daddy says that makes us special.

None of those children are my friends, and I don't have any friends at school either. That seems to concern Mommy and Daddy, but it doesn't bother me. I have Teddy.

Noreen's uncle, Frank, lives with her family. He is seventeen and always wears blue jeans and a white t-shirt with the short sleeves rolled up to show off his big biceps with their thick blue veins. He has dark hair, thick eyebrows, and the most unusual mouth I have ever seen. His upper lip is bigger than the bottom one, but it doesn't stick out; it's flat with two sharp points. Sometimes I want to lick it.

Frank has a 1939 Buick convertible that he's restoring. It's black, like our 1949 Ford, but unlike our gray fabric seats, the Buick's seats are bright red leather. Frank says it's a "Roadmaster." It has a funny grille that reminds me of Grandpa Dimora's black-and-white mustache, higher at the center of his upper lip and sloping on the sides. The Buick's spare tire is not in the trunk like most cars, but on the side, between the front wheel and the door.

Frank tinkers with the Roadmaster every evening after he gets home from work at a nearby gas station, and sometimes I watch him until Mommy calls me in for supper. I have seen Nadine and Noreen pester Frank with questions and how annoyed he gets, sometimes shooing them away, other times putting down his tools and going upstairs to his room to avoid them. I have learned to stand near Frank without saying one word.

ONE SUMMER EVENING, Daddy isn't home from work at the railroad. He's over an hour late, and I'm hungry, so Mommy gives me a bowl of spaghetti and a meatball. She says she will wait to eat with Daddy, but I know that it isn't because she's being polite; it's because she wants to make him feel guilty. We both know where he is, and it's not the railroad yard. He's playing poker or shooting craps with his buddies at Gernano's Grocery.

Just as I finish eating, Daddy comes home. Mommy dishes out their plates without saying a word. She is giving him "the silent treatment." If he were smart, he would eat his dinner without saying a word, just as I did, but Daddy has to speak.

"I work hard all day and have the right to spend some time with my pals."

"It isn't the time, and you know it." Mommy barely moves her lips. "I don't care about the time. It's the gambling."

The spaghetti sits on their plates getting even colder as they shout at each other.

"You're gambling away all our money!"

"Well, I'm the one who earned it."

I pick up Teddy and quietly go outside. Mommy probably notices, but she's too angry with Daddy to be concerned about me right now.

I see Frank bending over the Buick engine. I walk across the driveway and stand next to him, Teddy's ear in my mouth.

Frank looks at me, looks at my house, hears the shouting, and reaches over to a shelf in the garage and turns on the radio.

After a while, I say, "I like that song."

I shut my eyes, and slowly, the stiffness in my body goes away. I feel safe again, standing next to Frank and listening to Perry Como sing about chasing rainbows.

"MARY HAS TO go to the doctor tomorrow with her mother, and Mama Luisa can't babysit, so my dad is taking Anthony to The Sons of Italy tomorrow," Daddy tells Tony Tomasso, who is sitting in the front seat of our Ford. "His first time. Isn't that right, Anthony?"

I nod. I stand in the back with one foot on either side of the hump, my elbows on the back of the front seat.

"Is everything all right with Mary?" Tony asks. He's short and has a black mustache. Mommy says Tony has a mustache because he's going bald and wants people to look down instead of up. I don't think Mommy likes Tony, but Daddy says he's his closest friend, even closer than his brother Nick.

"She's fine," Daddy says. "Just some woman's thing."

"I have a lot of good memories from The Sons of Italy." Tony turns his head and smiles at me.

"I bet you do," says Daddy.

"What's that supposed to mean?" Tony wants to know.

Daddy gives a little jerk to his head, and I guess he doesn't want to say something in front of me. It must be a secret. Daddy and I have secrets we don't tell Mommy.

"It sure must be convenient having The Sons of Italy right next door to Mama Luisa's," Tony says.

"Maybe a little too convenient. I can't remember how many

times I'd come home from school and see my dad's car parked in Mama Luisa's driveway. I'd run in the house, but of course, he wasn't there. 'Where's Dad?' I'd ask, and Mama Luisa would sigh and say, 'Your dad's at The Sons of Italy,' as if he were in some exotic country and we never knew if he'd come back."

"I think women are jealous we have our own place where they can't go. We have *one* sanctuary where we can swear and fart with no wife or mother to frown, and they can't stand it." Tony lights a cigarette.

"Open the side vent so the smoke blows out."

"Oh, sorry. Do you want me to put it out?"

"No, but when you're finished, toss the butt out the window. I don't want Mary looking in the ashtray and thinking I was smoking. Say, do you remember my thirteenth birthday at The Sons of Italy?"

"How could I forget it? It's the first time I got drunk." Maybe Tony thinks he shouldn't have said that, because he turns to me. "It's a rite of passage for an Italian boy to go to The Sons of Italy on his thirteenth birthday."

Daddy says, "I remember my dad running into Mama Luisa's, all excited, waving a pink bakery box in front of my nose. 'I got sugar-coated fritters. I got sugar-coated fritters.' Mama Luisa gave him a funny look and asked how you can have a birthday party without a cake? Dad said he thought she'd bake one. And of course she had. Chocolate with fresh strawberries between the layers—my favorite. But she always has to get her digs into Dad. She told him the cake was for the family gathering, *not* for the Sons of Italy. And she didn't see how you could put candles on a fritter."

"I can just picture her in her apron with her hands on her hips," Tony says. "She always has to have the last word, doesn't she?"

"You got that right. But I love her. That night she cooked my favorite meal—veal with fried peppers—and I ate so much I felt sick. But I was excited, too."

I look in the rearview mirror, and Daddy raises his eyebrows just like Groucho Marx.

"I was finally going inside my dad's private club." He's telling me the story, now, not Tony. "Each lodge of the Sons of Italy has a name, and the one in Castleton is called *Trionfo Italico—Italic Triumph*—which sounds pretty grand, huh? I pictured a colorful mural of a brave leader wearing a gold-embossed cape, as I'd seen in a history book of Julius Caesar marching in triumph into Rome. Boy, was I disappointed. It was dark, as though the sun wasn't allowed inside. There were a lot of cheap, second-hand chairs."

"And the marble floor was cracked," Tony adds.

"But who cared? It was my birthday, and Dad's friends kept refilling my wine glass and shouting out toasts."

"To a long life!" Tony pretends he's lifting a glass.

"To a job that earns lots of money!" Daddy says.

"To sugar-coated fritters!" I say, and they laugh.

"It didn't matter what the toast was," Daddy says. "The point was to get me tipsy. It was like a sacrament. It was my little Triumph. And at the end of the evening, my dad said, 'Now you're officially one of us. A Son of Italy.'"

I look in the mirror, but Daddy turns away. His eyes are wet.

After a while, I lay down on the back seat. I figure that if Daddy thinks I'm asleep, he'll tell Tony the secret.

Tony smokes another cigarette. "What did you mean when you said I must have a lot of good memories at the Sons of Italy?"

I keep my eyes shut.

"Anthony?" Dad whispers.

"He's asleep. What did you mean?"

"Mama Luisa always said you were a nice, polite kid."

"I'm still nice and polite. I'm just not a kid anymore."

"Do you know what she calls your eyes? *Madonna eyes*. And you know, they do sort of look like those glass eyes on the statue of the Blessed Virgin at St. Michael's. And they sure as Hell can nail you if you don't do exactly what *you* want."

"So, if you don't want me to nail you," Tony says, "tell me what you meant. You know you want to."

"All right, all right. One night, when we were fifteen, you and I were playing cards with Dave Calvi and Rags Gernano, and after a bit, you said you had to use the head. I dealt out the cards for the next hand. Dave refilled our glasses. And you still had not come back. We all wondered what was taking you so long.

"'That's some leisurely dump,' Dave said.

"Rags said you were probably beating off, but I said you wouldn't do that. Not at the Sons of Italy. So I decided to go check, thinking maybe you were sick. I walked into the bathroom, and no one was at the urinals. I bent over and looked under the two stalls and saw your sneakers. And something else. I peeked in the crack between the metal door and the marble partition. A man was kneeling down in front of you, Tony."

"So I got a blowjob in the Sons of Italy. So what?"

I don't know what a blowjob is.

"The reason I remember it after all these years is not because I was shocked by what I'd seen but because I got an instant boner. I was horrified."

"You probably—"

"I know you're taking all these psych classes, but I don't want to know. I wish I hadn't told you. Sometimes it's better not to think too much about things. I just can't believe you got your cock sucked at the Sons of Italy."

Now I know what a blowjob is.

YOUNG BOYS ARE not usually allowed at the Sons of Italy, so before Grandpa Dimora takes me inside, I promise to not be noisy or ask any questions.

"It's good to want to know things," Grandpa says, "but this is one place where men can get away from the world and all its troubles. They like to just relax and not be bothered with questions."

I nod. I know how to be quiet from standing near Frank.

When Grandpa opens the door, I think we are in church. Sunlight glows through the dark shutters, making angles of light just like at St. Michael's. Grandpa says the floor is real Italian marble, not linoleum like we have in our kitchen. He says the wood walls are polished once a week, and the booths and chairs are covered with red leather, like Frank's Buick Roadmaster. The tablecloths are green-and-white checks. Grandpa says red, white, and green are the colors of the Italian flag. It looks nice, not all beat up like Daddy and Tony described.

Most of the men have mustaches, and they sit talking, and drink wine and beer, while smoking and playing cards. They greet Grandpa with friendly words, but a few frown when they notice me.

"He's a good boy and won't cause any trouble," Grandpa says. "Right, Anthony?"

I nod, determined to not say a word.

Grandpa pours himself a glass of wine and hands me a bottle of Coca-Cola, a real treat since Mommy won't let me drink sodas at home. He sits at an empty table in the back and pats his knee, wanting me to climb up to his lap. Three other men join us, and Grandpa deals the cards to play Pinochle.

I'm afraid I'll become too heavy for Grandpa; he'll tire of holding me. But every so often, he bends his face to my head and kisses my hair. Sometimes, when he wins a hand, he pinches my side. It isn't mean, like when Nick Junior does it, but almost like a tickle.

I feel so good, just like I do when I'm with Frank. I'm not stiff like I am at home, always wondering if I am going to do something that Mommy will not like.

I look up into Grandpa's eyes, a big smile on my face. He kisses my lips, his mustache tickling my nose.

I never want to leave.

Age eight

Taste

"INSTEAD OF SITTING inside and watching television, Anthony," Mommy says, "why don't you go outside and help your father rake leaves?"

"He didn't ask me."

"That doesn't mean he doesn't want you to."

"We only have one rake."

"Put on your jacket and go help your father. Now!"

I let the screen door slam even though I know it will make Mommy mad. I stand on the front porch playing with the zipper on my jacket.

I speak barely loud enough for Daddy to hear me. "Need any help?"

"Now you ask, when I'm practically finished."

Good. I can go back inside and watch *The Cisco Kid.*

"You can sweep the sidewalk."

I get the push broom from the shed and sweep the sidewalk. Then we load leaves into a rusty red wheelbarrow, covering the mound with a tarp so they don't scatter as we head to the backyard. We dump four loads next to a charred barrel.

"We'll burn a little at a time, so it doesn't get out of control." Daddy twists a piece of newspaper, strikes a match, lights the paper, and tosses it in the barrel. "How come you were so standoffish with Nick Junior yesterday? He's your cousin; you should try to get along."

"It wasn't me." I circle the bonfire to keep smoke out of my eyes. "He thinks because he's two years older that I'm still a baby."

"Nick treated me the same way when we were kids. Like father, like son, I guess."

I don't say anything.

"If you want to invite any friends from school over, it would be okay with your mom and me."

We toss more leaves into the smoking barrel.

"Do you have any friends, Anthony?"

I shrug.

"Don't you like any of the kids at school?"

"Not really. I like Frank."

"Frank? Next door? He's ten years older than you!"

I shrug again. "Most of the other boys play too rough."

"We could toughen you up a little."

I look away, toward downtown Castleton. Why do I have to be tough? What's wrong with the way I am?

"Come on, Anthony. I'll teach you how to wrestle. It'll be fun."

Not for me.

Daddy shows me the starting position, both of us on our hands and knees. I can tell he's going easy, explaining various holds and how to break them. Then he gets a little rougher. I like it when he grabs me tight, when he's on top of me, his body completely covering me. I let everything go, just surrender. Then, when he doesn't expect it, I fight back.

We start sweating, and Daddy takes off his coat. When I'm unzipping my jacket, Daddy surprises me and pins my shoulders to the grass. I smell the leaves burning, hear the fire popping. Daddy and I take deep breaths, almost panting like dogs. Except for our breathing, we are very still as he kneels over me. I can smell his sweat. A drop falls from his forehead right on my lips. Salt.

I look into his eyes. I turn my head and lick his hand.

"What are you doing?"

"Tasting your sweat."

"Well, stop it."

I lick the other hand.

"I said stop it!"

He presses his hands harder against my shoulders and sits back.

Uh oh. His bottom touches my penis. It is pointing straight up. He looks as though he doesn't believe it. He lets go of my left shoulder, reaches his hand behind him, and grabs my penis. It seems to get even bigger.

I stare into his amber eyes, wondering what he sees looking into mine.

He puts his hands around my throat.

I smile.

Daddy squeezes my throat tighter.

I stare at a vein swelling on his forehead.

I don't breathe.

"Go on, get out of here." He rolls off me. "Before I kill you."

THE FIRST NIGHT it's warm enough to eat outside, Nadine's dad grills hamburgers, and Mommy brings over macaroni and cheese. After ice cream, Daddy lights a cigar. It smells moldy.

Nadine and Noreen go inside to watch Red Skelton. I want to watch Gene Autry, but Noreen says it's their television and they can watch whatever they want. Red Skelton isn't funny like Milton Berle.

Frank walks by and, in a little while, I follow him upstairs. I walk past a blue bedroom, the girls' pink bedroom, the bathroom, and there it is. Frank's room. He has taken off his shoes and lies on the bed in white socks. I stand in the doorway. Of course, he has on his blue jeans and white t-shirt.

"How's Anthony doing?" He raises his thick eyebrows. "Come on in."

I've never been in Frank's room. The walls are yellow, and there are red shelves with trophies and model airplanes.

"You can touch them," he says. "It's okay. Just be careful."

I pick up a single-engine plane with a wing across the top.

"That's *The Spirit of St. Louis.*" Frank sits up. "Charles Lindbergh flew it across the Atlantic Ocean. He was the first man to fly from New York to Paris. Do you know those cities?"

"New York is where my parents were married."

Frank picks up another model. "This is a British *Spitfire.*"

He flies it around the room. He dips and rises, going in circles. I follow him with *The Spirit of St. Louis.* And trip over his shoes.

I land on my stomach.

"Are you okay?" Frank rushes to my side. "Are you hurt?"

I'm fine, but the plane isn't. "I broke it." Tears fill my eyes.

"It's nothing." Frank picks it up. "A propeller snapped off, that's all. It's easy to fix." He puts the pieces on the shelf.

He lifts me into his arms and kisses my cheek. "No tears, okay, pal?"

I run my finger along his upper lip, tracing the two points. He smiles and kisses my nose. I put my arms around his neck and kiss his lips.

He takes me downstairs. "Look what I found," he announces on the back porch.

"Anthony," Mommy says, "you shouldn't disturb Frank. Come on, we were just about to leave. It's past your bedtime."

When we get home, Mommy grabs my shoulders. "You are not to walk through other people's homes. It's rude. People will think I haven't taught you anything!"

AS SUMMER GETS hotter, Frank works on the Buick Roadmaster wearing only shorts and sneakers. No shirt. He bends into the hood, sweat dripping from the dark hair under his arms. I like how he smells.

One day, he's underneath the car with just his legs sticking out. They're completely covered with black hair. I sit on the driveway next to him, not saying a word, feeling happy but also something else I don't understand. I keep staring at his legs. The hair looks even softer than Teddy's fur. I close my eyes, trying to picture the doggie in the window that Patti Page is singing about on the radio. Almost without my knowing it, my hand touches Frank's hairy leg.

"What?" he says.

I run home.

The next day, there is a knock on our back door. Frank. Is he mad? Is he going to tell Mommy that I had touched his leg?

I stand behind her, holding my breath. Frank has on his dirty white sneakers, cut-off jeans, and a white t-shirt.

"Hi, Mrs. Dimora," he says. "I finally finished working on my car, and I wondered if Anthony wants to go for a test ride." He gives me a big smile.

Mommy warns him to drive slowly and "only around the block," but she lets me go.

Frank opens the door on the driver's side, and I scoot onto the seat, moving over to the passenger side. He gets in, reaches across, and pulls me next to him, one hand on the wheel, the other arm around my shoulder. The convertible top is down. Everyone can see us—Mommy standing at our front door, Nadine and Noreen sitting on their porch swing.

Frank stops at the end of the block, and I think, *That's it, just a little ride.* But instead, he slips his t-shirt over his head, hanging it behind him so his skin won't touch the leather. "Up," he says, and I know he means my arms. He takes off my striped t-shirt and places it behind me. Then he puts his arm around me again.

"Here we go!" he says and races down Hill Street.

I'm just tall enough that I can see out the windshield, but what I keep looking at is the black hair on Frank's legs.

We drive past Mama Luisa's house on Main Street. He takes the hill that leads to Grandma Peruzzi's. He doesn't turn onto her street but continues into the country. As he drives past the quiet farms, sweat rolls down his side and wets my skin. I run my finger along a drop of sweat and bring it to my lips. Salty like Daddy's.

How long do we ride? How far do we go? I'm too dazed to keep track.

"We better head back," he says, "or your mom will have my hide." At the top of our hill, he stops, and we put on our shirts.

Noreen jumps up and down as we approach, shouting, "Me next! Me next!" Frank tells her to move out of the way and pulls into the driveway.

In the cool darkness of the garage, he rubs my head.

We get out of the car, and he goes into his house.

I run home, the happiest boy in the world.

*

IT STARTS TO rain, and I come in from the backyard. Why is the house so quiet? Then I remember that Mommy has gone shopping. Maybe Daddy is taking a nap. I tiptoe toward their bedroom.

Daddy stands in front of the large, round mirror of Mommy's vanity. He rubs his chest, flexes his muscles, posing just like a weightlifter I saw on television. Only the muscle man wore a tiny swimsuit. Daddy is naked.

I slide down the door to the floor so that Daddy can't see me.

He spits in his hand and rubs his penis. He closes his eyes, and I rise on my knees so I can see better.

Soon, Daddy presses his penis against his stomach, and a white liquid shoots out, nearly hitting his chin. I almost scream, but quickly put a hand over my mouth. Daddy rushes into the bathroom and turns on the shower.

I tiptoe into the room and stand in front of the wooden vanity. A drop of the white liquid has fallen next to a perfume bottle. I scoop it up with my finger and take a taste. Sweeter than sweat.

DADDY SAYS IT's a caravan. Like stagecoaches heading out west or camels crossing the desert. Of course, Uncle Nick has to be first. His family is in a white 1950 Mercury Monterey ahead of us. I sit in the back of our black 1949 Ford coupe between Grandpa and Mama Luisa. Uncle Vic and Aunt Connie are behind us in a '47 Chevy with their three bratty girls—Coreen, Carmen, and Cindy. Uncle Larry and Aunt Anna come next in their new '53 Buick Riviera with Grandma and Grandpa Peruzzi in the back seat.

"It's called 'Reef Blue,'" Uncle Larry had said about the car's color, "and don't it look just like the ocean?" Everything in their house—from the carpet to the bath towels—is some shade of blue.

"I'd rather have a new car than children," he has said more than once, and every time he did, Aunt Anna hugged their tiny Chihuahua and said, "We have Cha-cha."

Although Uncle Larry's Buick is the newest car in our caravan, my favorite is Aunt Joan and Uncle Phil's black 1950 Dodge Woody, a station wagon with real mahogany on the doors. It is so long that their sons, thirteen-year-old twins Donny and Ronny, each have their own row, but today there isn't much room because of all the coolers and picnic baskets.

We are on our way to Lake Erie. It's the Fourth of July. We left early, but the shoreline is already crowded when we arrive, and we have to settle for a place where the sand is only a narrow stretch before it turns into pebbles.

By the time everyone in our group spreads out their sheets and towels, there is not much sand visible. The men stack the coolers in the shade. We'll have a picnic later.

Grandpa Dimora picks up his fishing rod and tackle box and walks away.

"Where are you going?" Daddy asks.

"To the pier to fish."

"This is supposed to be a family outing."

"I'll be back in time for the picnic."

Daddy's mad.

"Let it go, Rusty," Uncle Nick says. "You know what he's like."

"He can't even spend a few hours with his family on the Fourth of July," Daddy says. "But what did I expect?"

"Here, honey." Mommy hands Daddy a paper cup. "Have some ice-cold lemonade."

He waves it away. "I'll have a beer."

Mommy wears a one-piece yellow swimsuit with pleats and tiny ruffles. Daddy has on boxer trunks, white with drawings of black starfish and shells. Its drawstring is tied just below his belly button, which is covered with red hair. My swimsuit is maroon, like the chair in our living room.

Everyone but Grandma and Grandpa Peruzzi and Mama Luisa have worn their swimsuits under their clothes. Mama Luisa is in her usual black dress. Grandma wears a housedress printed with blue dots, but at least she removes her heavy black shoes. Grandpa doesn't. He sits on a fallen log and smokes Camels. Grandma and Mama Luisa gossip in Italian.

I am surprised that Donny and Ronny don't have swimsuits. They strip down to their white Fruit of the Loom underpants and run into the lake.

"Let me put some lotion on you before you burn," Mommy tells Daddy. I watch her spread Coppertone on Daddy's freckled shoulders. Then she turns to me. "You're next, Anthony."

I take the plastic bottle out of her hand and give it to Daddy. I offer him my back. He finishes too fast.

"Okay," he says, "you do the rest."

"You do it. Please."

I watch his big hand rub the white lotion into my chest and around my stomach. "That feels good."

He gives me the bottle. "Put some on your legs."

When I finish, I ask Uncle Nick, "Do you want me to do your back?"

"Thanks, but I think I'll keep my shirt on for a while."

He keeps it on even when he goes into the water.

Mommy opens her manicure kit and files her nails, then she paints them pale pink, carefully leaving the rising half-moons clear.

Lake Erie is dark and cold. Standing with just my feet in the water, I watch Donny and Ronny and Nick Junior, thigh-deep in the lake, toss a football back and forth. When Donny bends down to catch the ball, his underpants gets wet and I can see the outline of his penis. I hope Ronny gets wet too. He's usually nice to me, not a bully like Donny.

Coreen, who is eleven, starts splashing her cousins. When they splash back, she screams as if she's been stabbed. She swims underwater and pops up behind Donny, pushing his butt to try to knock him into the murky water. When that doesn't work, she swims over to Ronny and tries to topple him. The twins, without saying a word to one another, pick up Coreen—Donny by her feet, Ronny by her arms—and toss her as far as they can in the lake.

She comes up spitting out water. "I could have drowned!"

"Not if you'd shut your big fat mouth," Donny says.

With one last splash in the twins' direction, Coreen stomps back to the shore.

Being tossed in the lake looks like fun to me. I run toward my cousins, shouting, "Do me! Do me!"

The twins are only too happy to toss me in the lake. Like a dog chasing a stick, I can't get enough. I love sailing through the air and landing with a splat in the water. I love not knowing how far I'll sink before I have to surface. But most of all, I love being picked up by Donny and Ronny in their wet, white underpants.

While the women set out the food, the men toss the football on the sand. I'm glad it seldom comes my way, because I never catch it.

"Are you sure he's your son?" Uncle Vic asks Daddy. "You were basketball champ in high school, and your son can't even catch a ball."

"He's just a bit uncoordinated," Uncle Nick says.

"Yeah, he's not too good at football." Daddy gently tosses the ball to me. I surprise everyone by catching it. "He prefers wrestling, don't you, Anthony?"

I feel my face burning and throw the ball at Ronny so everyone will stop looking at me.

"You throw like a girl," Nick Junior says.

I go help Mommy unpack the food. I'm sure Uncle Vic wants me to hear him whisper, "Yeah, that's where you belong—with the women."

As we eat, a freighter, loaded with cargo, slowly moves along the lake.

"Looks like Long John Silver's out to claim more treasure," says Ronny, pointing to a large boat, its sails blowing as it chases the freighter.

"That pirate's dead," says Uncle Vic. "He never got off Treasure Island."

"Excuse me, Uncle Vic, but I just finished reading *Treasure Island*," I say, "and that's not what happens. Long John Silver sails with Jim Hawkins after they find the treasure, but at one of the ports on their way home, he jumps ship and is never heard of again."

"Yeah, well," replies Uncle Vic, "it's all a bunch of make-believe and foolishness."

"Sort of like you," I say.

"You got that right." Aunt Connie grins as her husband's face turns red.

Mommy gives me a look that says I am a naughty boy, but she smiles.

After the picnic, most of us settle down for a nap. I sprawl out next to Uncle Nick.

"How come men can take off their shirts but women can't?" I ask him.

"Because it's a state law."

"But why?"

"Because—because women have bigger breasts and they need to wear something to support them."

"Coreen and Carmen and Cindy and Rosa don't have big breasts, and they still wear a top."

"It's just the way it is, Anthony."

"How come you don't take off your shirt?"

"Because Lily thinks having hair on my back is 'embarrassing.'"

"I bet if your hair were feathers and you had wings, Aunt Lily would like it." I lift up his t-shirt and rest my head on the thick black hair covering his stomach.

"Come on, Anthony," Daddy says, getting up from his towel, "Let's go play Submarine."

Age nine

Child's Play

TOP OF THE eighth. Daddy's team is winning as usual.

As soon as the pitcher lets go of the ball, Uncle Nick, on second, takes off. He slides toward third, lifting his left leg and aiming his cleats at the baseman, who skips away just in time.

"Can I have the keys to the car?" I ask Mommy.

"What for?"

"I want to get my jacket."

The sun is bright. There isn't much of a breeze.

"Are you feeling sick?" Mommy reaches for my forehead. I back away.

"I feel fine, Mommy. Can I please have the keys?"

She takes them from her purse. I hop off the bleachers.

I roll down the car windows, lie on the back seat, and pick up *The Mark on the Door*, a Hardy Boys mystery. *I'll read just for a minute*, I think.

"What are you doing?"

I jump.

"I asked you a question." Mommy leans into the window.

"Reading."

She yanks the book out of my hand.

"Your father's batting next."

"We've already won the game, Mommy."

"That's not the point. Show your father a little support."

She opens the car door. I follow her back to the bleachers.

Daddy hits a triple. Mommy digs her knuckles into my side until I stand with the rest of the crowd, but I don't cheer.

AFTER BASEBALL SEASON comes basketball, and, of course, Daddy's on a local team. I don't have to go to many basketball games because they're during the school year, and I can say I have homework. But I still have to hear about them. Sometimes Daddy and his buddies sit around our kitchen table and go over a game, play-by-play.

"Did your father ever tell you about the time we played in the Lawrence County tournament?" Tony Tomasso has an unlit cigarette in his mouth. Mommy won't let him smoke in our house.

"No, he always tells me how you were all so poor that you didn't have a basketball hoop, that you just drew a circle on a wall."

"That's true." Uncle Nick belches. "You know, Anthony, I'm four years older than your dad, so we never got to play together in high school. But after Rusty graduated, we were eligible to play on the same team in the county tournament."

"You had to have a sponsor to enter the tournament." Rags Gernano never looks at me when he speaks. "We didn't have a sponsor. And we didn't have uniforms! So I convinced my mom to sponsor us. I told her if she bought our uniforms, she could put the name of our grocery store on the jerseys. Well, she coughed up the entry fee, but she would not pay for uniforms, the old cheapskate."

"But we had a team—the five of us." Dave Calvi points at

each one. "Your dad, Nick, Tony, Rags, and me. But you needed seven, two as relief players."

"So, we asked Sammy Piaza and Eddie Laurel," Daddy says. "They weren't good athletes, but we were in a bind."

"Eddie's short like me," explains Tony. "And if you're polite, you'd call Eddie's 'stocky' or 'heavyset,' but he's just plain fat, practically obese."

"Sammy's tall and thin, but he's a lousy player," adds Rags.

"Yeah, we were pretty mismatched." Uncle Nick cracks his hairy knuckles. "When we came out on the court for the first round, I could tell that the other team thought they could beat us with no trouble. But we walloped them."

"We slaughtered the next two teams, too," Daddy says. "There was only one team left, the Mahoning Town Tigers, who had won the tournament the year before—the reigning champs."

"What was your team called?" I want to know.

"The Castleton Crows," Tony says.

"We wanted to call ourselves the Italian Stallions." Rags looks into his beer. "But Mom said she wouldn't sponsor a team with that name."

"What's wrong with Italian Stallions?"

Mommy brings everyone another bottle of beer. "Nothing, honey. She just didn't like the name."

"Which is a shame." Nick's smile is wide. "Because it fit."

"Nick!" Mom slaps his shoulder.

"Anyway, it's the night of the big game." Daddy grabs a handful of peanuts. "We're doing real good, only your uncle Nick gets four fouls called against him. You get four personal fouls, and you're out."

"So, I like to play rough, so what?"

"So, we call in Sammy, who isn't much use," Daddy says, "but we're still in the game. Then, with two minutes left, Rags gets *his* fourth foul. We had only fat Eddie left. We never expected him to play. I mean, he wasn't even on the bench. He's up there in the bleachers in his street clothes. The game is tied, and if we don't have five players, we forfeit."

"Eddie tries on Nick's sneakers," Tony says, "but they're too small, and Rags are too narrow, so Eddie goes on the court in his socks."

"The crowd goes crazy, jumping up and down." Daddy's excited now. "I mean, here we are, this crazy team in mismatched jerseys with one really fat player in street clothes and socks, and we're up against the reigning champs. With just one minute to go, the Tigers foul. Tony gets the rebound, tosses the ball to me, and I dribble it halfway down the court before passing it to Dave, who makes a basket. And the Castleton Crows win by two points!"

"The fans ran down from the bleachers, hugging us even though we were all sweaty and probably stank to high Heaven." Nick sniffs his armpit and makes a face. "It seemed like half the town was there."

"Yeah." Daddy's not smiling anymore. "Everyone was there but Dad."

"YOUR FATHER'LL BE home soon. Better put those things away."

I look at the kitchen clock. Five-fifteen. Daddy doesn't know I have paper dolls. Even though Mommy said he wouldn't like it if I played with them, she gave me the Hedy Lamarr paper doll set she had as a girl. Mommy said Hedy Lamarr was a big movie star, but I've never heard of her. None of the paper outfits are costumes from her movies, but instead, they're mainly fancy evening gowns.

Noreen has paper dolls, too, but Mommy says I'm not to tell anyone about mine. All Noreen's cutout dolls are the same: Betsy McCall. Every month, Noreen's mother buys her a new collection. Betsy McCall has a tea party; Betsy McCall's Halloween; Betsy McCall goes to the country; Betsy McCall's Christmas. I think they are all childish.

I like grown-up, movie-star paper dolls. Besides Hedy Lamarr, I have Esther Williams. We saw her in a movie called *Dangerous When Wet*. My favorite paper doll is Marilyn Monroe. Besides all her beautiful clothes, she has a dressing table with a round mirror, just like Mommy's. We saw Marilyn in *Gentlemen Prefer Blondes* at the drive-in. My favorite scene was when Jane Russell sang in a gym, with lots of men wearing only tiny shorts that were almost the color of their skin, making them look naked. I heard Daddy tell Mommy that he thinks I don't understand Marilyn Monroe movies, but I know why diamonds are a girl's best friend.

I carefully fold Marilyn's dressing table, stack all her costumes, and put them in a white envelope. Each of my paper dolls has her own envelope, and then all three envelopes go in a larger yellow envelope with a metal clasp. I slide this envelope under the sofa, so Daddy won't see it. When the sofa is folded out for my bed, I like knowing that my paper dolls are sleeping right under me.

One Saturday, I come home from playing at Noreen's and hear Mommy and Daddy arguing, so I stay on the back porch.

"If they're so harmless, why is he hiding them under the sofa?"

"Because I knew you wouldn't approve."

"Damn right I don't approve. Boys don't play with paper dolls."

"But he likes them, Rusty. And maybe some good will come out of it."

"What possible good could come from my son playing with paper dolls? He's already too attached to that stupid stuffed bear of his."

"Anthony likes all the costumes, and sometimes he draws his own. Real extravagant outfits with feathers or fur coats with ribbons. Maybe one day he'll go to Hollywood and design costumes."

"You'd like that, wouldn't you? He gets those crazy ideas from all those stupid movie magazines you buy."

"I only buy one a month."

"I'm not begrudging you your magazines, Mary. I just don't think you should influence the boy with it."

"I don't tell him to read it. He picks it up on his own. In case you haven't noticed, he hasn't once looked at that new magazine you brought home. What's it called— *Sports Illustrated*? Why can't you let him do the things he's interested in?"

"He doesn't know the things he's interested in until he's tried them. Maybe he'd be interested in sports if he tried."

"How many times have you dragged him out to the backyard to play catch—and not one time has he expressed interest."

"Well, maybe that's because it's just the two of us. Maybe if he was on a team and there was some competition, he'd like it."

"What sort of competition?"

"I signed Anthony up for the peewee softball league."

"He's too small, Rusty! He could get hurt."

"He's not too small. That's why it's called 'peewee.' You're too soft on him. You're turning him into a sissy."

Mommy doesn't say anything.

"I bought him a mitt."

"Have you ever considered why he doesn't want to play ball?" Mommy says. "Maybe it's because he's not any good at it, and other kids tease him."

"Well, it's too late now. I already agreed to be the coach. How will it look if my own son doesn't play?"

I sit down on the porch step and repeat over and over in my head, *I don't want to play ball, I don't want to play ball.* Why is Daddy doing this to me?

I TELL MYSELF it doesn't matter that the other boys called me a sissy; they're not smart like me, and they don't get good grades. But I want the boys to like me. And I want to please Daddy, but I'm simply no good at any sport that involves a ball—I can't hit, catch, kick, or toss one. I'm uncoordinated, but there's something more, something I don't want anyone to know. I am afraid of the ball. They call it "softball," but that ball is still plenty hard, especially when it comes speeding toward me.

Daddy assigns me to right field, the least active position, since most batters are right-handed and hit the ball toward center or left field. Standing in mowed grass, I pray the ball won't come flying in my direction. Not that I can catch it if it does, even with my new mitt. At bat, I cringe as the pitcher launches the ball toward me. At every game, I strike out. Three times.

My teammates stare at me. "How can your dad be such a great coach and you be so awful?" They push me so hard I nearly fall down.

When a ball occasionally comes my way in right field, I throw it to the pitcher and hear the usual comment. "You throw like a girl." The other boys often say this with a sneer. This time, Daddy says it. In front of everyone.

When the inning is over, I walk toward the bench.

"You even walk like a girl," Daddy says.

I don't understand why he would embarrass me in front of everyone. I only know that sometimes I hate Daddy.

I'm an awful player, but the team doesn't need me to win. With Daddy and Uncle Nick urging the boys on, we have a good season and make it to the play-offs. We're behind one run when I take my last turn at bat. My teammates groan. Loudly.

"Strike one!"

The next pitch is too low. "Ball!" the umpire shouts.

Sweat drips under my arms. I don't care if we win. It's just a stupid game. But it would sure feel good to be the hero. I tighten my stance. Swing.

"Strike two!"

Inside pitch. "Ball!" And again. "Ball!"

I look toward the sideline. Uncle Nick jerks his head to one side. Puzzled, I frown. Uncle Nick jerks his head again.

I move closer to home plate. Uncle Nick nods, jerks his head sideways one more time. I move an inch closer to the plate. He gives me a thumbs-up.

The pitcher lifts his hands over his head; his right arm swoops in a wide circle; he releases the ball. I lean toward the plate. The ball scrapes my leg just above the knee.

Uncle Nick flashes me the "OK" sign, and I hear a few cheers as I walk to first base.

I never make it to second base. The boy at bat after me strikes out, and we lose. But this time, no one blames me.

"There's always next year," Uncle Nick says. He flings his arms around Nick Junior and me. "Let's go get pizza."

*

TONY TOMASSO PULLS up to our house in a brand new, 1955 Chevrolet Bel Air convertible. We all run outside to see it. Frank comes over, too.

"Wow, it's so different from the old Chevys." Frank walks around the car, bending over to look at the dashboard.

"I love the colors," Mommy says.

"Gypsy Red and India Ivory." Tony eyes Noreen, ready to slap her hand if she dares put a dirty finger on the dazzling chrome.

"I suppose," Frank says, looking at me, "now you won't want to ride with me anymore."

"Oh, Frank," I say, "this car has more chrome than a toaster. Your Buick Roadmaster is a classic."

Frank smiles and messes up my hair.

Mom stands in front of the car. "The hood ornament's ready to take off."

"And that's what we should do." Daddy looks down the street. "Oh, good, here comes Nick. Anyone need to use the bathroom before we head out? Now's the time."

I sit beside Tony on the white leather seat. Nick Junior and his sister Rose pout in the back. They wanted to be up front, especially Nick Junior, who said he deserved it because he was the oldest, but Tony said, "Oldest doesn't equal cutest. And if you don't stop complaining, you don't have to ride in the convertible at all."

Whenever I glance back at him, Nick Junior sticks out his tongue or makes a fist at me, meaning *I'll get you later*.

My parents ride with Uncle Nick and Aunt Lily. We are on our way to LeSourdsville Lake Amusement Park. There's a big swimming pool, but we want to go on the rides. First is the merry-go-round, but no one really enjoys that. It's too tame.

We head to the bumper cars. When an attendant unlatches the chain, everyone dashes for a shiny metal car with a wide black rubber bumper wrapped around it. I choose a red one.

Each car has only one pedal: *Go!* There is no brake.

As soon as the ride starts, Nick Junior rams into me, sending my car across the rink. Sparks fly as the metal bar rising from the back of my car streaks along the ceiling. I see Tony heading right toward me. I lift my foot from the pedal and take my hands off the steering wheel. When Tony hits me, I bounce and flop in my seat as my car skids in circles. In her yellow car, Mommy waves, her smile almost as big as mine.

Two teenage boys come at me from opposite directions. My car slams into a corner and spins, with sparks shooting.

Daddy scoots by, shouting, "Go after them!"

But I don't pursue them. Instead, I set it up so Uncle Nick smacks into me. Then Nick Junior, yelling like an avenging Comanche, hits me head-on. Even Aunt Lily and Rose, seeing an easy target, crash into me, too.

I love being pitched about, letting my body go limp. I shriek and squeal. I have never had so much fun. Too soon, the ride ends.

Out on the midway, Daddy grabs me by my shirt collar. "You're not supposed to let everyone toss you around like a rag doll. You should have been more aggressive and rammed the other cars."

"Rusty, everyone's watching." Mommy smiles at the staring faces.

Daddy sneers but lowers his voice. "Why'd you let everyone plow into you?"

I freeze. All the stiffness in my body is back. Why is Daddy doing this in front of everyone? I want to cry, but I know that will make Daddy even angrier. I stand rigid, looking at my shoes.

"It's unmanly." Daddy finally releases my collar. "You're embarrassing."

"You're the one who's making us all uncomfortable," Tony says. "Leave the boy alone."

"What do you know about raising kids?" Daddy raises his voice again. "You're just a—" He turns away.

"Come on, Anthony." Tony reaches out his hand. "Let's go on the world-famous Cyclone."

"Anthony will ride the Cyclone with Nick Junior," Daddy says. "And on the way back home, he'll sit between Nick and me. He's my son, Tony, not yours."

"I wouldn't be so sure." Tony's voice is such a whisper that nobody hears him. Except me.

Age ten

Truth

WHEN I WAS your age," Daddy tells me on my tenth birthday, "Mama Luisa said I was old enough to be her numbers runner."

We're sitting at the kitchen table. Daddy is drinking coffee, and Mommy is at the counter assembling my birthday cake. I got to pick what kind of cake I wanted, and I chose Boston Cream Pie, which is really a cake.

I have only one page left in my *Straight Arrow Indian Coloring Book*. It's a drawing of a charging buffalo. I left it for last because it's not very interesting. I liked coloring the Indians, putting bright stripes and circles on their bare chests. I'm hoping I'll get another coloring book for my birthday. I asked for *Cinderella*.

"What's a numbers runner?" I take the brown and black crayons out of the Crayola box.

"I would run around the neighborhood collecting bets that people made," Daddy says. "They would bet a penny or a nickel on what was called 'a three-number combination.' If they picked the right three numbers, they won $15."

"How did they pick the numbers?"

"Sometimes they'd have a dream, and Mama Luisa had a book that said what the dream meant. Each dream had a number, so they used that. Other people felt they had lucky numbers, so every day they'd bet the same three numbers, over and over again."

"Even when they didn't win?"

"Sounds like someone else I know." Mommy swirls chocolate icing on the cake. "So, besides being a midwife, Mama Luisa was a bookie."

Daddy frowns at her. "Each day after school, I crisscrossed the neighborhood collecting the bets. You know, not too many Italians have red hair, so people thought mine would bring them luck. The women stroked my head when they handed over their pennies. The men weren't as gentle. 'For luck,' they said and grabbed me around the neck before I had a chance to back away. Then their knuckles buzzed my head like a barber's shaver."

Daddy grabs me around the neck and buzzes my head.

"It stings."

"Imagine having that done to you over and over every day. Sometimes I felt my head was going to burst into flames."

I finish the buffalo and start on the sky. Since it's such a boring drawing, I'm going to make a colorful sunset rather than a plain blue sky.

"So, anyway, once Mama Luisa and I had collected all the bets, we took the money to this big fat man. I still remember his name. Mr. Rambaldi. He always wore a dark blue serge suit. If Mama Luisa gave him a hundred dollars, she got to keep ten. Then, when we walked back home, Mama Luisa would give me fifty cents."

"What's serge?" I ask.

"It's a heavy wool fabric," Mommy says.

"How were the winning numbers chosen?"

Mommy asks the question, but Daddy looks at me. "In New York, there's the Stock Exchange, where people buy and sell shares in a company. Every day, thousands of shares are traded. The person who correctly picked the last three numbers of how many shares were traded the next day was the winner. So, if 5,678 shares were traded, the person who picked 678 was the winner."

I don't really understand, but I nod my head because I know there must be more to this story.

"The best part of being a numbers runner was when I got to give someone their winnings. I always made sure I handed over some of the money in change. The women always tipped me, a dime or even a quarter. Some of the men tipped me, too, but most of them counted every nickel to make sure I didn't cheat them." Daddy whispers, "Sometimes I placed my own bets."

"I bet you did." Mommy rummages through the kitchen drawers.

"I even won a few times. I looked forward to collecting the bets. I had my favorites, hoping that Mrs. Costello, who always gave me a warm cookie, would win, and not Mr. Nardi, who always smelled of garlic. But running numbers was illegal, and one day there was a knock on our front door." Daddy knocks loudly on the table. "Standing outside was a cop. A big, burly man, over six feet tall. 'Get your hat, Mama Luisa,' he said. Everyone called her that, even the cops."

"Mama Luisa's not even five feet," Mommy says, "I bet they looked funny walking down Maple Street. Like a mismatched vaudeville duo."

"Yeah, well, I didn't laugh. I sat on the porch and cried."

Mommy holds up a small box of white candles. "Okay, I found them. Come on, you two, get your jackets. Everyone will be waiting for us. Grandma's serving your favorite, Anthony: rigatoni."

"Here's the funny part," Daddy tells Mommy as we get in the car to go to Grandma Peruzzi's. "Later I found out that the cops came for Mama Luisa about twice a year, just to make sure they got their part of the take." Then Daddy turns around and looks at me. "Don't tell Mama Luisa I told you that story. Nowadays, she walks around with her rosary in her hand and doesn't want to remember her past."

"DO YOU KNOW what Mary said when Anthony was born?" Daddy sips from a glass of Grandpa Peruzzi's homemade red wine.

"*I never want to go through that again,*" Mommy and Daddy say together.

"Well, what do you expect?" Mommy looks at her sisters sitting around Grandma's big kitchen table. "I weighed only ninety-eight pounds before I got pregnant. And Anthony weighed nearly nine pounds when he was born!"

"Eight pounds, twelve-and-a-half ounces, to be exact," Grandma Peruzzi calls from the pantry.

"Well, at least you got to be there." Mama Luisa carries dirty dishes to the sink.

"Let's not go through *that* again." Mommy shakes her head.

"All I'm saying is I am a midwife, and I should have been there."

"It's been ten years," Mommy whispers to Aunt Joan. "You think she'd finally accept that I only wanted my mother there."

"I got there practically at the last minute," Daddy says. "I was still in the Coast Guard and had to take the train from New York."

"And then to think," Mama Luisa says, coming in from the pantry, "the little innocent wasn't baptized for six months."

"Holy Mother of God," Daddy says, "here we go again."

"Don't blaspheme, Rusty." Mama Luisa makes the sign of the cross. "Anthony could've died and gone to Limbo."

I learned about Limbo in Catechism class. It's where babies who die before they're baptized go. I don't understand why God wouldn't let them into Heaven. It isn't their fault they died.

"I've told her a hundred times that Rusty had to return to duty right away," Mommy says. "And then he was shipped overseas for six months. I wasn't going to have my baby baptized without his father present."

I stand beside Daddy, who puts his arm around my waist.

"Mary wanted to name you 'Carlo Dimora III.' But I said no son of mine was going to be The Third. All the other boys would tease you."

I don't tell him that most of the boys tease me anyway, including Donny and Ronny, sitting across the table and sticking their tongues out at me.

"Only a sissy has a number after his name," says Uncle Vic.

"Kings have numbers," Aunt Connie says.

"So do popes," Aunt Joan adds.

"Well, if Anthony grows up to be a king or the pope," Grandpa Dimora says, "then he can put a number after his name."

"You were named after me," says Tony Tomasso, standing in the doorway. Mommy had said that only family should be invited to my birthday party, but I wanted Tony to come because he's always so nice to me.

"Sorry, Tony, but Anthony wasn't named after you," Mommy says. "Although I admit that's what I thought when Rusty suggested it. After all, you were his best man at our wedding."

"So, how did I get my name?"

Daddy says, "My mother was born on St. Anthony's feast day."

*

AFTER DINNER, I want to open my presents, but Mommy says not until after we have cake and ice cream. Everyone groans and says they're too full, so we take a break. Daddy and Tony Tomasso go out to the front porch and sit on the swing that hangs from the ceiling. I sit on the steps and look through a photo album. There is one of Daddy on his eighth birthday, holding a plate with a piece of cake. He looks like he is going to cry. There's another one when he's a teenager wearing shorts and holding a basketball, and his hair is long and wavy. But I like best the one of Daddy in his white Coast Guard uniform. He has a holster with a gun.

"Have you heard from Nick?" Tony asks Daddy. Last month, Uncle Nick moved his family to Ohio.

"Yeah, he got a job at Wright-Patterson Air Force Base. He's making good money." Daddy takes a sip of Grandpa Peruzzi's wine. "Nick keeps raving about Dayton's 'booming economy' and thinks I should move there too."

Move? I wouldn't mind leaving Castleton. Sure, I'd miss Grandma Peruzzi and Frank, but I don't have any friends my age at school. And I'd get to see Uncle Nick again.

"Do you want to move away?" Tony asks Daddy.

"I don't think so. I do wish I had a better job and made more money. But all my friends are here, and I'd miss them if we left. I'd miss everyone except my dad." He takes a bigger sip. "I'm surprised he came tonight. I guess he did it for Anthony. He certainly wouldn't do it for me."

"Maybe it's time you cut your old man some slack."

"Is that what you learned in all those psych courses?"

"Only one more year and I'll get my degree." Tony lights a cigarette. "You going to be my first patient?"

"Being on the couch isn't for me, but you sure are easy to talk to. You always have been."

"So, talk. I know something's on your mind. I can always tell."

"It's nothing important. Just that I was thinking about Anthony's baptism, and how that day changed everything."

"In what way?"

"I remember it very clearly."

I stop looking at the pictures and just listen.

"When we got back here from church, Nick and I inserted two leaves in the dining room table—we didn't eat at the kitchen table that day. This was an important occasion. Mrs. Peruzzi was barking out orders, and Mary's sisters were flitting around like they were getting ready for a visit from the Pope. They drove me crazy—still do—so I went to the basement to play cards with the other men."

"Why don't you like Mary's sisters?" Tony asks.

"I always found the Peruzzi sisters shrill and unattractive except for Mary. She was petite and beautiful. Still is. You know, we were living in this house when I finally got out of the Coast Guard. Well, it was on that day, the day of Anthony's baptism, that I promised myself that as soon as I could, I would get my son out of that gaggle of women. And that's why I say it was that day that changed my life. I just knew I couldn't be a part of that big, loud family. I had to go my own way and take Mary and Anthony with me."

"Maybe you aren't so different from your father, after all. He always seems to go his own way."

Mommy comes out carrying an old milk bottle filled with Grandpa's wine. "How you guys doing out here?" She refills their glasses, then stoops down beside me. "What do you have there?"

"A photo album."

"It looks like Mama Luisa's. How did you get it?"

"She gave it to me. She saw me looking at it at her house and said she'd give it to me on my birthday."

"Why didn't you wait to open it with your other presents?"

"It wasn't wrapped. She just handed it to me."

"Well, you take good care of it. Those are precious pictures."

"Mary, maybe you ought to take Anthony inside. It's getting chilly."

"I don't want to go in. I want to stay here."

"Come on, Anthony." Mommy stretches out her arm to me. "I think the boys want to talk about their war stories in private."

I follow her inside, but not into the kitchen. I sit on the floor in the living room behind a chair where no one can see me. The window is open just a little bit, but if I concentrate, I can hear Daddy go with his story.

"Right after Anthony's baptism, I asked Mama Luisa if Mary and the baby and I could move into her house. We stayed in one cramped room for nearly six months until Mary found a duplex on Uber Street that we could afford to rent."

"I don't think your living arrangement is the reason you wanted Anthony to go inside."

"Yeah, you're going to be a great psychiatrist."

"Psychologist," Tony says.

"What's the difference?"

"I'll explain some other time. Go on with your story, Rusty."

"Okay, enough stalling. There's something that happened when Anthony was a baby, and I hadn't really thought about it for a long time, but lately it keeps popping into my mind. It wasn't long after we moved to Uber Street. Mary was busy in the kitchen, and Anthony was fussing, so she asked me to check his diaper. Anthony was such a good baby. Hardly ever cried. Just ate and slept. And shit. Everyone said he was 'such a big baby,' but to me, he was tiny. After I changed his diaper, I touched his lips, and he sucked my finger. I felt his warm breath. And I don't know, I almost felt like crying. Here was a living person I helped create, and he was so precious, so fragile, so... *helpless*. I promised then that he would have everything he needed. I would protect him and teach him. We would play ball together—baseball, basketball, and even football if that's what he wanted—and maybe, just maybe, one day my son would be what I wasn't: a star player on a professional team."

Daddy takes a deep breath before he continues. "I put my finger in Anthony's hand, and he squeezed. He had such little fingers with such tiny nails. And little toes. Ten tiny toes. And his penis. Like a toy. 'He's so cute,' I thought, 'I could eat him alive.' I kissed his pudgy belly, blowing raspberries with my lips. Then I opened my mouth and—and I put his penis and balls in my mouth. I froze. I mean, what was I doing?"

"I know you think what you did is shocking," Tony says, "but you aren't the only parent who gets overwhelmed with emotion, especially when the baby is so totally dependent on them. Fortunately, the child is too young to remember anything, so there aren't any repercussions. Except for the parents' guilty feelings."

"I did feel guilty. I stayed very still, listening, making sure Mary was in the kitchen and hadn't been watching. And I've never told anyone. Not even the priest in Confession."

"Why do you think you're telling me now?"

"I don't know. It still embarrasses me. I guess I just wanted to show you that I did love my son. At first."

I don't stay behind the chair to hear what else Daddy tells Tony. I run upstairs to the bathroom, afraid I'm not going to make it in time. I vomit chewed-up rigatoni.

Daddy must be so disappointed in me, that I'm a lousy ballplayer.

"Anthony, are you up there?" Mommy yells. "We're ready to have cake and ice cream. Everyone's waiting."

All my aunts, uncles, and cousins sing "Happy Birthday" to me.

When I blow out the candles, my wish is for Daddy to still love me.

I KNOW THE words by heart and spell out his name in the singsong rhythm. M-I-C-K-E-Y M-O-U-S-E!

Every day after school, I watch *The Mickey Mouse Club* on television as a parade of cartoon characters follows their leader, a singing mouse with big, round ears.

But he's not the one I care about.

I like the one marching out of line.

Donald Duck!

He jumps above the crowd, shouting his name. I shout with him.

Mickey has a squeaky voice, and his "aw, shucks" attitude makes me frown. Even though the mouse is at the front of the parade, I don't see him as a leader. He wants everyone to fall in line and for everything to stay the same. I prefer Donald, who seems willing to try something different, to go his own way. He's the one for me, even if nothing ever seems to go right for him. At the end of the song, Donald strikes a gong. It cracks and falls to the floor.

The Mickey Mouse Club features singing, dancing, newsreels, and cartoons, and I enjoy them all. It starts at 5:00, and Mommy will only let me watch it if I've already finished my school homework and set the table for dinner during the commercials.

One Monday, head Mouseketeer Jimmy Dodd introduces a serial called *The Adventures of Spin and Marty*. It takes place at The Triple-R Ranch, a summer camp for boys. On the first day, the boys say goodbye to their parents. Most of the boys are cute, although one is very tall and doesn't have much of a chin, another is short, and another is almost fat. Spin Evans is the most popular and "the best at everything." He has slicked-back hair like Frank.

A long car driven by a chauffeur pulls up, and out steps young Martin Markham, who shouts at three boys on a horse to move out of the way.

Spin sneers at Marty as the episode ends.

The next day, my homework is finished, and the table is set a half-hour before the next episode is on. I sit on the floor as close to the television screen as Mommy will let me.

When Mr. Burnett, the Triple R camp counselor, says, "Hello, Marty," the new boy corrects him.

"Excuse me, sir, but my name is Martin."

"Oh, didn't anybody ever call you Marty before?"

I understand how Martin feels. No one calls me "Tony." I'm "Anthony."

I'm not rich like Martin, and I've never been to a summer camp. But like him, I don't enjoy baseball or football. He wears a bow tie. So do I, on Sundays when we go to church.

Mr. Burnett says, "I'll straighten that boy out if it takes up my whole summer."

I know that Marty's different from the other boys. I'm different, too. But does that make me *wrong*?

In episode three, Mr. Burnett tells Marty that if he's interested in them, the boys will be interested in him. But I know that's not true. What Marty says is the truth. "They're just mad because I don't do silly things like they do."

I can't pretend to enjoy sports or throwing water balloons at girls. That doesn't mean I don't want the boys to like or admire me. It's like Marty says. "I'll show them! I'll show all of them!"

The awful thing is, just like most of the boys at the camp, I don't like Marty either. I like Spin.

Thursday's episode opens with a boy hunting frogs with his shirt off. His jeans are so low that it looks like he's not wearing underwear.

I watch every single day.

There's singing around the campfire and rides along the trails. A hungry bear chases a couple of the boys up a tree. Marty breaks his wrist. The climax is a rodeo. And, of course, in the end, Spin and Marty are best friends.

Television is *not* like school.

I AM ALREADY in my pajamas, watching *I Married Joan*, when Daddy walks by and rubs my head.

"Rusty," Mommy says, "Please don't go out again tonight."

"I'm just going to have one drink with the boys."

"*Just one drink*," Mommy says, like she's making fun of him. "*Just for an hour.* But it's always three or four drinks, three or four hours before you return. Broke."

I stare at the television but hear only the voices in the kitchen.

"You knew I liked to gamble before you married me."

"And you know I don't mind you playing once in a while, but you want to do it every night. We can't afford it."

"I'm making enough money."

"And you're losing it on cards. If I pay the rent this month, there'll be nothing left for groceries. Do you want me and Anthony to go without food?"

"You're always exaggerating."

Mommy runs past me into their bedroom, shouting, "Don't you dare move," and I don't know if she is talking to Daddy or me. She comes back, opening her purse. "You're the accountant," she screams, tossing money at Daddy. "You count it. There isn't enough."

I get up and stand in the kitchen doorway as Daddy picks up some of the money and stuffs it in his pocket.

"I forbid you to gamble again tonight." Mommy guards the back door.

"Who do you think you are to forbid me anything?"

"I'm your wife, and—

"That's right, you're *my* wife. I'm the husband. I'm the boss. I'm the one who says what goes on around here."

Mommy looks ready to cry. "You think you're so smart. Well, you don't know everything."

"And I suppose you do."

"I know enough. I know things you don't know."

"Like what?"

"Like how your mother really died."

Daddy grabs Mommy by her shoulders. "What are you talking about? She died of pneumonia."

Mommy doesn't say anything for a long time, then she takes a deep breath. "Your mother died from an abortion."

I don't know what that means, but Daddy's furious.

"You bitch! How dare you say such a horrible thing to me?"

"It's true. Lily told me."

"Lily's a liar. Mama Luisa wouldn't have lied to me all these years. She raised me as if she were my real mother."

"Mama Luisa performed the abortion."

Daddy slaps Mommy.

I stand there with my mouth open. I think Mommy will cry, but she looks right up at Daddy and says, "Mama Luisa raised you because she killed your mother."

Daddy pushes Mommy away and rushes out the door. He slams it so hard it shakes the wall.

I run to Mommy and hold her. She cries without making any sound.

In a little while, she takes my hand, and we go into the living room. She unfolds the sofa and makes up my bed. She doesn't say anything, just pats the bed, and I crawl under the sheet.

She goes into her bedroom without turning off the television. I watched the end of *My Little Margie*. Mommy comes back in her pajamas and gets in bed beside me. We watch *Masquerade Party*, then *I've Got a Secret*. I've never stayed up this late on a school night.

Mommy gets up and turns off the television, then goes into the kitchen. I hear her open the back door. She closes it but doesn't lock it. She leaves the little stove light on, then she comes back into my bed, cuddling close to me.

DADDY COMES HOME while I'm eating my cereal. Mommy doesn't eat breakfast, just a cup of coffee. She doesn't look at him.

Daddy pours himself a cup of coffee. "I slept on Tony's couch." He stands behind her chair. "I'm sorry I took my anger out on you."

Mommy doesn't say anything.

"I am very, very sorry I slapped you. I lost control. I promise you it will never happen again."

The kitchen is so quiet, I am afraid to chew.

"What do you want?" Daddy says. "I said I was sorry. I don't know what else I can do."

Mommy turns around and looks at Daddy. It is that stern face, like when I do something wrong. She wants you to do or say something, but she won't tell you what it is.

But Daddy knows what she wants, because he says, "Okay. I promise I won't gamble anymore."

"Go take a shower," Mommy says. "I'll fix your breakfast."

"Here," Daddy says, handing Mommy a wad of money. "I actually won last night."

I smile at Tony the Tiger on my cereal box and eat my Frosted Flakes.

DADDY SITS DOWN at the table with his hair still wet, and Mommy places a dish in front of him. Two fried eggs sunny-side-up, just the way he likes them, and three pieces of bacon.

"Anthony, honey," she says, "go brush your teeth and change out of your pajamas."

I leave but stand just inside the doorway so I can still hear them.

"I'm sorry I had to tell you, Rusty," Mommy says. "I didn't mean to hurt you, but I was desperate. I was frightened of what would happen if you lost any more money. I had to stop you, and that was the only way I knew how."

"I know. I'm sorry I put you through that."

"I don't hear any water running," Mommy says loudly, so I go into the bathroom.

After I brush my teeth, I take off my pajamas and carry my clothes into the living room, and stand by the doorway getting dressed.

"Late last night I phoned Nick, and he said Dad told him when he was fifteen how our mother died," Daddy says. "He said Dad never told me because I didn't live with him, so it all goes back to me deciding to live with Mama Luisa instead of Dad and his new wife. Of course, if I had known what Mama Luisa did, I—"

Daddy sounds like he's crying.

SOMETIMES WHEN MOMMY and Daddy go to bed, they shut their door. If I haven't fallen asleep when they do this, I get out of bed and tiptoe to the window. I look up at Frank's window, but he never looks down at me. Tonight, the bedroom door is open, and I can hear Daddy whispering.

"Every time I think about it, I get sick to my stomach. I don't think I can ever face Mama Luisa again. How could she have done such a horrible thing? And how could my father have let it happen?"

"It's going to take some time," Mommy says, "but one day you'll be able to forgive them."

"I don't want to forgive them. I want to kill them."

"Don't say that, Rusty."

"Why? It's true. I nearly killed my father today."

"*What?*"

"I went to the railroad yard before he got off work. I'm sure Nick called to tell him I knew what had happened, but Dad didn't say anything. He didn't even step out of his shed when he saw me approach. He just sat there on his stool, running his finger down a train schedule. Finally, I said, 'I know how my mother died.' He said, 'I told you how she died. I never lied to you. Rosa did not die from an abortion.'"

I don't understand. A portion of what? I take Teddy and

quietly stand by the door. I know Daddy's talking about his mother, that she died when he was very young, but now it seems like the story is changing, that someone lied.

"Dad said my mother was never very healthy, and that after I was born, the doctor said she shouldn't have any more children, that another pregnancy might kill her. He said they took precautions, but she got pregnant anyway."

"Did he say why they asked Mama Luisa to perform the operation?"

"She was a midwife. She knew what to do. He said it wasn't her fault that my mother died, that she was already weak and got pneumonia."

"He must have been devastated. They both must have been devastated."

"I asked him how he could face Mama Luisa knowing what she did, and you know what he said? 'She did what she thought was right.' How could he think what they did was right? His own mother murdered his unborn child and his wife."

Murder? I bite Teddy's ear.

"It wasn't *murder*, Rusty."

"That's exactly what *he* said. He called it 'a medical procedure.' Then he picked up his goddamn switching tool, said a train was coming, and he had to switch the tracks. I followed him across the yard and screamed, 'You accept it so easily.' He said it wasn't so easy back then. 'Time heals.' Time heals! What a bunch of crap!"

"Honey, don't get yourself all worked up again."

"I haven't finished."

"What else happened?"

"I asked him about the Church, and he said, 'What about it?' I said abortion is a mortal sin. 'So are lots of other things,'"

he said. 'The Church sets up rules to protect innocent people—'
That's when I shoved him. 'Innocent as an unborn child?' I
said. I could hear the train coming in the distance. He kept
talking. He had his rationalizations all worked out. He said,
'You sin, you confess, you're forgiven.' How could he be so
cavalier? I watched him put the tool in the switching device.
I told him I didn't know who he was. 'Maybe if you had lived
with me, you would,' he said. So, we were back to that, that
I had chosen Mama Luisa over him. God, he made me so
angry! I pushed him so hard he fell in the gravel between the
tracks.

"Jeeze, Rusty—"

"Then I stepped on his hand, which was on the rail. The
train was heading right toward us. I could hear the whistle
shrieking. It was so damn loud, like it was coming from inside
me. I shouted at him. 'You and Mama Luisa killed my mother!'
Then I ground my foot into his hand, and over the whistle, I
heard something crack."

"Oh my God."

I think I'm going to pee, right there in the doorway, but
then they'll know I'm listening, so I just squeeze Teddy tighter.

"I turned the tool and switched the tracks so the train
headed for the station. Dad sat in the gravel holding his wrist.
He said, 'I loved Rosa more than anything in my life. If she
had another baby, she might die. It wasn't just my decision.
She and I talked it over. We did what we had to do. I was willing
to sacrifice another child for my wife's life, but God took her
anyway. Maybe it was my punishment. All I know is that I
loved her, and she was gone. I still miss Rosa. Even on the day
I remarried, I missed her.' I asked why, if he missed her so
much, he got married again. He said he needed a companion.

Then he said he did it for me, too. He said Nick was old enough to be on his own, but I needed a mother to look after me. I said I didn't want another mother, and he said, 'No, you wanted Mama Luisa. You loved her so much that I could never tell you how Rosa died, even when you got older. Sometimes I thought of telling you, but I saw how much you loved Mama Luisa, and I didn't want to break that bond. Even when it hurt me. Even when I knew you loved her more than me.' He started crying. 'You didn't pick me,' he said, and the goddamn bastard was crying."

It sounds like Daddy is crying, too. I imagine Mommy is holding him just like she holds me when I cry.

Then Daddy says, 'I'm still not picking him. I'm not picking any of them. I'm going to take that job at the cement pipe company in Dayton that Nick told me about, and we're getting out of this rotten town."

"What about Mama Luisa? Are you going to talk with her?"

"She can rot in Hell."

"WHY DO WE have to clean the house if we're moving?" I want to know. "We've been scrubbing for two days."

"It isn't nice to leave a dirty house for the next family." Mommy dips her sponge into a soapy bucket. "And we don't want them to think I'm not a good housekeeper."

They haven't even met you, I think, but don't say anything.

Later, I carefully wrap each dish with thick white paper Mommy got from the butcher and place it in a cardboard box. We eat dinner on paper plates with plastic forks and drink out of paper cups.

The next morning, we load our mattresses into a rental

truck that holds the rest of our furniture and boxes. Tony Tomasso will drive it to Dayton, Ohio. Daddy, Mommy, and I will follow in the Ford, the backseat loaded with houseplants.

"I'll be right back," I say and run out the back door before Mommy can stop me. I don't even knock, I just run up to Frank's room. "It's time."

He kneels so he is my height. "If it gets too tough, you think of me and Perry Como." He hugs me as tightly as I hug him. Then he turns me around and pushes me toward the door. I know if I glance back, I'll cry, so I walk down the stairs looking straight ahead.

Mommy walks through the house one last time. She checks every closet, each cupboard. Nothing is left behind except half a roll of toilet paper.

"They might not know what box they packed theirs in," she says. "And we don't want them to think we're so poor we have to take the t.p."

Daddy toots the horn, and we run out to the car.

He drives down Hill Street and turns on Main. Mama Luisa stands on her porch. She is in black, like she always is, but it is her Sunday dress, even though it is Saturday. Her yellow-white hair is twisted around her head. Her hands are crossed in front of her. She looks so tiny standing alone on the big white porch.

Tony honks the truck's horn three times. Mommy rolls down the car window, and I crawl across her.

"Goodbye, Mama Luisa!" I wave. "Goodbye! Goodbye!"

She blows me a kiss.

Daddy keeps his eyes straight ahead.

*

I'M GLAD TO move away from Castleton. Like Mommy says, "It's a fresh start."

I don't have to sleep on the foldout sofa anymore. I have my own bedroom, but we're only in our rented house for a couple of months.

Uncle Nick buys a new home in a new subdivision. He says the builder declared bankruptcy, so the houses are going at "bottom-level prices." Daddy wants to buy one too, but Mommy is worried they may not be well-made. Uncle Nick said they're "top of the line, that's why the guy went bankrupt." He tells Daddy it's stupid to pay rent when he can buy a house for almost the same monthly payment. So, Daddy puts down a deposit on a brand new "ranch-style" house on Dundee Circle across the street from Uncle Nick.

This means I'm going to change schools. *Again.* When we moved to Dayton, Mommy wanted me to go to Catholic school, but it was filled, so I had to go to the public school—for six weeks—until there was an opening at Holy Family. Come September, I'll be going to another school, St. Helen.

And moving means we have to pack everything again, but before we do, there's a lot of work to do on the new house, because none of the "finishing work" was done once the builder went bankrupt. Nick adds woodwork to both our homes. Daddy, Mommy, Aunt Lily, Nick Junior, and I do the painting, inside and out. I picked daffodil yellow for my bedroom.

There are no trees or shrubbery in our yards. There isn't even a blade of grass. Daddy says we have to lay sod soon, or our sloping backyard will erode in the next rainstorm. Even though Uncle Nick has a flat yard, he gets the first truckload of sod and has men from the Air Force Base lay the grass.

Our load is dumped in our driveway on Saturday. Daddy

works half a day on Saturdays, so Mommy and I start positioning the grass blocks. Showers are predicted, so I think we should start in the backyard, where the dirt could turn to mud in the rain and roll down the deep slope. But Mommy wants to do the front first. It's smaller, more manageable, she says, and it's what the neighbors see.

We finish the front lawn by one o'clock, just as Daddy pulls in the driveway. Mommy fixes bacon and eggs for lunch. I'm surprised that Daddy has not come to help us, but has instead changed into his baseball uniform.

"You guys are real troopers." He dips toast into a yolk. "My little boy's quite a man."

I don't look up from my plate. I want him to skip the dumb game and help lay sod before it rains.

"It's starting to cloud over, Rusty," Mommy says. "Maybe the game will be postponed."

"If it is, I'll come straight home and help you, but if it just sprinkles, we'll still play. It's for the play-offs!"

"Maybe Nick Junior can help us," I say.

"He's going to the game with his dad." Daddy kisses Mommy on her forehead and heads out to the baseball field.

Mommy doesn't waste time washing the dishes.

I stare at the mountain of sod. "It barely looks any smaller." I fill the old red wheelbarrow and dump the load next to Mommy, who's on her knees and will arrange the blocks of grass like a tiled floor. I dump three loads along the back of the house, then join Mommy in shoving the blocks together.

I wheelbarrow three more loads. Then three more. We lay row after row. Sweat streaks down our dirty faces. We have done less than a quarter of the backyard—only the flat part closest to the house—when the sky turns a menacing gray. The slope has started, but we are achy and have slowed down.

When we reach the halfway mark, we feel the first raindrops. At first, the drizzle feels cool and clean. But it turns into a downpour, and the dirt beneath Mommy's knees becomes mud. The wheelbarrow sticks. The sopping bricks of sod get even heavier.

We don't talk.

As it gets even darker, we finish the steepest part of the slope. Then, when there are only a few yards at the bottom of the hill left to cover, Daddy pulls into the driveway.

"We won!" His uniform is completely wet and sticking to his body. "We're in the play-offs!"

Mommy doesn't look up. Her hair is flattened against her head. Her clothes are covered with mud.

I push the wheelbarrow up the hill for another load.

"Did you hear me?" Daddy says to me. "We're in the play-offs!"

With a flat shovel, I lift a wet block of sod into the wheelbarrow. I can't look at Daddy. I squeeze the shovel tightly, afraid I might bash his head with it. Rain and sweat wash down my face. Tears, too.

MOMMY HAS THE same name as the Blessed Virgin Mary. I understand the blessed part. Daddy says Mommy's a saint for laying all the sod in the rain. I'm not so sure about "virgin." I know from the Catechism that the Immaculate Conception means Mary was born without original sin. The part about Jesus being conceived by God, not by Joseph, has me stumped.

I know that mommies carry babies in their stomachs, but I don't know how they get there. When I ask Mommy where babies come from, she says, "God." I know Mommy won't lie to me. It's a sin to lie. But I know there's more to it.

One afternoon after school, Mommy and I sit at the picnic table in the backyard and draw. She has torn out a small ad from her movie magazine. It shows a sketch of a woman's head. The headline says, *If you can draw this, you can become a commercial artist.*

I make my drawing the same size as the one in the ad, a little bigger than a matchbox, but Mommy's drawing fills up her whole page.

"That's really good," I say. "It looks just like her. Are you going to send it in like the ad says?"

"Oh, no, Anthony. I'm just doing this for fun."

"Wouldn't you like to be a commercial artist?"

"I'm happy being a mother."

On Saturday, when Daddy and Uncle Nick are off playing golf—their new "hobby"—Mommy and I go across the street to Aunt Lily's. I want to stay home and watch *The Pinky Lee Show* on television, but Mommy won't let me. She won't even let me bring Teddy.

I go up to Nick Junior's bedroom. He is just as thrilled to see me as I am to see him. For a long time, I just sit on the carpet while he reads a comic book on his bed. When he's finished, he gets a deck of cards from his desk drawer and sits down opposite me. He doesn't say a word, just deals the cards. We play War.

After a while, Rose comes in and, in a very prissy manner, announces that my mother is ready to go. I put down the cards and go downstairs. Mommy doesn't like to be kept waiting. She has told me, several times, how I had been two weeks late in being born, how she had to carry me in the hot, sticky heat, and that I was never to be late again.

Mommy stands by the back door listening to Aunt Lily, who doesn't seem like she's ever going to finish her story. I wait by the kitchen counter. On the dining room side, shelves are filled with dusty Italian figurines. There are delicate ballerinas and fancy-dressed women sipping tea. The biggest piece is the Last Supper, with Jesus and the Apostles. My favorite piece is one labeled *Ben-Hur*. I rub my finger along the body of a nearly naked man in a chariot, whipping his horses. I roll the dust into a ball.

"What are you doing?" Mommy glares at me.

"Nothing."

"Oh, those figurines haven't been washed since before we moved here." Aunt Lily holds out her hand for the dust ball. I drop it into her palm, and she tosses it over her shoulder into the sink.

"Well, I've got to get home and get some chores done," Mommy says, yanking my arm. As soon as the door closes, she cuffs the back of my neck with her hand. "How could you embarrass me like that?"

I try to never do anything wrong. If I upset Mommy, I feel I have to return to "go," just like in Monopoly, and start over to win her love.

Sometimes when she and Daddy get into an argument, she barely speaks to him for several days. She just says what's necessary, like, "Dinner's ready."

I know what day of the week it is by what's for dinner. On Monday, we always have baked chicken. Dad likes the legs and wings. Mommy and I each have a breast, or "white meat," as she calls it. She and I both like the liver, and I always suggest we cut it in half.

"No, I want you to have it."

So why doesn't she simply put it on my plate when she serves us? Why is there always a discussion even though we know who's going to eat it and who's going to be Mother Martyr?

I love Mommy, but sometimes she can be so annoying. One Saturday afternoon, I'm at the kitchen table drawing cars with sweeping fins, and she suddenly stops sewing a new skirt for herself. "It's too hot up here." She grabs the fabric, a thin paper pattern, pinking shears, and a red velvet box stuffed with spools of thread, needles, and pins. "Let's work in the basement. It'll be cooler. Carry down the sewing machine for me, Anthony."

"It's too heavy." It's a brand-new portable Singer. "I'll drop it."

"No, you won't. You're a big boy. Come on, help Mommy." She looks exhausted.

I place the pale aqua plastic lid on top of the black metal motor, but don't clamp it shut. Mommy has left a needle on the table, and I put it on top of the lid. I lift the machine—it isn't *that* heavy—and hold it close to my chest. There are twelve steps, and I count them as I go down. I stumble on number nine. I land on my stomach on the concrete floor. The lid flies off, and the machine comes down on top of it.

Mommy steps over me and picks up the plastic lid.

"It's cracked!"

"I'm so sorry." I pick up the needle lying next to me.

"I can never have anything new!"

Her eyes look like they're about to pop out. I know what's coming. A slap. I quickly get up and start running. She follows me across the basement, and when I look back and see her right behind me, I swing my hand around to protect my butt from her blow.

She hits me anyway. And the needle goes into my palm.

I stop howling, and Mommy removes the needle. There isn't much blood, but the needle has gone in deep.

"It might get infected." Mommy doesn't apologize for slapping the needle into my palm.

We ride the bus to the doctor's office. "The doctor doesn't have to know all the details," Mommy says. "Just tell him you fell when you were carrying a needle."

So, Mother Mary lies. Now I feel she's just like everyone else.

SPLAT! Another belly-smacker. It stings, but I like the shock.

Daddy frowns. I don't see why everything has to be a lesson. Why can't he let me dive on my own? I was just watching some older boys on the diving board, and thought I would give it a try, and right away, Daddy had to come over and show me "the right way" to do it.

"Bend your knees like this." He poses with his toes hanging over the pool.

I try to concentrate, but Daddy's always adding one more thing. I bend my knees. I point my hands. I tuck my head. I lift off. And go too deep.

I hit my head against the bottom of the pool.

"Don't cry," Daddy says when I surface. "Take it like a man."

I don't cry, but I don't make another dive either. I lie on my towel and watch the lifeguard sitting high above everyone. Why doesn't his chrome whistle get hot and burn his skin? He has blond curls. Mommy says they're not natural, that he probably squeezes lemon juice on his hair. I think they're pretty. I guess all the girls do too, because they're always hanging around him.

In the locker room, I get dressed like I always do, but Daddy stops me.

"Don't tuck everything into your underpants. You're supposed to just tuck your undershirt into your briefs. Then you tuck your outer shirt into your jeans."

"Well, tuck you!" Nick Junior says, and Uncle Nick laughs. I do too, but I don't know what's so funny.

ALL SUMMER LONG, Daddy, Uncle Nick, Nick Junior, and I work at St. Helen to get the new grade school ready for September. I'm the only one who can tell the nuns apart or at least remember their names. The principal, Sister Eileen Thérèse, wants everything done exactly as she says and complains that everyone is too slow. Sister Anna is no taller than me, and she looks very old and frail, but she pushes desks into neat rows in the classrooms. Sister Robert Marie is young and chubby and told me that the white scarf covering her forehead is called a wimple. I think that's funny. She does too.

One day, she and I unpack books in a storage room without any windows.

"It's really hot in here, Sister."

"Hell's hotter!" She flaps her arms in front of her face, fanning herself. "At least you get to wear shorts and a t-shirt. I'm stuck with this heavy habit—and it's black, too."

"Aren't you used to it?"

"I just got out of the convent, where we wore white."

I stack erasers and boxes of chalk on gray metal shelves.

"Your father's a nice man. He's been very helpful. But he seemed so disappointed that the school doesn't have a gym."

"He likes sports."

"I think the Cleveland Indians are going to win the World Series, but your dad doesn't believe me. What do you think?"

I shrug.

"You more of a football fan?"

"I don't like sports."

Sister Robert Marie's eyebrows disappear into her wimple. "Do you have any brothers?"

"No. No sisters, either."

"What do you like to do?"

"Read. And I'm not just saying that because you're a teacher."

She smiles. "What do you enjoy reading?"

"*The Hardy Boys.*"

"What about Nancy Drew?"

"She's okay. I like the boys better."

The eyebrows disappear again. We work in silence for a while.

"What grade are you going to be in?"

"Sixth."

"Oh, then I'll be your teacher."

Daddy sticks his head in the doorway. "The other nuns have gone back to the convent for dinner. The principal told me to get you. Anthony and I'll walk you home."

At the end of the school parking lot, Daddy and I wait for the traffic light to change, but Sister Robert Marie dashes into the road.

"Sister, cars are coming!"

"They won't hit me. I'm a nun."

Age eleven

No More Daddy

SCHOOL IS EASY. I always listen the first time Sister Robert Marie teaches something new, but she repeats the same lesson over and over, so I draw cars with high fins and lots of taillights. She seems surprised when she calls on me, and I know the answer.

Many of the nuns know me from working with them this summer, but once again, I'm the new kid, and most of the other students are already in a group of friends. Girls like me—they say I'm cute—but I don't really care about them. One boy in my class, Philip, wants to teach me to play chess. Philip's a sissy and cries when the other boys take his hat and toss it back and forth. I feel sorry for him, but I don't want to be his friend. I don't want the boys to think I'm a sissy, too.

I want Jim Sweeney as my friend. His blond hair is buzzed on the sides, but he has thick, long bangs. No one else in my class has a haircut like that. The boys must wear ties, but during recess, Jim takes off his shirt and tie and plays ball behind the school in his white undershirt. He rolls up the sleeves just like Bud Anderson on *Father Knows Best*.

The kids not playing ball hang out in the empty parking lot, which is divided in half: boys by the street, girls by the school. Between the two sections, Sister Anna walks back and forth in such a straight line it's as if it's painted on the blacktop. Sometimes I walk behind her, my head slanted just so to the right, my hands folded in prayer and pressed against my lips, exactly like the nun. Everyone laughs, and when she turns around, I stand there innocently. One day, she coughs, and I see blood on her handkerchief. I don't make fun of her after that.

I usually stand right on the edge of Sister Anna's invisible line and talk to a couple of girls about what we watched on television the night before. Or about Jim Sweeney, who's always getting into trouble.

One day in class, I drew a picture of him with his bangs across his eyes. I think it looks pretty good, but then I'm afraid someone will see it, especially Jim, who sits across the aisle from me, so I tear it into tiny pieces and stack them at the corner of my desk. When Sister Robert Marie turns her back to write on the board, Jim reaches over and brushes the pile of scraps off my desk. Snowflakes flutter to the floor just as she turns around. Sister Robert Marie stops talking, and when the last little scrap has landed, she tells Jim Sweeney to pick them up.

The whole class watches him kneel next to me. My heart beats very fast. I think he will threaten me, say something like, "I'll get you, Dimora," but when he looks up at me, his eyes are wet behind his blond bangs. I bend over and help him pick up the tiny pieces of paper.

Every so often, the boys behind the school get tired of playing ball. Then they go after Philip. Five or six boys chase him into the trees as he screams like the Bride of Frankenstein. They hold him down, then Jim Sweeney opens Philip's belt buckle and unzips his fly. Jim and another boy pull down Philip's slacks. Then Jim yanks down Philip's underpants.

"Still no hair," Jim says. Then he and the other boys run away laughing.

I wonder if Jim has hair. I don't.

Philip's skin is as white as his shorts. I offer a hand and help him up. He dresses and walks away without saying "thank you."

I lean against a tree and think of Jim Sweeney pulling down my pants.

UNCLE NICK BUYS a Lionel train set. He wants to build a miniature village in his basement with the tracks twisting along streets and through a tunnel. It's supposed to be a father-son project, but Nick Junior isn't interested. He'd rather zoom through the neighborhood with the other boys on their bikes. Once Uncle Nick sees how careful I am, he lets me paint the little houses he builds out of balsa wood. He even lets me select the colors. I paint pale blue houses with dark blue doors and shutters, white ones with dark green trim, yellow with black, and tan with brown. Only one house in the village has a red door.

"Who lives there?" Uncle Nick asks.

I shrug my shoulders, but I know that's where Jim Sweeney lives.

Uncle Nick buys flashing lights and guard posts that go up and down when the train crosses a street. He buys plastic miniature trees and shrubs, a herd of cattle, and six chickens. He buys toy cars and trucks, stop signs, and billboards. One day, he brings in a bag of tiny pebbles, and we build a wishing well in the village square. Just when I think we're done, Uncle Nick buys another train set and lays more tracks.

Now that there are two trains with separate controls, Nick Junior and his friend Jack race the trains around the turns until one of them derails. After they leave, I fix the damage before Uncle Nick comes home.

Jack, who lives down the street, and Nick Junior are already teenagers, two years older than Nick Junior's sister, Rose, and me. Jack's sister Kimberly is twelve. Sometimes, when our mothers have coffee downstairs, the five of us play Monopoly in Nick Junior's bedroom. He always sits close to Kimberly and presses his knee against hers. She doesn't seem to mind. When I press my knee against Jack, he moves away.

One day, I buy Park Place after already owning the utilities and a railroad, and Jack says he's tired of playing.

"Let's go around the board one more time." I'm ready for my turn.

"Naw, I quit," says Nick Junior.

"You don't want to play because I'm winning."

"I don't want to play because it's boring." Nick Junior sweeps his hand across the board, scattering the houses and hotels.

I see something pink peeking out of his shorts. "You aren't wearing any underwear!"

"Yuck!" screams Kimberly, and she and Rose run out of the room.

"Now look what you've done," Nick Junior says.

"I didn't do anything. You're the one who's flapping his—"

"My what? My *pee-pee*? Is that what you still call it? Can you say 'penis'? How about 'dick'? Or 'cock'?" He shoves my shoulder.

"I think he wants to see it," says Jack.

I feel my face turn red.

"I think he wants to suck it," Nick says, and pushes me flat on the floor. He kneels over my chest, pulls up the leg of his shorts, and points his penis at my mouth. "Do you want to suck my dick?"

"Anthony!" Mommy calls from downstairs. "We're leaving."

Nick Junior hops off my chest. "Saved once again by your mama."

Before I can get up, Jack flops on top of me. I expect him to be heavy, but his weight feels nice, like an extra blanket when it's cold. He puts his mouth right next to my ear and whispers. "I don't think Anthony wants to be saved."

"Come on, Jack." Nick Junior jabs his sneaker in Jack's side, then he runs out of the room and down the stairs. "Mom, I'm hungry!"

Jack pats my cheek, then hurries after his friend.

I lie alone on the floor in Nick Junior's bedroom. Panting.

"SIT DOWN, ANTHONY. I have some exciting news!" Mommy takes my schoolbooks out of my hands and puts them on the kitchen table.

I don't care how exciting the news is. I'm home from school and want my cookies and milk. Mom pats my chair, and I sit down.

"You're going to have a little brother or sister." She has put on fresh lipstick, and her lips are very red. "Isn't that wonderful?

"I guess so."

She looks disappointed I'm not jumping up and down. "What's wrong? I thought you'd be happy."

"Where will the baby sleep?" I have my bedroom just the way I want it. In the top drawer of my desk, I've lined up all my color pencils like a rainbow. On the bulletin board above my desk, I pin all my drawings of cars.

"For the first few months, the baby will sleep in your old bassinet in Daddy's and my room. I'll have to feed him every few hours. But when he's older, we'll put a crib in the sewing room."

"When will the baby come?"

"In seven months. After Christmas."

For a while, nothing changes except Mommy's stomach keeps growing. I don't see what's so exciting about feeling the baby kick. It's weird.

ON SUNDAYS, I'M an altar boy. St. Helen has two Masses. At eleven o'clock is High Mass, with incense and twelve tall candles burning. Even though it lasts an hour, most of the altar boys like to serve at High Mass because there are four of them, and Father Kaiser can't tell which ones don't know the Latin responses. I know my Latin and always serve at six-thirty Low Mass, when there are only two altar boys. We light two short candles, and there's no incense or choir. The best part is it's over in thirty minutes.

We live only two streets from St. Helen, and I usually walk to church in the dark. It's a little spooky, but I pretend I'm one of the Hardy Boys.

One Sunday, it snows while I walk to church, and it's still snowing after Mass, but now the wind is blowing, so I keep my head down. I'm almost at the end of the parking lot before I see our Ford parked across the street. I run across the street. Daddy's come to pick me up!

When Mommy opens her door, I push against her seat to tilt it forward so I can crawl into the back. But she doesn't budge.

"Your mom's having the baby," Daddy says. "I'm taking her to the hospital. Go over to Nick and Lily's. She'll make you breakfast. I'll call as soon as the baby's born, but it could be a while."

"Be a good boy, Anthony." Mommy looks like she's in too much pain to smile.

I run all the way to Uncle Nick's house. After I eat a bowl of Rice Krispies, I go outside and build a snow fort. Rose says it's too cold to play outside, and Nick Junior spent the night at Jack's, so I have the whole front yard to myself. I build the walls so high that when I sit inside, no one can see me, but I carve out three small windows so I can look out. When I see Nick Junior and Jack coming down the street, I stay real quiet, but they come into the fort anyway.

"Hey, that's pretty neat."

I can't believe Nick Junior says something nice to me.

Jack takes off his gloves and pats the wall. "It's too bad it's going to melt so soon."

"No, it won't, Jack." I point to the sky. "The sun's not shining, and it's too cold for it to melt."

"We don't need the sun to make it melt."

Jack unzips his fly and pees on the wall. He makes a big yellow *J* that indents the snow. Nick Junior makes an *N* on another wall. I know they expect me to beg them to stop and to cry when they won't, so instead, I make an *A*.

After supper, Nick Junior does his homework. I already did mine on Friday, so I lie on the floor and draw while he sits at his desk. He takes off his sneakers and throws them at me. I toss them right back.

I wonder where I'm going to sleep tonight. Nick Junior has only one twin bed.

"I hate homework. I hate school." He slams his book shut. "Let's play monster."

"How do you play that?"

"I'm Godzilla, and you're the town, and I destroy you."

"That doesn't sound like much fun."

"Not for you.... Hey, I'll show you something really neat, but you gotta promise not to tell anyone."

"I promise."

He shuts his door, then opens the bottom drawer of his desk and takes out a magazine from underneath a stack of comic books. It's called *Playboy*.

Nick Junior lies next to me, flipping the pages. There are lots of pictures of women in underwear. One woman with blonde hair wears black panties with ruffles. She holds something up to her chest that's also black. I squint, but I can't tell what it is.

"What's she got in her hand?"

"You aren't supposed to be looking at her hands, dummy!"

There's a knock at the door. Nick Junior quickly slides the magazine under his stomach as Aunt Lily walks in.

"You have a baby brother," she says. "His name is Robert."

I DON'T THINK "Baby Bobby" is cute. He's red and tiny and cries too much.

Aunt Lily comes over and helps with housework and cooking, but she doesn't cook as well as Mommy. And she won't let me lie quietly next to Mommy when she's taking a nap.

One day, when I come home from school, Mommy tells me to sit down at the kitchen table.

"Are you going to have another baby?"

"No, Anthony." She smiles just for a second. "Daddy wants me to talk to you."

"Did I do something wrong?"

"No, honey, but you're growing up, and he thinks that you're too old to keep calling him 'Daddy.'"

I look at the Aunt Jemima cookie jar on the counter. "What does he want me to call him?"

"'Dad.'"

"What should I call you?"

"'Mom,' I guess." Mommy—Mom goes to the refrigerator, pours out a glass of milk, and puts it in front of me. She lifts off Aunt Jemima's head and takes two oatmeal cookies, puts them on a napkin, and places them next to the milk.

But I don't eat them. "When Bobby starts to talk, will he be allowed to call him 'Daddy'?"

"He'll probably say 'Dada' at first, but little boys take after their big brothers, so he'll probably say 'Dad,' too." She sits down in the chair next to me. She looks at her hands, at her chipped fingernail polish. Then she looks in my eyes. "Your father also thinks you're too old to kiss him anymore."

Why is she telling me this? Why isn't Daddy telling me himself? "What do *you* think?" I ask.

She twists her lips. "I don't think a child is ever too old to kiss his parents. But that's what your father wants, so you must obey him." She pushes the cookies closer to me. "There's one more thing. Your father also thinks you're too old to play with your Teddy bear."

So, I'm too old to call him 'Daddy,' too old to kiss him, and too old to have a Teddy bear. Grown-ups have a lot of rules. "Do I have to throw Teddy away like I did my paper dolls?"

"No, honey. Just keep him in your closet so Daddy doesn't see him."

"You mean so *Dad* doesn't see him." I eat my cookies.

That night, when I go to bed, I kiss Mom but not Dad. I don't even say "good night" to him.

Age twelve

Growing

"MARY! Anthony! Come see this."

We hurry into the living room. Dad picks up Bobby and stands him in the palm of his right hand, holding Bobby's chest with his left hand. He slowly moves his right arm away from his body, and when it is outstretched, he takes away his left hand. One-year-old Bobby stands in the middle of Dad's hand and smiles.

"Rusty, he's going to fall." Mom's face is wrinkled with concern.

"No, he won't." But Dad takes Bobby in his arms.

When Uncle Nick comes over, Dad shows him his "little trick with Bobby." He shows Aunt Lily. He shows Nick Junior and Rose. He shows anyone who will watch. Anyone who will clap.

Every evening when Dad comes home, he asks the same question. "Did he take a step today?"

Dad stands Bobby on the floor in front of the sofa. Then he backs away and reaches his hands toward him. "Come to Daddy."

Bobby drops down and crawls to him.

Dad positions Bobby on his feet and lifts his legs toward the ceiling, swaying back and forth, playing Airplane, just like we did when I was a baby. I wonder if they will play Submarine someday.

Finally, one day, Bobby takes a step. Then two. Three. He's walking.

It doesn't take Dad long to start tossing a ball at him.

I'm glad. Now Dad can make Bobby his sports star, and I can stay inside and read. We don't have the big maroon chair anymore. Now Dad has a La-Z-Boy recliner in tan vinyl. He holds Bobby in his arms, and I sit cross-legged on the floor while we watch *Leave It to Beaver*.

I don't mind losing Dad. But I miss Daddy.

"ANTHONY, HELP YOUR mother set the table."

"It's okay, Rusty," Mom says. We're fine. Let him watch his movie."

Dad whispers to her, "Why do you have to contradict me in front of my friends?"

"They're in the backyard. I'm sure they didn't hear."

Tony Tomasso and Rags Gernano have come from Castleton to visit Dad and Uncle Nick.

"Well, they're hungry," Dad says. "How much longer is it going to be?"

"I just put the rigatoni in." Mom's voice is as impatient as Dad's. "Do you think your pals can wait fifteen minutes?"

Dad scoops up Bobby and takes him outside.

"Don't you drop him!" Mom shouts after him.

Mrs. Gernano, Aunt Lily, and Rose set the table. When Mom says dinner's ready, Dad yells for me to turn off the television and come to the table.

"But, Dad, there's only ten minutes left."

"Your mother has spent all afternoon preparing this meal, and my friends have driven all the way from Castleton, so the least you can do is come to the table when it's ready."

"No one will care if I'm not there."

"I said to come to the table, and I mean it!"

"It's Alfred Hitchcock, Dad. I want to see the ending."

"I don't care if it's Bishop Sheen." Dad stomps to the TV and turns it off. I walk toward the dining room with my head down. Dad slaps the back of my neck. "Don't pout."

"Rigatoni. My favorite," Tony says. "Bet you can't guess why."

"Because it ends with –*toni*. I'm twelve, not four."

"I thought your favorite was cannelloni," Rags says to Tony. "It's so long and creamy."

Nick Junior giggles.

Tony sprinkles Romano cheese on his pasta. He has more hair on his knuckles than Uncle Nick. "What movie were you watching?"

"*Lifeboat.*"

"Oh, I remember that one," says Aunt Lily.

"The first time I saw *Lifeboat* was with your dad when we were in the Coast Guard," says Tony. "It's quite a doozy."

I look at the man sitting next to me. "Do you like Alfred Hitchcock?"

Before Tony can answer, Rags says, "He likes all kinds of—"

"Rags!" Mrs. Gernano frowns at her husband.

"I watch *Alfred Hitchcock Presents* every Sunday night," Tony says. "Sometimes I even figure out the ending before it happens."

"There's no murder mystery in *Lifeboat*. It's not like *Suspicion* or *Spellbound.*"

"No, but it's suspenseful. Hitchcock's known as 'The Master of Suspense,'" Tony says. No one else at the table is paying attention to our conversation. They're shoving food into their mouths. "*Lifeboat* was made during World War II. If I remember correctly, there's a lot of anti-German propaganda."

"What's 'propaganda'?"

"It's like lying on a mass scale, like spreading Communism."
Tony pats my hand. "Tell you what, Anthony. After dinner, you
and I will go for a walk, and I'll tell you how *Lifeboat* ends."

"I have to dry the dishes."

"Okay, you dry, I'll wash."

"The ladies will do the dishes," Dad says.

"They've been slaving over this delicious meal while we've
been in the backyard drinking beer," Tony says. "Anthony and
I can do the dishes. We don't mind, do we, kid?"

Dad gets a look on his face like he's about to explode, so
Mom asks Mrs. Gernano what's been happening in Castleton.
Rags asks Nick Junior what sports he's playing.

Homemade apple pie is the dessert, and although everyone
is "stuffed," they each have a warm slice topped with melting
vanilla ice cream. Mom puts Bobby to bed, while Rose and Mrs.
Gernano clear the table, and Aunt Lily puts away the leftovers.
Then Tony shoos them out of the kitchen.

"You ladies put your feet up and watch television."

Dad and Rags go over to Uncle Nick's house for cigars and
brandy. Nick Junior takes off on his bike.

"I don't know what's gotten into my dad," I tell Tony when
we're alone in the kitchen. "I can't seem to please him anymore.
Everything I do annoys him. Last Saturday, we were watching
Perry Mason, and during a commercial, I said the sister did it
and even explained why, and it turned out I was right. Dad said
it was just a lucky guess. He seemed furious I had figured it out."

"Fathers are funny sometimes. They want the best for their
kids but resent it when the kids do better than they do."

"Is your father still alive?"

"Oh, sure, but we don't see much of each other, even though we live only a few streets apart." Tony winks. "So how far did you get in *Lifeboat*? Was Tallulah's typewriter tossed overboard yet?"

MR. and Mrs. Gernano sleep at Uncle Nick's. Tony sleeps on our foldout sofa—my old bed. During the night, I wake up and go to the bathroom. The TV is on in the living room, Tony is sitting up, his head silhouetted against the blue glow. It's the same color as my pajamas.

I softly clear my throat so I won't startle him. "What are you watching?"

"*Casablanca*."

"You have the sound so low, how can you hear what's going on?"

"I've seen this movie half-a-dozen times. I don't need to hear it to know what's happening."

"I like black-and-white movies."

"Sit down." Tony pats a spot next to him. He's not wearing a pajama top. Black hair hides his chest. "Watch with me until you get sleepy."

I lift the sheet to get in beside him. "You're naked!"

"I haven't worn pajamas since I was a teenager. I don't even own a pair. And I hate sleeping in underwear I've worn all day. I always sleep in the nude. Don't tell your mom, or she'll boil the sheets."

We sit staring at the screen, our hands folded on our laps.

"Tony, can I ask you a question?"

"You just did."

I nearly say, "Can I ask you another question?" but realize that's one too.

"What do you want to know?"

I exhale. "I know babies grow inside a woman, but how do they get started?"

"How old are you?"

"I'll be thirteen next month."

"No one's talked to you about this at school?"

"I go to a Catholic school."

"Right. And your father never said anything?"

"He talked about the woman's egg and the man's seed, but he never said how it gets inside her."

"Do you think you know the answer?"

I nod.

"And you just want someone to confirm what you're thinking?"

I nod again.

"Well, Anthony, it is what you're thinking, but just so there isn't any confusion, I'll spell it out."

I watch the piano man silently sing "Time Goes By" as Tony talks softly.

"Do you have any other questions?"

"No. I'll go back to bed now. Thank you."

When I get to my room, I take off my pajamas. The sheets cool my burning skin.

MY BIRTHDAY PRESENT arrives early.

Dad, Uncle Nick, Rags, and Nick Junior drive to Cincinnati to see the Red Sox play. Tony and I go to a movie. Not having to go to a stupid baseball game is a wonderful gift, but that's not my present.

Even though Tony's old enough to be my father, he doesn't

treat me like a kid. We talk about all sorts of things, including religion. I'm surprised he hasn't gone to Mass in thirteen years. He said he stopped when he was overseas during World War II and never felt the need to go back.

I suggest we see *Vertigo*, even though I've already seen it, because I didn't really understand it, and we both like Alfred Hitchcock; but Tony's also seen it and has another idea. "Do you like musicals?"

"I like the singing, but I don't care that much about the dancing."

"Well, there's a movie playing here that hasn't come to Castleton yet, and I'd really like to see it."

"What's it called?

"*Gigi.*"

"I read about it in Mom's movie magazine. It has that old lady with the weird name. I saw her on the George Gobel show. She's funny."

"Hermione Gingold."

After the movie, we go to Farmers for ice cream.

"Do you want my cherry? I don't like them." I hold it up by the stem, and Tony snaps it between his teeth like a fish taking the bait.

"My favorite song was 'The Night They Invented Champagne.'" Tony digs into his butterscotch sundae. "Which one did you like best, Anthony?"

"The one where Hermione puts down that snooty Frenchman, who got everything wrong. He thinks they met in April, and it was June. He thinks it was sunny, and it rained. He says she wore a gold gown, and it was blue."

"That 'snooty Frenchman' is Maurice Chevalier and probably France's most beloved actor."

"Yeah, well, he's a ham." I scoop up a spoonful of my banana split. "How much older than Gigi do you think Gaston is?"

"About ten years, I guess."

"Oh, so not old enough to be her father."

Spending the afternoon with Tony is very nice, but that isn't my birthday present either. I find it when I take off my clothes in the bathroom. Three black curly hairs right above my penis. I stand under the shower and twist them around my finger, careful not to pull them out. Pubic hair at last! Well, at least a start. Happy birthday to me.

I keep turning down the cold water so the hot beats on my chest. It nearly scalds me, but it feels good, like the stinging of belly flops in the pool. I push my penis forward and let hot water pound it as it gets harder and bigger. Soon a white gooey liquid shoots out. It feels incredible.

I remember watching Daddy. I mean Dad.

Age thirteen

Grandmothers

"I WANT TO go home for Christmas, Rusty."

"This is your home." Dad doesn't look up from the *Dayton Daily News.*

"You know what I mean. I want to go to Castleton." Mom hands him a plate of waffles. "I miss my sisters, and I haven't seen Connie's new baby."

"Fine, we'll go to Castleton." He pours on maple syrup. "I can see some of my old buddies."

"Don't you want to see your family?"

"You know my family isn't close like yours."

"Anthony wants to visit your father and Mama Luisa."

Dad looks up at me. I nod eagerly.

"So, you and Anthony visit them."

"It's been more than three years, Rusty," Mom says. "Isn't it time you talk to them again?"

Dad turns to the comics.

Mom sighs. "I don't understand how you can go to Confession every Friday and take Communion every Sunday and yet still not forgive your father and grandmother for something that had happened more than twenty-five years ago."

Dad holds up his coffee cup. "Is there more coffee?"

"It's in the pot." As she leaves the room, Mom raises her

eyebrows at me.

Mom knows how to get what she wants. Early Christmas Eve morning, as we drive to Pennsylvania, Dad leads the Rosary. We each have our own set of beads. Mom and I made them years ago.

"Hail, Mary, full of grace! The Lord is with thee. Blessed art thou among women and blessed is the fruit of thy womb, Jesus." Dad nods his head.

"Holy Mary, mother of God," Mom and I respond, "pray for us sinners, now and at the hour of our death."

"Amen," we all say, even Bobby, who's two years old.

Of course, I know the words by heart. I watch the road for new-model cars. I want to see a 1958 Chrysler DeSoto. The 1957 model is beautiful, much sleeker than the '56. Just like the ads say, it has "The Forward Look," the most futuristic car on the road with its smooth, soaring fins. And forget two-tone. The DeSoto has *three* colors: the main body, the roof, and a "sweep" on the side. The '58 model isn't changed much—four headlights instead of two, new side paneling—but so far, I've only seen pictures.

I'm stuck in the back seat of our same old 1949 black Ford. Once we're done with the Rosary, I read an Agatha Christie mystery.

"You'll get a headache," Mom warns.

We eat fried-egg sandwiches that Mom packed. Dad sips coffee from a thermos. Bobby and I have a treat: small cartons of chocolate milk. Dad had said we were in no hurry, we'd have a leisurely drive, but he races along the highway and stops only twice for "potty breaks" on the five-hour drive.

That evening, we have Grandma Peruzzi all to ourselves, but on Christmas, Mom's sisters join us. Aunt Joan, Uncle Phil, and the twins, Donny and Ronny, drive in from their farm. Aunt Connie and Uncle Vic bring their three girls and the new baby. Aunt Anna and Uncle Larry arrive next with their new Chihuahua, Pedro. Mom gets lots of hugs and kisses. She's the only Peruzzi sister to have moved away from Castleton.

Since the last time I saw my cousins, they have grown out of being mirror twins. Now fifteen, they have far-apart brown eyes with thick brows, but Donny's lips are thicker and his smile wider. His face is longer, and Ronny's ears stick out too far. Mom says Donny is now a bit taller than his brother.

"That's because I'm older," he says.

"By three minutes." Ronny rolls his eyes, as if they've played this scene as many times as a couple of old vaudeville comics.

Donny is also thinner. Maybe they don't like being identified as twins because they have different haircuts. Donny's is thick and greased back like Elvis Presley, while Ronny's is shorter and parted like Tab Hunter. They're both as cute as Billy Gray on *Father Knows Best*. Ronny says "hi" to me and gives Mom a hug. Donny heads to the refrigerator without saying a word to me.

Eating some grapes, Donny tells everyone a sow at the farm gave birth to four piglets last night. Aunt Coreen's girls want to go see them. I'd like to be with Donny, but the last time I visited the farm, I was miserable because of allergies, probably because of the hay and the animals, so I stayed at Grandma's. At exactly noon, the women start preparing for the big meal. I help Aunt Joan put pads on the dining room table. We spread out a white tablecloth, then placed a lace one on top.

"Your grandmother crocheted this by hand," she says. "It took her a year."

"It's pretty," I say, even though I think it's old-fashioned. "But I like modern furniture."

"You mean all that plastic stuff and blond veneer?" Aunt Joan scrunches her nose.

"I like the simple, smooth lines," I explain.

She takes out "the good china" from a display cabinet and wipes off each piece with her apron before handing it to me to put at each place. These are not thick, heavy plates made at the Shenago factory, but so light that if I hold one up to the window, the sun almost shines through. The border of each plate is a circle of raised roses in a rainbow of reds.

Aunt Joan opens the bottom drawer of the sideboard and lifts out a heavy leather case. "Grandma was given this on her wedding day by her mother, who was given it by *her* mother. I hate to think of the fight over who will get this when she dies." Aunt Joan makes the sign of the cross and stares at the box as if it contains a religious object, but when she opens it, all that's inside is silverware. The handles are decorated with more roses. "Count out ten pieces each," she tells me. "Knives, forks, and spoons."

I place the silverware next to the plates. "Was Grandma born in America?"

"Yes, in Jamestown, Virginia. But when she was about five or six, her family went back to Italy. Her mother was homesick and never liked it here." She watches me. "It's amazing, you know what side of the plate the forks and knives go on. If I let my boys have their way, they'd eat everything with a soup spoon. Or their hands!"

"I always set the table at home. Did Grandpa and Grandma meet in Italy?"

"Yes, we did." Grandma stands in the doorway, wiping her hands on a hand-embroidered dish towel. "We met in San Marco Evangelista, outside of Naples, when I was sixteen, and we got married in less than a year."

"When did you come to America?"

"They came for their honeymoon and never left," Mom says. She carries in a tray of napkins that she's folded into swans.

I carefully place a napkin in the center of each plate. "Where'd you spend your honeymoon, Grandma?"

"In New York City," she says. "We landed at Ellis Island, and New York was right there, so we stayed a few days. We didn't have money to stay very long. Then we took the train to Castleton." She smiles at me. "Joan, if you're finished in here, grate the provolone. I'm going to start the pasta, and everyone better be back from the farm on time, if they want it *al dente*."

"They'll be here," Mom says. "They know not to disobey you."

"Anthony," Grandma says, and I snap to attention. "Do you want to finish making the antipasto?"

On my way to the pantry, I see Aunt Connie and Aunt Anna setting the kitchen table, where the children will eat. No lace tablecloth for us. We get the everyday china and paper napkins.

"Anna, fill all the glasses with water," Grandma commands. "Connie, slice the bread—and don't get crumbs all over the floor."

"What about Mary?" Aunt Anna pushes her orange-blond hair behind her ears. Mom says it's dyed. "All Mary's done is fold silly napkins."

"Mary, would you toss the salad so that Anna doesn't get in a snit?" Grandma nods toward the sink. "Connie, wash your hands before you cut the bread."

Carrying four trays of ice cubes, Aunt Anna rushes to the sink. "Don't splash hot water on the ice," she says, elbowing Aunt Connie.

"Then wait 'til I'm finished." Aunt Connie pushes her sister away with her hip.

I put three kinds of olives on a large platter with salami, anchovies, lupini beans, and chunks of asiago cheese. Suddenly, there's a lot of noise on the back porch. They've returned from the farm.

"I'm starved!" Donny rushes into the pantry. "What'd you make for me?" He stuffs a piece of salami into his mouth. And pinches my butt.

AFTER DINNER, EVERYONE leaves to drop off Christmas presents at their other relatives, but they return in the evening to Grandma's. That's what we call the large redbrick house. Grandma's. Not Grandpa and Grandma's. Aunt Joan describes Grandma as "the magnet of love."

The adults sit around the kitchen table talking. Grandpa is at his regular seat by the window, drinking his homemade wine. Whenever there is loud laughter, he turns to Grandma, who tells him, in Italian, what's so funny. He chuckles and takes another sip of wine. Grandma opens the refrigerator behind her and puts out grapes. Grandpa stretches his crooked fingers, and she pushes the plate closer.

In a little while, Grandpa shuffles down to his wine cellar in the basement. Donny and Ronny follow him. I go after them.

Lining the two longest walls of the small wine cellar are wide shelves holding four wooden barrels of homemade wine. Grandpa pours wine into small juice glasses and hands them to us. I wonder if he realizes I'm only thirteen.

"*Centellinare*. Sip," Grandpa says when Donny chugs his, but he refills the glass.

Grandpa rolls a cigarette. Donny takes a crushed cigarette out of his back pocket. He straightens it, lights up, and inhales deeply. Then he hands the cigarette to Ronny, who takes a puff. They're fifteen, and I know they will think I'm a baby, but I shake my head when Ronny offers it to me. Cigarettes smell good when they're first lit, but I hate the smell of stale smoke. I don't want it on my clothes, especially my new sweater from Grandma.

Grandpa sits on a stool in the center of the narrow room. Ronny leans against one of the barrels. Donny sits on a shelf, one leg crossed over the other. His sock is down to his ankle, and between it and his pants, I can see bare skin. Except it isn't bare. It's covered with black hair.

I wonder if Ronny's legs are just as hairy. Do they have hair on their chests? Do they compare who has the most? What else do they compare?

I suddenly wish I had a twin.

Ronny asks Grandpa how old he is.

"As old as the century."

"Do you know why Italians are called *wops*?" Ronny looks at me.

I shake my head.

"Because they came to Ellis Island without any papers. You know, like birth certificates. So their immigration cards were stamped *WOP* for *With Out Papers*."

"But *without* is one word, not two."

"Well, they couldn't stamp it *WP*, because that could mean *With Papers*." Ronny shrugs. "Anyway, that's what my dad told me."

I ask Grandpa why he settled in Castleton.

"Because I had a *cugino*, a cousin, who lived here. He could help me find work."

"Did you live in San Marco Evangelista like Grandma?"

"No. In Caserta. Nearby."

"I saw pictures of your wedding. There were a lot of people there."

"We both have big families."

"*You* have four daughters," Donny says as he puts out his cigarette in a tin ashtray already overflowing with butts. "Do you ever wish you had a son?"

"I had a son," Grandpa says. "He died when he was eight. Burst appendix."

Donny finishes his wine. "Are any of your relatives in the Mafia?"

Grandpa stands up, glaring at Donny as if he's going to slap him. "*Basta domande*! Enough questions! Enough wine! Upstairs!"

Donny stands up.

They're only small wine glasses, but I've had two, and I feel woozy. I sway toward Donny. He puts up a hand to stop me, but I keep going forward. I lean against his chest. I lift my head and kiss his neck.

"You're drunk." He pushes me away from him.

I stumble up the steps, giggling.

"CAN WE VISIT Tony Tomasso?" I've thought about him a lot since he stayed with us. I've slept "in the nude" ever since, but I still put my pajamas in the laundry hamper, so Mom won't know.

Sitting in front of a mirror in Grandma's guest bedroom, Mom pins on a pale blue hat. "I don't think we should drop in on Tony."

"We could call first."

Mom doesn't wear the hat correctly. I've seen it in a magazine. It has a veil that's supposed to cover the eyes, but Mom rolls up the lace so that it's like a headband. "I don't think it's a good idea to visit Tony."

"Why not?"

"I just don't think we should."

"But why not?"

"Because he doesn't live alone." She rummages through her purse, and I know she's hoping I'll just drop the subject, but I won't.

"Who does he live with?"

"Another man."

"What difference does that make?"

Mom glares at my reflection in the mirror, her anger as red as the lipstick she applies. She blots her lips with a Kleenex. "Why can't you find a friend your own age? First, it was Frank; now, it's Tony Tomasso. He's old enough to be your father."

"And he treats me like a son."

"What's what supposed to mean?"

"He asks me about the things I'm interested in, like books and movies."

"Everyone's interested in books and movies." She puts on white gloves.

"I've never seen Dad read a book."

"Your dad's busy."

"Yeah, playing basketball."

"Get your coat and go see if Grandma has Bobby bundled up. Your father's ready to drive us to Mama Luisa's."

"Is Dad really not going to come in with us?"

"He's going to the Sons of Italy to have a drink with his pals. Maybe Tony Tomasso will be there, and when we're ready to leave, you can go say 'hi'."

Mama Luisa has a buffet spread out on her dining room table. "Who knows," she says, "who might drop by?"

A lot of people bring presents. They fix a plate and drink eggnog. Mama Luisa isn't up and down like Grandma Peruzzi, who always puts out more dishes, always coaxes you to eat one more anise cookie. Mama Luisa never moves from her green velvet armchair by the window. She smiles and nods. She offers advice. And all the while, she glances out the window. I know who she's looking for.

"What was my dad like when he was a kid?" I ask her.

"He was a good boy. He seldom got into trouble at school. Once in a while, he would swear, trying to impress the older boys, but I took care of that." She slaps her hand in the air, and now I know where Dad learned to cuff me in the back of my neck. "He was smart and got good grades, and his teachers liked him. I knew other boys teased him for being the "goodie," but he never came crying to me. He always defended himself. And he was good at sports, right from the beginning. He loved playing with the older boys. He made a lot of friends that way. They'd play football with a tin can."

I know boys picked on Dad because of his red hair, but I'm surprised they teased him about being good. "Is it true he was a numbers runner?"

"Anthony!" Mom is talking with one of the neighbors, but she's keeping an eye—and ear—on me.

"It's okay, Mary." Mama Luisa looks out the window while she talks. "That was a long time ago. Some of the neighbors said I was corrupting him, but I didn't see the harm in Rusty collecting the bets. He learned about money and people. And I needed someone to help me. It was just me and Rusty. His father wasn't much help, not once he remarried. And I wanted Rusty to have nice things. I made sure he had nice clothes. They weren't hand-me-downs. I probably spoiled him."

"What was it like during the Depression?"

"Mama Luisa doesn't want to talk about those dark days," Mom says.

"Why not?" Mama Lusia smiles. "I survived them. It was a rough time, but we never went on relief. Sometimes people would trade food for my services. You know I was a midwife, don't you?"

I nod.

"We were one of the few families who owned a radio. On Friday nights, I'd put it in the front window, and our neighbors would sit on the porch and hear the fights. Fighting was big then." Mama Luisa finally turns away from the window. "Here come the Parones from across the street. Let them in, will you, Anthony?"

There are at least eight of them, and I take advantage of the noise to whisper to Mom. "Can I go to next door now?"

"Yes, and tell your father I'll be ready to leave in half an hour."

When I walk into the Sons of Italy, everyone looks at me.

"Over here," Dad calls. He's drinking beer with Rags and Tony.

Tony asks if I want a Coke. I shake my head. Rags tells a dirty joke, looking at me to see if I get it. I do, but it isn't funny, just crude. Like Rags.

Light floods in as the door opens. Everyone looks to see who's arrived. It's Grandpa Dimora. Heads turn toward Dad, then back to Grandpa. It's like a Western, with everyone expecting a duel. I guess they all know that Dad broke his father's wrist four years ago, and they haven't talked since.

Grandpa walks right by our table.

Afraid no one will talk, I say, "Hi, Grandpa!"

"Hi, Anthony. Did you have a nice Christmas?"

I nod. Dad doesn't say anything.

"Come tell me about all the presents you got."

Grandpa sits at the next table, his back to Dad.

While Grandpa and I talk, I watch Dad drink three glasses of beer, one right after the other. Then he walks over to our table.

"Anthony, go talk with Tony." He sits in my place, facing Grandpa.

When I sit down, Rags moves to another table. I'm glad.

"How about that Coke now?" Tony asks.

"Do they have root beer?"

Tony goes to a small bar in the back.

I look at the photographs on the wall, pretending not to eavesdrop. Grandpa and Dad haven't said anything about what happened four years ago. They talk as if they just saw each other last week.

"I can't remember my mother," Dad says. "I see the wedding photo, but I can't see *her*."

"You were just over a year old when your mother died," Grandpa says. "You can't expect to remember her."

"What did she look like?"

"Rosa was beautiful. Her hair was red like a blood orange. She didn't wear it up, like most Italian women. It was thick and wavy and reached halfway down to her waist."

"But she was Italian?"

"Of course she was. Her family was from Torino. Near France."

"When did they come to America?"

"I don't remember exactly. Around the turn of the century. Rosa was born here in 1903. First generation."

Tony puts a frosty glass in front of me. "*Auntie Mame* opens in Pittsburgh tomorrow. Do you think your folks would let you go see it with me?"

"I don't know. I asked Mom if we could visit you on this trip, and she said no."

"Did she say why not?"

"Because you live with another man, but I don't see what that has to do with anything. Is he here at the Sons of Italy?"

"He's not Italian. He's Irish." Tony sips his wine. "Listen, we'll go to a movie some other time." He traces a finger along the green checks of the tablecloth.

"Aren't you going to visit Mama Luisa?" I hear Grandpa ask Dad.

"Next trip," Dad says. "I can't see her right now, okay? I'm afraid I'll say something I'll regret."

"She misses you. You were more of a son to her than I was. She's an old woman. Go see her, Rusty. I just came from there, and she's sitting by the window praying you'll come by."

"Next time."

THERE IS NO next time. Dad gets a call from Tony.

"Mama Luisa died," Dad says after he hangs up the phone. "She had a heart attack. The funeral's Thursday."

Driving back to Castleton, just two months after we had been there, we recited the Rosary once again. Dad dedicates it to Mama Luisa.

It seems as if the whole town has come to pay its respects. The funeral home is crowded, and there are no empty seats in the church. The caravan to the cemetery is nearly a mile long. There are flowers everywhere.

Standing in front of the open grave with the casket on top, a priest speaks about Mama Luisa's good works. I hear sobbing behind me. Several people wipe their eyes and sniffle.

The Dimora men stand in a row on either side of me. Grandpa Dimora. Uncle Nick. Dad. Nick Junior. They stare straight ahead. Not one tear. They won't cry. Not in front of everyone. Not in front of the other Sons of Italy.

Age fourteen

Suddenly

"YOU KNOW WHAT I gave your father for his fourteenth birthday?" Uncle Nick asks me a few days after my fourteenth birthday. He rolls beige paint on a wall. He likes to do the big areas, and I do the trim. This is the fourth house he's bought to fix up and rent. He pays me fifty cents an hour to help him.

"No, what did you give my father for his fourteenth birthday?"

"A prostitute!"

Uncle Nick enjoys shocking me. "You may not believe it, but your dad was a shy kid. Mama Luisa taught him good manners. He was her 'best little boy'—meaning she really had him under her thumb." Nick smiles. "Not like me."

"You didn't live together, did you?"

"We all lived at Mama Luisa's for a while, but when our dad remarried, I went to live with him and my stepmom. But I was very independent. Nobody told me what to do. And if they did, I didn't pay any attention."

"And the prostitute?"

"Oh, yeah. So, even though Rusty was real good at sports, I thought he was a bit of a wimp and would never get a girl on his own. So, when he turned fourteen, I drove him to this tobacco shop down by the train station in Castleton. They did sell cigars and cigarettes, but it was just a front. Upstairs there were a couple of girls, and for two bucks, you could have one for fifteen minutes."

"Had you been there before?"

"Oh, sure. Not that I was a regular or anything. I always had plenty of girlfriends. Anyway, when we got to the tobacco shop, I said your dad was fifteen, because that's how old you had to be to go with one of the girls. Your dad was real nervous. Practically shaking. There were two guys there—the manager and his big bouncer—and the manager looked at me and said, 'You sure he knows what to do?' That made Rusty even more nervous. I thought he was going to faint. But he went upstairs, and as soon as the men heard the door shut, they looked at their watches."

"Why'd they do that?"

"They were timing him. First-timers never take much time."

"Did Dad say anything afterwards?"

"Yeah, I remember he said she was old enough to be his mother, but that he liked it that she undressed him."

"Does my mom know all this?"

"No, and don't you tell her. Or your Aunt Lily."

"I won't. I can keep a secret. Did you take Nick Junior to a prostitute when he turned fourteen?"

"I didn't have to." Uncle Nick smiled like the wolf in *Little Red Riding Hood*. "Do you want me to take you to a prostitute?"

"Not this year."

"Yeah, I didn't think so."

DAD'S NOT SUPPOSED to play on the amateur Air Force basketball team since he doesn't work at the base, but Uncle Nick "worked it out." He's good at that.

For a while, Mom and I went to almost every game. Mom has seen Dad play on teams for years, so I was surprised by how excited she still got, standing up and shouting when Dad dribbled the ball down the court, and his team made a basket. I didn't care who won or lost. I just wanted it to be over. Once Bobby was born, Mom stopped going to the games, and so did I. But lately, I started going again with Dad. I still don't care about the game, but I like the locker room.

"Hi, sport!" Uncle Nick rubs my head as I walk in. He's only wearing a white jockstrap. His chest hair is slick with sweat. "Quite a game, huh?"

I say hello to Dad, then take my spot next to a stack of towels. The men on the Castleton team were all Italians with hairy legs and asses. Here, there are all kinds of players. One tall blond man has no chest hair, and his skin is almost as white as the towels. All of them are taller than Dad, who's the only redhead. Each man smells different. It's funny to watch them sniff their armpits as if their sweat is a rare perfume.

After they shower, I hand towels to the dripping men. One night, only Uncle Nick is left still showering.

"Hey, Anthony," he shouts and spins around. He has an erection. His penis is very dark, and it pokes straight out of a mass of thick pubic hair. He laughs, turns off the water, and walks toward me.

My hand shakes as I offer him the last towel.

He winks as his penis goes down.

A week later, Dad, Uncle Nick, Nick Junior, and I drive to Cincinnati to watch the Reds play. During the third inning, the fans jump to their feet and cheer.

Running through possible clues to a murder mystery I had been reading at home, I haven't been paying attention to the game. "What happened?"

"He hit a home run," Dad says. "Didn't you see it? It sailed right over the fence."

"What fence?"

"The green one."

"I don't see it."

"You don't see *300* painted on a green wall?" Dad points beyond center field. "Those letters are six feet high, Anthony!"

I WANT TORTOISESHELL frames for my eyeglasses, but they're too expensive, so I have to settle for black plastic. Walking out of the optician's office, I'm amazed at how clearly I can see the people across the street.

Mom treats us to hot fudge sundaes at White Castle. Sitting across from her, I tell myself I will not taste the whipped cream until I ask the one question that has been bothering me for two weeks. I fidget, afraid to look at her. Maybe she won't know the answer. She hadn't seen what happened in Lake Erie. She hadn't seen Dad try to strangle me when we were wrestling.

"What's the matter, Anthony? Why aren't you eating your sundae? I thought hot fudge was your favorite."

I let out a deep breath. "Does Dad love me?"

"Of course, he loves you! We both love you. Why would you ask such a silly question?"

"When we went to see the Reds, I went to the bathroom, and when I came back, I heard Dad talking to Uncle Nick about me."

"What did he say?"

"He said that when I got glasses, he hoped I'd be a better ballplayer. He said he wished he had a son like Nick Junior. He said, 'Maybe Bobby will be the son I've always wanted.'"

I stuff whipped cream in my mouth.

"He was talking about sports. You know how good Nick Junior is at sports—that's all Dad meant. He wishes you liked to play ball like Nick Junior does. It does *not* mean he doesn't love you."

"Sometimes I wish Dad were more like Uncle Nick. He doesn't care if I like sports or not." I swirl the hot chocolate in circles.

"That's because you aren't his son." She reaches across the table and rubs my hand. "Come on, eat up. We'll miss our bus."

When we're riding back home, she says, "You shouldn't go to the bathroom by yourself at the ballpark."

That night, after carefully wiping my new glasses with a special cloth and placing them in their black case, I lay in bed thinking about what happened at Lake Erie.

IT'S NINE O'CLOCK at night and still so hot my Popsicle drips down my hand. There's no breeze, not even on the porch.

"Where are you going?" I call to Uncle Nick as he leaves his house with his toolbox.

"I have to fix a leaky shower at the pool." He's on our subdivision's board and does most of the repairs. "Want to tag along?"

The pool is three streets over, and although it's almost too hot to walk, I decide to go. Maybe we can go swimming and cool off.

"I don't ever remember a September being this hot," Uncle Nick says. He takes the showerhead apart and inserts a new washer. I walk around the women's locker room. It's just like the men's, except there are no urinals. And there's a plastic chaise chair in one corner.

"Want to play Submarine when you're finished?" I try to sound casual, but my heart is beating so fast.

"Where'd you learn that game?"

"Dad taught me."

"Rusty and I played Submarine as kids. I'd stand in the water, and he'd swim through my legs."

"Didn't you ever swim through his?"

"No, the oldest always has to be the bridge."

"Did other boys play Submarine?"

"Yeah. Tony Tomasso got a kick out of it. He was a funny kid. When I started growing chest hair, he wanted to count it to prove that he had more than I did."

"Who won?"

"I did, of course. I *always* win."

"I hope I grow lots of hair like you, Uncle Nick."

"Some people don't like it."

"Yeah, I remember you telling me Aunt Lily thought it was 'embarrassing' to have it on your back. Why'd she marry you if she didn't like your hair?"

"People get married for all sorts of reasons. Besides, I have other assets." Nick gathers his tools. "Well, I didn't bring my swim trunks, so we'll have to play Submarine some other time."

"We could swim in our underwear," I say, although I really wish we could swim naked.

"A dip would be nice in this heat."

Uncle Nick strips down to pale blue boxer shorts. I have on white briefs. He switches off the lights. "Do you think you can find your way in the dark? It will be better if no one knows we're using the pool this late."

He dives in the water, barely making a splash. I swim laps. Uncle Nick swims beside me, but after two rounds, he stands in the shallow end breathing heavily.

"I'm getting old."

"Old enough to be my father." I dip underwater and swim toward him. I place my hands on his hairy legs, spread them apart, and swim through.

"I forgot to put up my periscope." I make a circle and dive underwater. Opening my eyes, I swim toward him. I raise my right hand. I glide my fingers into his fly.

Uncle Nick grips my wrists as tight as a vise. I hold my breath, hoping he'll let go, but he squeezes tighter. When I come up for air, he glares at me without saying a word. He gets out of the pool and goes to the locker room.

I stand in the water shivering. I can't stay here all night, and I certainly can't walk back home in my underpants. I have to go into the locker room and face my uncle.

We haven't brought towels. Uncle Nick dries himself with his undershirt. With his back turned, he lowers his boxers and steps into his khaki shorts. I take off my briefs and quickly put on my clothes over my wet body. Even though I am afraid of what Uncle Nick might say or do, I feel excited wearing my shorts without underpants.

Uncle Nick stands by the door as I put on my sneakers. I don't bother to tie them. Just as I'm about to walk past him, he pushes me against the cinder block wall. He grabs my wrists again and holds them over my head as if they're handcuffed. He pushes his knee into my groin.

"You're lucky I don't tell your father." His face is only inches away from mine.

I have tears in my eyes. Not because he's hurting me, but because I feel confused and rejected. "When I handed out towels after the basketball game," I say, "you pointed your—your erect cock right at me. Why'd you do that?"

"I thought it was funny."

"Ha ha!"

He looks like he's going to slug me. "I saw where your eyes were looking when the players walked to the showers, and I thought I would shock you. I was just clowning. It didn't mean anything."

It meant something to me.

He pushes me out the door and locks up.

We walk home in silence. Our underwear drips a trail behind us.

"NOW THAT YOU are in high school," announces Brother Hayes, standing in front of the class, "the first thing you must do is forget everything the nuns ever taught you."

I look around the room. None of the boys seems shocked by this statement. A couple nod in agreement; some smile, but most look as though they weren't even listening.

"The nuns are very sweet, but they don't really get out in the world," Brother Hayes continues. "They don't know what it's really like. Here at Chaminade, you'll have the usual high school subjects such as algebra and biology, but in my homeroom, you'll also learn the truth of the world and how you fit in." He stares directly at me. Maybe because I'm the only one who's frowning. I like the nuns and don't want him to put them down.

Brother Hayes looks very young. Maybe he just got out of the seminary. I used to think of becoming a monk. Not because I'm religious. What appealed to me was the solitude and silence of a monastery.

Brother Hayes has blond hair and blue eyes; his skin is almost pink. He is short and very thin. He doesn't wear a cassock, like a priest, but a black wool suit. It's too large on him, as if it were handed down from a bigger brother. He also wears a white shirt and a narrow black tie. His shoes are extremely plain, no design of any sort, but almost as shiny as patent leather.

"All right, everyone, gather up your things and stand in the back of the room," he says. "I find the easiest way to learn my students' names is to have them sit in alphabetical order. You will all sit in the same place each day, so remember where that is." He looks at a sheet of paper and points to the front desk in the first row. "Daniel Adamo." A chubby boy with curly hair scurries to the desk. Brother Hayes moves down the row. "John Brown. Michael Czarnecki. Anthony Dimora."

I take my seat behind Michael Czarnecki. He has the biggest nose I've ever seen. It sticks out from his face like the handle of a coffee mug. His tiny, round mouth is too small for his long face. His eyebrows are slanted down toward his ears. He has black straight hair falling across his forehead.

Brother Hayes stands in front of his desk, looking around the room. His eyes settle on Michael and me. "I sense I'm going to have trouble with you two. You're like two peas in a pod."

How can he say that? During the summer, I grew four inches and lost all my baby fat. I'm much better looking than Michael Czarnecki!

We stay in the same room all day. Every hour, another brother or priest comes in to teach us math, history, religion, science and Latin. The only time we leave the room is for lunch and gym class.

Brother Hayes is also our English teacher. Our first assignment is to write a one-page story based on a recent headline. I am sure he hopes each of us would select a significant event, such as the United States launching two monkeys into space or Alaska becoming the forty-ninth state or Pope John XXIII opening the Second Vatican Council.

The next day, Brother Hayes asks for a volunteer to read his story in front of the class. When no one comes forward, I raise my hand. I chose a headline from one of my mother's movie magazines: *Liz Steals Eddie from Debbie!*

As I read my story about Elizabeth Taylor running off with Debbie Reynolds' husband, Eddie Fisher, several of the boys snicker, and one of them sends a paper airplane in my direction. Brother Hayes tosses a piece of chalk at him.

"That was well written, Anthony," Brother Hayes says, "but not an important subject matter."

When I return to my seat, Michael Czarnecki turns around and says, "I liked it."

Our next assignment is to write a two-page story that is a fantasy or science fiction. We turn in our papers, and in a couple of days, Brother Hayes hands them back and picks who will read his story aloud. I wrote something stupid about robots. I get an *A-*, and he doesn't select me. He calls on Michael Czarnecki. While Michael reads a fantasy about Elizabeth Taylor and Debbie Reynolds both ditching Eddie Fisher and running away together, Brother Hayes stands next to my desk. He puts his hand on my shoulder. His thumb makes circles on my neck so tiny I feel they are our little secret.

Michael invites me to eat lunch with him and his friends. Holding my tray, I look across the room and see "the cool boys" sitting together. They are all so natural. I bet they don't worry about what the other boys think about them. Or even what the teachers think. They all have their ties loosened. I have mine tight against my Adam's apple. So do Michael and his friends.

If Michael hadn't asked me, I would never have sat at the same table as Jerry O'Connor. I'm used to boys calling me a sissy, but I'm not anywhere near as prissy as Jerry. He's small for his age. Maybe he isn't fourteen like the rest of us. He seems very smart, so maybe he skipped a grade. His hands are as delicate as a doll's. The skin is so white, I wonder if he wears gloves outside. If my dad saw Jerry walking down the school hallway, his books clutched to his chest rather than held at his side, he would shake his head in disbelief.

The other boy at the table is Lino Torres, who is from Spain. His skin is darker than any of the Italians I know. I wonder if that is what makes his teeth look so white. His lips don't disappear into a thin line when he smiles, but stay plump. He speaks English with a slight accent. I noticed in gym class that his legs are very hairy. He even has hair on his toes. He also has the only uncircumcised penis in gym class.

After that first day that Michael asked me to join them, the four of us have always had lunch together. Jerry usually does the most talking, his hands darting around like a bee. Lino doesn't say much, but sometimes I catch him looking at me. One day, I quietly press my knee against his leg under the table so Michael and Jerry don't see. Lino doesn't move away.

Since Chaminade is in downtown Dayton, there is no room for a sports field, which means we don't have to play football or baseball. But there is the gym, so there's basketball. Of course, I'm not any good at that, but no one teases me, because there are other things I can do. I climb the thick-coiled rope all the way up to the rafters. Unfortunately, I slide down, peeling the skin off my hands. Well, at least I don't have to go to gym class until I heal.

*

"WHY DOESN'T CHAMINADE have any art classes?" I ask Brother Hayes as I erase the board after the last class of the day.

"We don't have anyone to teach it." He gathers up our latest essays and puts them in his briefcase. "What sort of art are you interested in? Painting?"

"Oh no. I don't want to be an artist. I want to design record albums and book covers. Do they have courses for that in college?"

"At some schools. It's not too early to send away for some college catalogs, Anthony." He takes the eraser out of my hand and puts it on the ledge. "I could help you find out what universities have good art schools."

We stand facing each other. I can't believe I'm as tall as my teacher.

Brother Hayes takes my right hand and turns the palm face up. He stands there for the longest time, looking at my hand covered with white chalk. I wonder what he's thinking. I close my eyes and remember the wonderful, forbidden feeling of his thumb drawing tiny circles on my neck. I think of him drawing circles all over my face, touching my eyes, my lips. I feel like I'm in a trance, but his voice wakes me up.

"Maybe you should go wash the chalk off your hands."

"I don't have time. I have to catch my bus."

As he places my hand on the lapel of his black suit, a little puff of white chalk rises up like a miniature cloud. Even through the wool jacket and starched white shirt, I can feel his heart beating. He closes his eyes and puts his other hand over mine. I think of leaning into the space separating our faces and kissing his beautiful lips, but he opens his eyes. They are wet with tears. He lets go of my hand. "Run," he says. "Run and catch your bus."

*

MICHAEL CZARNECKI AND I don't live in the same neighborhood, so every Sunday evening we watch *The Loretta Young Show* in our separate homes. The program always begins with Loretta sweeping through a door in a different dress. Loretta subtly moves her hands so the full skirt flares as she twirls to shut the door. The stories that follow are okay, but it's the dress that matters. At 10:30, Michael telephones, and we talk about the show until Mom reminds me there's school tomorrow. When I don't pay any attention, Dad demands that I "get off the damn phone."

Sometimes that's the most Dad says to me all week. At breakfast, if I say "good morning," he'll reply with "morning," but he never greets me first. And we don't say "good night." At dinner, Mom has stopped encouraging me to tell him what happened at school. He doesn't want to hear, and I don't want to tell him. He reads the paper. I don't know why he's so angry all the time. He's even stopped playing with Bobby.

But I don't think about Dad much anymore. For the first time, I have a real friend. Michael Czarnecki isn't popular at school, but he doesn't seem to care. He doesn't play sports, but nobody teases him. He isn't beautiful like the cool boys, but he has the same sense of naturalness, as if he likes his body, big nose and all. He's interested in all the same things I am—movies and mysteries, reading and writing. But the best thing is he likes being with me. Having a friend like Michael changes everything. I like having a friend, feeling like I belong somewhere. I smile all the time.

Even though we are in the same class and eat lunch together, Michael and I talk on the phone every day. We're excited about Elizabeth Taylor's new movie, *Suddenly, Last Summer*. In the ad, Elizabeth crouches in the sand. Her thick black hair is wild, and she's wearing a revealing, white swimsuit with the straps nearly falling off her shoulders. She looks up at a man standing in front of her. We see only his lower half, starting with two deep dimples just above his skimpy swimsuit, which is so tight it looks stuck in his ass. He has long legs with muscled calves. As much as I like Elizabeth, I can't stop staring at those legs. Next to the photo, it reads ...*suddenly last summer Cathy knew she was being used for something evil!*

I desperately want to see the movie, but my parents won't let me go because the Catholic Church condemned it. Michael's folks don't care, and he suggests we go together.

"Come on, Anthony. It will be an adventure," he says. 'Certainly, you've disobeyed your parents before."

I shrug. "How would I get to the theater?"

"Tell your mom you're spending the night at my place. My mom will drive us to the theater and pick us up afterward."

"Maybe." But in the end, I don't go. Mom always knows when I tell a lie.

So I make Michael promise to tell me all about the movie. The next day, after lunch, he and I find an empty classroom, and he relates the plot.

"Katharine Hepburn wants Montgomery Clift, who's a doctor, to operate on Elizabeth's brain so she will stop saying horrid things about Sebastian, Katharine's son."

"Is that the man in the poster?"

"Yes," Michael says. "And that's all that's ever shown of him. We never see his face. Anyway, Elizabeth confesses that she had lured men on the beach by wearing the white bathing suit Sebastian bought her." Michael does a perfect imitation of Elizabeth's raspy whisper: "*When it got wet, I looked naked.*"

Michael describes how Elizabeth, hysterical and falling to the ground, cries out that she was not attracting men for herself but for Sebastian.

"He was," Michael says, "a homosexual."

"What's that?" I ask.

"A man who loves other men."

I don't see what all the fuss is about.

Age fifteen

Biology

I AM AFRAID to see if it's listed in Chaminade's library, so one day after school, I go to the public library in downtown Dayton and look up "homosexuality" in the card catalog. There are not many books. *Sexual Behavior in the Human Male* by Alfred Kinsey is in a special reference section, so it can't be checked out. There are three novels: *Giovanni's Room* by James Baldwin, *Advise and Consent* by Allen Drury, and *The City and the Pillar* by Gore Vidal. I decide on *Advise and Consent* because it recently won the Pulitzer Prize.

As I look for the book on the shelves, a librarian walks by and says, "You should be in the teen section." But she doesn't linger, and I ignore her.

At the front desk, I hand over the book and my library card.

"You can't check this out," the woman at the desk says.

"Why not? My card hasn't expired."

"This book is for adults only."

"But I've checked out other adult books. Just last month, I read *Exodus*, and it's in the same section of the library."

She puts *Advise and Consent* on a shelf behind her. "If you don't have any other books to check out, please move on. Other people are waiting."

I stand by the front door, zipping up my jacket and putting

on my gloves, when a man with white hair comes up to me.

"Excuse me. I was in the line behind you," he says, "and saw that nasty busybody wouldn't let you check out the book you wanted. *Advise and Consent* is a good book, and I don't think you're too young to read it. It's out in paperback, and you can find it in the book department at Rike's Department Store." He looks around. The woman at the desk is watching us. He reaches into a pocket and takes out several coins. He hands me two quarters. "Here. Consider it a gift from your fairy godfather."

He hurries out the door before I can say "thank you."

I catch the bus home in front of Rike's, so I don't even have to go out of my way to buy the book. I stuff it in my schoolbag. If the librarian doesn't want me to read it, my mom probably won't either. She's going to be furious that I'm late. I've missed my regular bus and have to catch the next one. It will be dark by the time I get home. I can't wait to call Michael and tell him about my fairy godfather.

A man in a Navy pea coat comes out of Rike's. He has a crew cut and no hat. I guess he doesn't feel the cold because his coat isn't even buttoned. He has on very tight jeans and an argyle sweater. When he walks by me, he licks his lips. At the corner, he turns and looks back at me. I'm too scared to smile.

He crosses the street, opens a black door, and goes inside. There's no sign, just "237" stenciled in white on the door. Waiting for the bus, I watch several other men walk through that door. I wonder what's on the other side.

DAD WAS PASSED over for a promotion—the reason he's been so angry—so he finds another job, still as an accountant but with more responsibility and higher pay. The new company is a cement pipe manufacturer near Pontiac, Michigan, so once again Mom and I pack all the family possessions for the move. This time, there's Bobby's possessions to pack, too. He doesn't understand what's happening.

Dad finds a split-level home on a small lake in a new subdivision in Drayton Plains. This time we don't have to lay any sod or paint the house—all the rooms are already beige.

I tell Mom I no longer want to attend a Catholic school, and I want to enroll at the brand-new Kettering High School. I thought she'd be upset, but she has a different outlook.

"There will be girls!"

I don't say her enthusiasm is misplaced. I think I'm homosexual. I read *Advise and Consent* in two days, and I wish Senator Anderson hadn't killed himself just because he went to bed with another man.

The priests at Chaminade never said one word about homosexuality. They only warned about the danger of getting girls pregnant and "self-abuse," although Brother Hayes implied masturbation wasn't even a venal sin. When I went to confession and admitted that "I abused myself three times in the past week," the penance was only three Hail Marys.

Soon after moving to Drayton Plains, Mom and I went shopping for new school clothes, now that I don't have to wear a tie. No more white or pale blue shirts! I select an orange-and-yellow plaid.

I think because Kettering is a new school, no one will know each other yet, but many students are already friends, not just from the old high school, but also from elementary school. They have their little cliques, and I don't fit in any of them. I want to call Michael Czarnecki every day, but because of the long-distance charges, Dad will let me phone only once a week.

It doesn't matter to me that Kettering is co-ed, but the girls like me and say I'm "cute." I know a couple of them wish I'd ask them out, but I'm not interested, although I enjoy hanging out with them during lunch hour. They tell me all about their boyfriends.

Chaminade students stayed in one room all day, and teachers moved from classroom to classroom. At Kettering, the teachers have their own rooms, and the students do the shuffling. My English teacher, Mr. Jaffe, doesn't sit us alphabetically as most of the other teachers do. He doesn't even have his desk at the front of the room like in all the other classes. Instead, it is turned at a ninety-degree angle facing the door, and a student desk in the far front of a row abuts Mr. Jaffe's desk.

"Ray Hutton," he calls out, pointing to the desk smack up against his own, "sit here. Anthony Dimora, you're behind Ray. The rest of you can sit wherever you want."

Ray Hutton has the most beautiful hair I have ever seen. It isn't blond, and it isn't red. It's as shiny as a topaz and changes color in the sunlight just like the jewel. Ray probably wears his hair long because he knows how beautiful it is, just enough to curl at his ears and dance across his forehead.

His skin tone is not ashy like many redheads and blonds, but a pale golden rose. Freckles cross his long, sloping nose like a bridge. His eyes are—*oh, no*—amber like my father's. His eyelashes are unforgivably long. His lips are chiseled like a statue, and his cheekbones are carved at a perfect angle for a camera. I could stare at him for hours.

Mr. Jaffe is the polar opposite of Ray Hutton. Our English teacher is as short as the shortest student in class, and he has the shape of a D'Anjou pear.

Did he sit Ray Hutton next to his desk because the boy is so beautiful? So why did he position me behind Ray?

Ray shows no interest in me. Every day, he sits staring straight ahead, his neck rigid. I wonder what he would do if I drew tiny circles on it. Probably punch me.

I like all my classes, but English is my favorite. Mr. Jaffe has a rule: if you get a grade lower than an *A* on a composition, you have to rewrite it. I always get *A*s, but one day I got an *A-* for my latest story. I slowly read it, looking for grammatical errors. Finally, I raise my hand.

"Mr. Jaffe, I've read my essay over three times, and I can't find a mistake."

All the students, even Ray Hutton, turn toward me as Mr. Jaffe walks over to my desk and picks up my paper. He points to a sentence about halfway down. "That comma is not needed," he says. "When in doubt, leave it out. And that applies to sex, too."

Students giggle, and I feel my face turn red.

"He got you!" Ray says.

I'm embarrassed, but who cares? Ray Hutton spoke to me.

ONE WEEK, I don't call Michael Czarnecki. And he doesn't call me. Another week passes, and no call, and I realize that Michael has never called me, that I only call him. I place one more call. I want to tell him about Ray Hutton, but I'm afraid of his reaction. Our conversation is stilted, and after that, there are no more phone calls.

While the rest of my class has study hall, Ray is on duty as a hall monitor, sitting at a blond-veneer desk at the intersection of two wide corridors lined with lockers. One day, I get a pass excusing me from study hall to go to the library.

I show him my pass, and he nods, but instead of going to the library, I sit on the floor beside him. He looks down at me but doesn't say anything. I bet he can't stay quiet as long as I can, and I'm right. In less than a minute, he says, "Aren't you going to the library?"

"No."

"So, why'd you get a hall pass?"

"I finished my homework and thought I'd come sit here."

He gives me a *you're-strange* look.

"Are you going to the Sadie Hawkins Dance?" I ask.

"Yes."

"Who asked you?"

"Betty Weber."

I wait, but he doesn't ask me if I'm going. Maybe he thinks none of the girls would ask me. Maybe he knows I wouldn't go even if I had been asked.

I change the subject. "Have you seen pictures of the new Corvette? The whole rear end is new. You can hardly see the taillights."

I found the right subject. He's excited now, going on about horsepower, cubic inches, and fuel injection. The only part I understand is *V-8* because my dad explained it to me once.

I wish Ray Hutton would shut up and just let me stare at him.

But why? Why am I so drawn to this Adonis? I thought I was going to faint the first time I saw him naked in the gym locker room. He has no hair hiding his pink, budding nipples. His chest is not overly muscled but as quietly defined as Tony Curtis' in *Spartacus*. Golden hairs circle Ray's belly button, forming a path to a mass of topaz pubic hair. The head of his penis is the exact pink of his nipples. And then there are the legs. From the back, they remind me of the man in the *Suddenly, Last Summer* poster, with their shapely calf muscles, except Ray's legs are lavishly covered with shimmering gold hair.

I stare and stare and stare. I am so drawn to him, I *must* be homosexual, but I don't fantasize about *doing* anything with Ray. I don't lie in bed at night and dream of Ray's penis in my mouth. Or anywhere else.

And then it hits me: I don't want to merely lie on top of him; I want to sink into his body.

I want to *be* Ray Hutton.

But I still want my own mind.

Age sixteen

Discovery

RAY AND I are in only one class together in our senior year. Fortunately, it's gym, so I get to stare at his beautiful body. And wrestle.

I'm not too bad at wrestling. I guess Dad's early lessons sunk in. I long to get on the mat with Ray, but Mr. Greene, the gym teacher, always selects the partners, and since I don't have muscles like Ray, we aren't paired. Until one day, when half the school seems to be out with the flu, Ray and I finally face each other on the mat.

I hope I don't get too excited when we touch. Ray is all business. He grabs me under my arms and yanks me toward him, my back pressed against his chest in a bear hug. I smell my sweat mixed with his. I tilt my head back and rest it on his neck.

"Come on, Dimora!" Mr. Greene shouts. "Fight back. He's your opponent, not your boyfriend."

I hear one of the other boys laugh, and I turn my head to see who it is. Ray takes advantage of my distraction and does a leg sweep, so I fall. He soon pins my shoulders to the mat. I lose. I don't care. Ray Hutton is straddling me. It's everything I want. His face is only inches from mine. He smooches his lips and makes a kissing sound. He winks and hops off me.

I have one thought: *Everyone must know.*

*

MY DIARY IS not how I left it in my desk drawer.

I reread the last few pages—all about Ray Hutton, his beautiful, hairy legs, and my feelings for him. And there it is, in blue, fountain-pen ink, in my own handwriting: *homosexual.* Underlined. Twice.

I'm sure Mom read it. I can tell by the way she avoids looking at me. She's probably worried about what the neighbors will think if they find out she has a queer son.

The next day, she insists I run an errand with her. Bobby's in the back seat chattering away, but Mom and I are silent. She hasn't told me where we're going. She pulls into our church parking lot and says, "I made an appointment for you with Father Kaiser. He's waiting in his office."

Father Kaiser is old and smells of stale cigarette smoke. We sit facing each other in cracked black leather chairs with fat armrests. He talks about God, the Church, high school, sports— everything except homosexuality. Finally, he says, "Your mother told me that you seem to be interested in boys. It's a sin. Put it out of your mind."

Then he asks me to kneel beside him and recite the Lord's Prayer.

What a jerk.

TWO DAYS LATER, Dad takes me for a drive, something he has never done before. "We're very concerned," he says. "You know we only want what's best for you. Your mom and I have talked it over, and we think you should burn your diary."

I look out the window. *Burn my diary?* It's supposed to be private. No one's supposed to read it but me.

"We're worried about what might happen when you go away to college." He puts his hand on the back of my neck. "I understand these feelings, Anthony. I was in the Coast Guard."

I start crying.

This is the first time Dad has touched me since I was ten years old.

I drop my head onto his lap.

He strokes my hair.

Two thoughts flash through my mind: *I can either press my hand against his foot and hold the gas pedal all the way down so we crash and die, or I can unzip his pants.*

Age seventeen

Sad Song

I SING ALONG with Little Peggy March on the radio in my bedroom while I draw with color pencils a carefully arranged pile of dead leaves.

"It's common practice," Dad says, walking in without knocking, "for a man to change the pronouns when he sings a song written for a woman."

"*I will follow him.*"

"Shut it off. I've got some bad news. We just got a call from your Uncle Phil. Grandpa Peruzzi died. He had a heart attack. Your mom's pretty upset. Pack a suitcase. We're leaving for Castleton as soon as we can get ready."

"Will we be back in time to go to work on Monday?"

"No. I've already talked to my boss. He'll explain to your supervisor, and things will be fine. Come on, get moving."

Mom wears sunglasses the entire trip, even though most of the time it's raining. She doesn't want anyone to see her red eyes, but it's just Dad, Bobby, and me in the car. Bobby's six, and I'm not sure he understands what's going on. My job is to keep him quiet in the back seat. Just as I run out of games to play, he falls asleep on my lap. I read *City of Night* by John Rechy. The book is racy, but it thrills me more that I am reading about a male hustler while my parents are in the front seat.

The funeral parlor is packed.

"We lost Grandpa," Grandma Peruzzi says to everyone who approaches her. I have a feeling she's not going to miss him very much. She keeps her eyes on the door, making sure everyone signs the guestbook.

Dad says I don't have to go up to the coffin, but I'm curious. Why'd they put all that makeup on Grandpa? It doesn't even look like him.

The day after the funeral, I tag along when Dad goes to the Sons of Italy. Anthony Tomasso's there. It's been five years since I've seen him. He's shorter than I remember. Not stocky but compact. His wavy black hair shines with Vitalis. His white sleeves are rolled up to his elbows; thick black hair covers his arms and springs out of his collar.

"Anthony! I almost didn't recognize you. You've really grown." He extends a hand. "Do you remember me? Tony Tomasso."

"How could I not remember you?" I smile. "You told me the ending to *Lifeboat*."

"So, are you still called 'Anthony'? No one ever calls you 'Tony'?"

"Not more than once."

Tony asks if I'm going to college and what my major is. I'm polite and say art, but I don't care about any of that stuff right now. I want to ask him a question, but I can't do it in the Sons of Italy, not in front of all his friends.

"You always drove such neat cars, Tony. What are you driving now?"

"A 1960 Oldsmobile Ninety-Eight. It's three years old, but I think it looks more modern than the new models."

"Oh, I agree. Especially the way the roof looks like it's

floating on glass."

Dad is engrossed in a poker game. I don't think he's gambled since we moved out of Castleton. I bet he's going to be here for a while.

"Say, Tony, I haven't had an Isley's ice cream cone in years. How about we go get a scoop?" Tony looks around, as if he can't decide. I make the decision for him. "I'll tell my dad we're going."

Tony's car is right next door. "You know I bought Mama Luisa's house, don't you?"

"Yeah, I heard."

"I set up my practice downstairs and live upstairs." He's standing beside his car.

"What kind of practice?"

"I'm a psychologist."

"You know, Tony, I haven't been in Mama Luisa's house since she died. Maybe you could show me how you changed it." And I'll find the answer to my question.

He's partitioned the front room in half and made part of it into a reception area. The old dining room is his consulting room. The sparse furniture floats in the large space: a leather couch, two wing chairs, and a few small tables. He's added an outside door so a client can leave after a session without running into the next client in the waiting area.

"I didn't think there'd be much demand for a psychologist in Castleton."

"You'd be surprised."

He shows me his small, private office—the other half of the divided front room. It's crammed with bookshelves, filing cabinets, and an old-fashioned kneehole desk. It's upstairs I want to go. Upstairs I'll find my answer. But he doesn't move out of his office.

"My dad said he lived upstairs for a while. Can we see that?"

"It's a little messy, but sure." I follow him up the steps. "This is my room."

There's a double bed. But that doesn't answer my question.

"There's not one single family photo in this room."

"What are you looking for, Anthony?"

I guess he's a good psychologist. "Signs of *him*."

"Signs of who?"

I think my body's going to start shaking. I think I'm going to cry. But I have to get it out. "Five years ago, Mom wouldn't let me come visit you because she said you lived with another man."

"Oh, *him*." He walks over to a small bookcase and pulls out a photo album. He flips the pages, then points to a photo of Tony and a handsome, dark man with their arms over each other's shoulders. "Jack Carlyle. He left two years ago. He couldn't take the pressure of living in a small-minded town like Castleton. He went to New York. I haven't heard from him in a while."

He puts the album back on the shelf. I sit on his bed. It's covered with an Indian blanket with two narrow gray stripes and a wide bright red one. My left leg is moving up and down, up and down, like it's operating an old sewing machine.

"Have you always known about me?" I ask.

"Probably before you did." He stays on the other side of the room.

"So, you're alone now."

"Most of the time."

"I'm tired of being alone, Tony."

He doesn't say anything. I grab my leg to stop it twitching. The room is so silent. There aren't even any songs playing in my head.

I take off my sports coat and start to unbutton my shirt. "I've been working out. Want to see my muscles?"

"I told you I'm a psychologist," he says.

"What does that have to do with it?"

"What you're suggesting may not be ethical."

"I'm not your client."

"Maybe you should be." He sees the hurt on my face. "I didn't mean that the way it sounded. I meant if you were my client, there would be no doubt in my mind. Besides, you're underage."

"You're not seducing me. I'm seducing you. Or at least I'm trying."

My leg takes off again. My shoulders start to shudder, but I hold back my tears. "*Please,*" I whisper.

"You should do this with someone your own age."

"They're all too scared. They probably don't even know what to do."

"Do you know what to do?"

"I think so. I'd like to learn."

"I'm old enough to be your father."

"I like that you're my father's age," I say. But I don't tell him what I'm thinking: *It erases Lake Erie.*

I REST MY face in Tony's soft, furry chest. He looks at his watch. "Your father's probably wondering where you are."

"Not if he's losing."

"Well, we should get dressed. We haven't gotten that ice cream cone. What flavor do you want?"

"Vanilla." I caress his chest. "Don't get up yet. I like just lying here."

"It's hard for me to just lie there when you're in my arms. Excuse the pun." He gets out of bed, and I see he's erect again. "I'll put on some music."

He stacks 45s on a turntable. The first record drops as he hops back in bed. "Hello, Stranger" by Barbara Lewis.

"I'm surprised you like music like this," I say.

"I like the love songs. 'Hey Paula' and 'Our Day Will Come.'"

"I like the sad ones. 'The End of the World' by Skeeter Davis is one of my favorites. But maybe I won't be singing sad songs anymore."

Tony looks deep into my eyes. "We'll always be singing sad songs."

He moves his thumb around my nipple. It feels so good to be touched. But I have questions. "Is it hard being homosexual in a small town like Castleton?"

"It isn't easy being homosexual in a big city. Jack wanted me to move to New York with him, but I'm just perverse enough to like it here. I know people talk about me behind my back, but they also respect me."

"Do you know other homosexuals here?"

Tony crosses his arms behind his head. There's a whiff of sweat. I like it.

"Every town has homosexuals," he says, "but I don't hang around with most of them. I have two friends I pal around with. Strictly platonic. It helps to have someone you can be open with. But you know, Anthony, there's more to my life than being queer." He kisses my forehead.

I put my head back on his chest. "Do you remember when we went to an amusement park and rode the bumper cars? I was about nine."

"Sort of."

"My father was furious that I let people plow into me with their cars. He said I should've been more manly. You stuck up for me, and he said to mind your own business, that I was his son, and you said, 'I wouldn't be so sure.' I always wondered what you meant by that."

"Not what you think. I suspected you were queer. All I meant was that you were more like me than like him. Disappointed?"

I shrug.

"Would you have liked it if I were your father?"

"To be honest, I wanted Perry Como to be my father."

"You know, he's from Pennsylvania. Not too far from here."

"Yeah, I know."

"Why Perry Como?"

"He seems calm. And I felt he'd like me and give me hugs."

Tony squeezes me. "I like you."

I kiss him. "I hate to disappoint you, but you weren't my second choice either."

"It seems like you gave this a lot of thought."

"Oh, yeah. I often thought about having a different father."

"So, who was number two?"

"My uncle Nick."

"You went from Perry Como to Nick Dimora? Como is probably nice to everyone, and Nick's a tough prick who always has to be first."

"He's always been nice to me." It's difficult to concentrate on the conversation with Tony massaging my neck. "Nick never made me feel bad because I was lousy at baseball, like my dad did."

"Okay, I guess Nick can be a nice guy when he wants to be."

"I saw him at the funeral, and he's still sexy."

"I'm glad I'm not your father because then I couldn't be in bed with you."

My body tenses. Tony turns my face, so I have to look right at him. "Did something happen between you and Rusty?"

"What if I wanted something to happen?"

"It's okay, Anthony. You can tell me. You can tell me anything."

Nestled in Tony's arms, I close my eyes and tell him about swimming through Daddy's legs in Lake Erie.

"You won't tell Dad I told you, will you?"

"No," Tony whispers in my ear. "It's just between us."

I roll over on my stomach. We lie still, Tony massaging my back as we listen to Jay and the Americans sing "She Cried."

"When my dad found out I was homosexual," I say when the song is over, "he never said it was wrong or anything. We were in his car, and I remember exactly what he said. 'I understand these feelings. I was in the Coast Guard.' What do you think he meant by that, Tony?"

"Did he say anything just before that?"

"'We're worried about what might happen when you go away to college.'"

Tony presses his hand in the small of my back. It feels warm. "Tony?"

He stares at the ceiling. "Your father and I enlisted in the Coast Guard together, but it wasn't until after the war that we were on the same ship. We sailed all the way to New Delhi. The ship was full of Hindus, who had served on British ships, and we were taking them back to their homeland. We were at sea a long time, and you can imagine how horny everyone got. Even some guys who would beat up a faggot, just for the fun of it, back on shore, fooled around. But not your father. He said it was a sin and an abomination in the eyes of God. I said bullshit. Well, it got around on board that I was, shall we say, 'available.'

Frankly, I was having the time of my life, and maybe I got a little overconfident."

"You mean you got 'cocky'?"

Tony slaps my butt. "Smart ass. Anyway, one day I approached the wrong guy, and he started slugging me, then several of his buddies joined in. Hell, I had been with two of them, but I guess they wanted to look tough in front of each other. Your father saw what was going on. I called out to him for help—and he just turned away."

"That's awful, Tony."

"Yeah, your father's one hell of a guy." He nearly spits.

"But you're still his friend."

"Maybe not after today." He stares into my eyes, as if looking will make the pain disappear. He blinks. "Anyway, I think when he told you he understood those feelings because he was in the Coast Guard, he was probably thinking about how those guys beat me up on that ship. I think he was worried about your safety." Tony caresses my ass. "You keep it up, you're going to be as hairy as me."

"Or Uncle Nick."

Tony presses a finger between my cheeks.

He opens a nightstand drawer and takes out a jar of Vaseline.

I've never felt anything this good. I whisper in Tony's ear, "Shoo-bop, shoo-bop, my baby, ooooh."

Then I look up and see Dad in the doorway.

I DON'T MOVE. Dad's face is twisted with disgust. He flees.

Tony lifts his head from the pillow. "What's wrong?"

The front door slams shut.

"Dad saw us."

"Shit."

Tony looks out the window. "He's sitting in his car across the street."

I reach for my clothes.

"Do you want to take a shower?"

"No, I'd better go."

"Do you want me to go with you?"

I shake my head. Tony kisses my forehead. I run down the steps. But I don't run to Dad's car. I don't know how I know it, but I realize these are the most important steps of my life. I walk across the street with my shoulders back, my head up. I open the car door and sit down. I smell Tony all over my body.

Dad starts the car. He says, "You're breaking your mother's heart."

I'm breaking my mother's heart? She didn't see Tony and me together. And I'm certainly not about to tell her. But Dad obviously will. I wonder why he can't keep our little secret. Like other little secrets. Maybe he thinks it will make her love me less.

MOM'S JUST AS cheery and chatty with her sisters as she always is, but she hasn't looked at me all day. She hasn't said one word to me.

The day before we leave, Grandma Peruzzi announces she wants to make our favorite dishes. I ask for gnocchi. Dad wants braciole. Bobby goes for zabaglione, although he can't pronounce it. Grandma says it's the easiest dessert to make, and maybe he'd like something a little more complicated, but it's what he wants. Mom says she doesn't want Grandma to go to any trouble for her.

"This is the last time I'm asking, Mary," Grandma says. "Do you want something special or not?"

"Well, since the entrée and dessert are already selected," Mother Martyr says, "I'll pick an appetizer. How about mozzarella and tomatoes?"

She doesn't even like mozzarella and tomatoes! Dad likes it. And I know Mom is not going to let Grandma make it. Mom will fix the dish, with just the amount of basil that Dad likes.

Early the next morning, Grandma rolls the braciole and sets it to simmer in tomato sauce. Then she and I go to the basement. She mixes the dough for the homemade pasta, rolls it into long tubes, and I cut it into bite-sized pieces.

"Do you have a girlfriend, Anthony?"

I shake my head.

"Have you ever had a girlfriend?"

Another shake.

"You don't like girls very much, do you?"

I shrug.

"That's okay, Anthony." Grandma puts her hand, white with flour, on mine. "As long as you don't hurt anyone, it's okay."

I kiss her shoulder. Why can't my parents be more like Grandma?

She told her other daughters that tonight's dinner is just for Mary and the Dimoras, and we sit around the kitchen table enjoying our favorite foods. Sipping his homemade wine, we give a toast to Grandpa. Mom has tears in her eyes, and I know they're for me as well as her dead father.

After we finish dessert, Mom's sisters come by to say goodbye to us.

We leave early in the morning, and once it's just the four of us, Mom drops her cheerfulness. It takes nearly four and a half hours to drive from Castleton to Drayton Plains. No one turns on the radio. We don't even pray the Rosary. Even Bobby is surprisingly quiet.

There's about a month to go before I can leave home and move into a dorm at the University of Michigan. I sort through my books and other possessions, deciding what I want to take with me. I write a long letter to Tony, telling him how much what we did meant to me and how sorry I am that I didn't get to say goodbye. I ask him not to write back until I have an address in Ann Arbor. I don't trust my mother to not open my mail.

She finally brings up the subject, one Saturday when Dad is playing golf. Carrying my clean laundry in her arms, Mom sits on my bed.

"If you just meet the right girl, Anthony, your problem will disappear."

"It's not a 'problem' to me."

She looks at me as if she's trying to decide what happened to the son who was so obedient and never caused any trouble.

"I shouldn't have let you play with paper dolls."

"That was a symptom, not the cause." I put the laundry in the drawers.

"I don't know why you want to put your family through this."

"This isn't about you. It isn't about the family. It's about me. About who I am." I wish my voice didn't sound so pinched.

"We just want you to be happy." She twists her hands.

"What if I told you, *I am happy*? That when I was with Tony, it was the *happiest moment of my life*."

She covers her ears with her hands and walks out of my room.

The house is even quieter than usual. The only one who shows any joy is Bobby. I had bought him a toy piano for his sixth birthday. He plays it all the time, until I am sick of its tinny sound. I spend some of the money I've put aside for college on a miniature "baby grand": only thirty keys, but a big improvement. I swear Bobby's teaching himself to read sheet music.

Dad doesn't bug Bobby to play sports as he did me. He must have surrendered to the idea that he simply isn't going to have a son who's a star athlete. But he installs a basketball hoop over the garage door, and he, Uncle Nick, and Nick Junior shoot baskets every evening until it gets dark.

During the week, I ride with Dad to work. In the morning, we listen to the news. On the drive home, it's the financial report. Most days, I lean against the window and shut my eyes. But I don't want to fall asleep, because then I'll see the rubber O-rings I make, hour after hour. I cut a long strip of rubber to the right length, put the ends in a hot, round vice, pull a lever, and the ends fuse, making a circle. O-rings are used as washers to connect the concrete pipes when they're laid for sewer systems. It's a dirty job, and I wish I didn't have to do it.

On Saturdays, whether it needs it or not, I mow the lawn with my shirt off. I want my tan to last all winter. On Sundays, I bicycle through our neighborhood, the next one, and the one after that. I exhaust myself.

I soak in the bathtub, reading *Ship of Fools*. The water cools, and I let most of it out, then turn on the hot full blast. The bathroom fills with steam. The water's almost painful. My skin is pink. I put down the book, lean my head against the white porcelain and stroke myself. I think of Tony and all the things we did. I see Uncle Nick flash his erection when I'm handing out towels after the basketball game. I rub my chest and see Nick Junior kneeling over me, flapping his dick in front of my mouth. I see my cousins Donny and Ronny in the wet white underwear in Lake Erie. And Daddy.

Spread your legs.

I'm coming through, Daddy.

I'm coming.

MOM NOTICES I don't take Communion at Mass. The next Saturday, she announces we're going to Confession. Bobby hasn't even had his First Holy Communion, but she insists we all go as a family. At least she lets Bobby bring a book; he's reading *The Little Prince*. Again.

Dad goes into the confessional first. Mom's next. Then it's my turn.

What am I supposed to confess? That I jacked off thinking about men? I stopped confessing that "sin" three years ago. I guess Mom wants me to confess that I had sex with a man. Dad wants me to—what? Denounce homosexuality completely? Not be who I am?

Father Fleming coughs behind the screen separating our faces.

"I've been with a man. But I don't think it's wrong. I don't think it's a sin."

"In the eyes of the Lord," Father Fleming says, "it is a grievous sin. You must ask forgiveness."

"I'm not sorry. It seems like I waited my whole life for it to happen, and I loved every moment of it. I really don't believe it's a sin."

"It's not up to you to decide what's a sin. And I cannot grant you absolution unless you show repentance."

"Then don't." I walk out of the confessional.

On Sunday, I refuse to go to Mass.

WITH ONLY ONE week left before I leave for the University of Michigan, it's time to ask the question that has been circling my brain. I lower the radio as Dad drives us to the cement pipe plant.

"Tony Tomasso said when you two were on board a ship during the war, he got beaten up and you didn't help him; you just walked away. Why did you do that?"

"He deserved what he got." Dad stares at the road. "He was asking for it."

"Because he gave sailors what they wanted? He wasn't hurting anyone."

"He was hurting himself."

"How?"

"He was condemning his soul to Hell."

I put my head in my hand. "You think homosexuals are going to Hell?"

"It's a mortal sin. It's against God, and it's against nature." Dad squeezes the steering wheel tighter. His fingers turn white. "And if you don't change, Anthony, you're going to Hell with the rest of them."

I am stunned. But why should I be surprised? It's what the Catholic Church teaches. But I don't accept it.

"I think I've always known right from wrong." I look at Dad, even though he doesn't even glance my way. "I've never needed the Church to tell me what's wrong. I think a person knows inside." I point to my chest. "And I don't feel that I've done anything wrong."

"Well, you have." He pulls into the parking lot of the factory. I open the door, eager to get away from him. "Hold on a minute. I have a couple of things to tell you. I was going to wait until next week, but I might as well tell you now." He finally looks at me. "I think I failed you as a father. It's something I have to live with, and even though you may not believe it, I am truly sorry." He doesn't look contrite. He looks smug. Self-satisfied.

"You failed me, alright, but not in the way you think."

He sneers. "I've paid your tuition this first term, but that's the only one I'm paying. From now, on you'll have to cover it yourself." His eyes focus beyond me, out the window. "I'm not going to make the same mistake with Bobby." He says it softly, as if a vow. Then he stares right in my eyes, and I understand what hatred really looks like. "Once you go back to college, I don't want you coming home anymore."

"What?"

"You heard me. I don't want you to influence Bobby with your ways."

"Does Mom know about this?"

"I'll handle your mother."

"Don't you think she'll want to see me?"

"She can visit you in Ann Arbor."

"And after I graduate?"

"Don't come back home. Ever."

Age eighteen

College

ANN ARBOR IS only about an hour's drive from Drayton Plains, but I feel I'm on another planet. A world without parents. Without priests. Maybe a world with people like me.

My roommate at the dorm is named Gary. We're told that when roommates were assigned, they were paired with similar interests, but I can't figure out a thing Gary and I have in common. He's studying engineering. Within our first hour of meeting, we discover we've not seen any of the same movies, read any of the same books, or liked any of the same songs. All we have in common is that we're freshmen. We share the same room but go our separate ways. We don't even eat together in the dorm cafeteria. I'm the only guy in my entire dorm who is studying art.

I'm probably too picky about choosing what guys to talk to at the dorm or in my classes. I don't want to be friendly with someone, then find out he's boring and not know how to end the friendship. I'd rather be alone.

In high school, not many boys took art class. I guess they didn't think it was masculine, even though most famous artists are men. It's the same at college; there are very few male students studying art.

When we turn in our first assignment for Color and Form, I am surprised by how awful most of the students' work is. It looks dashed off in an hour the night before. I spent three days on my illustration.

"You look more disappointed than the teacher," a girl sitting next to me whispers.

"Your work is cool," I tell her. "It's almost three-dimensional on a two-dimensional surface. But a lot of the stuff the other students did is ghastly."

"Most of the girls are here to find a husband."

"In art school? They outnumber the men five to one."

"They're just studying art to be at the university. They date law students or pre-med."

"How do you know this?"

"I'm from New York City. We grow up fast."

"I'm from the Midwest. Most of us never grow up." I'm pleased she smiles. "Doesn't it bother you that these husband-seekers are taking up class space?"

"Not really. The teachers know right away who's interested in art and who's not. Some of them may flirt with the girls who are looking for husbands, but they'll devote their time to the students with talent." She gathers up her art supplies as the class ends. "Do you want to grab a coffee?"

"I don't drink coffee." She looks more shocked than disappointed. "But I can have a cocoa."

We walk to Dominick's, just down the street from Art School. She's as tall as I am but a bit chunky. Her name is Ruth Roman.

"Like the actress?"

"What actress?"

"Ruth Roman. She was in *Strangers on a Train*. It's a Hitchcock movie. One of his best. And please don't say, 'Who's Hitchcock?'"

"I know who Alfred Hitchcock is," Ruth Roman says. She

has frizzy red hair and a nose so tiny it barely holds up her glasses. "*Psycho. The Birds.*"

"He's my favorite director. I've seen almost every one of his movies. The early ones he did in England aren't shown much."

"Which one's your favorite?"

"*Dial 'M' for Murder,* but I've seen *Vertigo* three times. I'm going to keep watching it until I understand it."

"Maybe we can go to a movie together sometime."

I silently sip my cocoa.

Ruth Roman says, "I'm not looking for a husband."

PETER BRANT'S DORM room is across the hall from mine. His shaggy blond hair is almost white. He has a huge smile with two too-big front teeth. He's always smiling.

Peter's brought weights with him, and almost every day he lifts a barbell with his shirt off and his door open. He has a beautiful body, and I think he knows it. He wears gray gym shorts, white socks, and tennis shoes. His chest is hairless, but his legs are covered with white down. When he sees me watching him, he flashes that huge smile.

"Come in." He waves me over. "You should work out with me. It is always better to have a partner. My roommate is not interested in improving his body." He picks up a weight in each hand. "Start off slowly. This is the Hammer Curl. It's good for the biceps." He demonstrates, lifting the dumbbells straight out from his sides. "Now you do it."

I lift the weights in perfect form.

"You have done this before." His English is formal—no contractions—and he has a strong accent.

"I have some weights at home," I tell him.

"Why did you not bring them?"

"I thought maybe I'd join the university gym."

"It is too crowded."

That's exactly why I want to join—the chance to meet other guys. But maybe the guy I want to meet is right across the hall from me. "So can I work out with you?"

Peter shuts the door. "Now that we will be workout buddies, there is no need to keep the door open." He yanks on my shirt. "It is better without this. That way, you can see if you are working the right muscles."

When I toss my t-shirt on one of the beds, I notice a photograph of a beautiful young woman on a nearby desk. "That is my girlfriend," Peter says. "Amanda. She goes to school in Ypsilanti."

"She's very pretty."

"Yes. I think that is true."

"Where are you from?"

"Denmark. I have lived in your country one year." He lifts the barbell. "You are very hairy. It will be hard to see the definition. Maybe you want to shave?"

"I like my hair."

"Yes, very manly." He smiles, but I can't tell if he's being snide.

We work out for thirty minutes.

"Next time, wear shorts," Peter says. "We will work the legs."

"When is next time?"

"Tomorrow. Three o'clock."

"I have a class."

"What time is it over?"

"Four o'clock."

"Okay. 4:15."

When I am at the door, he says. "What is your name?"

"My name is 'Anthony,' Peter."

The broad grin. Peter catches that I already know his name.

"What are you studying, Anthony?"

"Art."

"Ah." He nods his head, puts lots of meaning in that one word, but I'm not sure how to interpret it. "I am studying political science." He shakes my hand. "Okay, see you tomorrow, Anthony. In shorts."

"JUDY GARLAND'S NEW TV series started last Sunday," I tell Ruth in class, "but I couldn't watch it, because the guys at the dorm watched *Bonanza*. Do you think the girls in your dorm would agree to watch Judy?"

"I don't know. But my dorm has two community rooms, so if they're watching *Bonanza* in one room, we can go to the other. We'll work it out."

Judy's guest that week is Barbra Streisand.

"I first read about Barbra in *Time* magazine," I tell Ruth during a commercial. "The article said she sang 'Happy Days Are Here Again' as a sad song. Well, I just had to hear that, so I went to the record store and asked the clerk, 'Is there a Barbra Streisand album?' and he handed me *The Barbra Streisand Album*. That's what it's called. And her next album, which came out in August, is called *The Second Barbra Streisand Album*. Isn't that cool?"

Ruth rolls her eyes. She's wearing very tight jeans and a baggy black t-shirt that still manages to show she has huge breasts.

"When I played the first album on my parents' stereo, my mom said, 'I like her. She can sing. Not like that awful Bob Dylan you listen to. He can't even carry a tune.' And you know what? I was annoyed. I didn't want my mother to like Barbra Streisand. I wanted the singer all to myself. Isn't that strange?"

"Not really. Each generation has its own idols. Our moms' generation had Sinatra. We have Dylan. And I guess some of us have Streisand."

"Judy Garland is cross-generational. Our parents like her, and so does our generation."

"I don't think so, Anthony. Look around this room." Ruth spreads her arms. "There are just two people here: you and me. Everyone else is watching *Bonanza*. You're the only one who likes Judy. And Barbra."

"You don't like Judy?"

"I like you."

I stare intently at the advertisement on the television, as if I'm seriously considering smoking Lucky Strikes.

Judy and Barbra sing a medley of 'Happy Days Are Here Again' and 'Get Happy.'

After the show, Ruth says, "I want to ask you a question."

Oh, God, I think. *Here it comes.* And I'm right.

"Are you a homosexual?"

There it is. The first time anyone has asked me—other than Grandma's allusion. I've thought about this a lot. What I'm going to say. What I want to say. I'm not ashamed of being queer. But I know it's taboo in our society. If I admit it, will I lose the only friend I've made in Art School? Will she tell everyone, and I'll be shunned? I don't look at Ruth when I answer. "No."

I grab my jacket and zip it up to my chin.

"I'll walk you out," she says.

"That's okay. I know the way." I don't want her to expect a kiss on the doorstep.

"Actually, it's a rule that we have to escort guests out."

She holds the door open, but it doesn't look like she's even thought about a kiss. I look into her eyes and know Ruth Roman is someone I can trust.

"Yes," I say.

"I thought so." She nods her head up and down several times. "There's a guy in Art School I want you to meet. I'm going home for my sister's wedding, but when I get back, I'll introduce you. I think Jason Johnson is exactly what you need."

That must mean he's queer too. Thank God! So far, the only guy I've met whom I like is Peter Brant, and he has a girlfriend. Maybe Jason's one of the cute students I've seen walking around Art School that I've been too shy to approach. *Jason. Jason. Jason.* I dance all the way back to the dorm. Happy days are here again.

The next weekend, with Ruth in New York, I'm reluctant to go to her dorm and ask if I can watch Judy Garland's show. But I am not about to suffer through *Bonanza*, so just before nine, I go to the drug store to console myself with a Baby Ruth. The middle-aged woman at the cash register barely notices me when I pay for the candy bar. She has her eyes raised, looking over my head, and when I turn around to see what's engrossing her, it's Judy, on a small black-and-white set.

"Do you mind if I stay here and watch with you?"

"Knock yourself out."

I sit on a stack of unsold newspapers.

"Could you turn up the sound a bit?"

"HE'S THE ONE at the corner table in the black coat," Ruth says when we walk into Dominick's. "Oops, he's seen us, so it's too late to change your mind."

Jason Johnson isn't handsome or good-looking. He's not the cute boy-next-door Judy Garland sang about in *Meet Me in St. Louis.* He's the neighbor nobody notices. His eyes and mouth are slightly too small in proportion to his nose, not that he has a bigger-than-average head. And there it is. Exactly what Jason is: average.

He stands as we approach. Average height. Average weight. We shake hands after Ruth introduces us and sit opposite each other. Ruth says, "I have a class." And walks away.

"At six o'clock? I thought you were joining us for pizza," I call after her. Without turning around, she waves her fingers above her shoulder.

Jason puts his hand on mine. "I like romance, but I'm not looking for a boyfriend."

"I like pepperoni but not anchovies."

"Oooh. Ruth's right. We *are* going to get along." Jason picks up a menu.

His hair is brown. The most common color. He parts it in the middle.

I don't know why beauty's always the first thing I look for in a person. Maybe it's because I wish I were a knockout. What would it be like to walk into a room and have everyone desire you? Well, it's not going to happen to me. And it's not going to happen to Jason Johnson.

We decide on mushrooms and black olives. Jason's a vegetarian.

"I'm starving," I say. "Medium or large?"

"The pizza or my dick size?" He winks. "That shade of red looks good on you."

I look at my shirt. It's blue. "Oh, you mean I'm blushing." I learned at Chaminade that you don't dismiss someone just because he's not attractive. Michael Czarnecki had that huge nose, and I liked him. He was my best friend. Of course, he didn't make me queasy and excited the way Ray Hutton did. And neither does Jason Johnson. Why can't he look like the unavailable Peter Brant?

He sips his Coke. "What are you majoring in?"

"Graphic design. What about you?"

"Photography."

"What dorm do you live in?"

"You know what I hate most about meeting someone new?" He looks in my eyes as if he's about to say something profound. "It's always the same questions."

"Sorry."

"It's not your fault." He puts his hand on mine again. "How else are we going to get to know one another? Maybe I'll print cards with the ten most pertinent answers and just pass them out. Anyway, I don't live in a dorm. I live in a house on South State Street, near the stadium."

"How'd you manage that? I thought all freshmen had to live in a dorm."

"I'm a sophomore."

"That explains why you're not in any of my art classes."

"But I didn't live in a dorm as a freshman either, because my family lives in Ann Arbor. Well, at least my Mom. My parents are divorced. Dad's in Flint."

After we finish the pizza, Jason asks, "Do you want to go to The Flame?"

"What's The Flame?"

"The only bar in Ann Arbor where men of a certain persuasion are not harassed."

Jason drives a 1963 Studebaker Avanti. It's probably the coolest car ever made. The Flame is downtown, on Washington Street, but I wish it were in Detroit, just so I could be in the car longer.

I've never been to a bar before, but I'm sure The Flame would be classified as a dive. Two men with two stools separating them look up when we walk in, then slouch back on their elbows on the bar; they've probably been here since the place opened. We sit at a booth with cracked red vinyl seats and a table that looks like it hasn't been wiped off in a while. Two guys and a girl are in a nearby booth.

"She's a drag queen," Jason says. "You know what that is, don't you?"

I nod, and he orders two beers. The bartender doesn't ask for IDs, although I have a hunch Jason has a fake one claiming he's twenty-one.

I wish the bar weren't so dark. A guy walks in who looks like he might be attractive—at least he's not old or fat—but it's so dark I can barely make out his features. He sits at the bar, far away from the two men already there. Three older guys amble in, and when they pass our booth, one of them makes kissing sounds as he looks at me.

"Do you come here often?" I ask Jason. He looks like I've said something snide. "What?"

"I'm trying to figure out if you're really naïve or if it's an act."

"It's not an act, and I never lie."

"Why not?"

"It's too hard to keep track of lies. It's easier to tell the truth." I sip the beer. It's too bitter. "So *do* you come here often?"

"You only want the answer to that question so you can judge me."

"Or maybe I just want to know if you're lonely."

"I come here maybe once a week. Sometimes when I'm lonely, but usually when I'm horny."

"So when you see a guy you find attractive, how do you strike up a conversation? What's the first thing you say to him?"

"*Do you come here often?*"

"Oh. Now I see why it's funny." My eyes have adjusted to the darkness, and I look again at the men. None of them is appealing. I don't think I'd come here if I were feeling lonely or horny.

Jason chugs his beer. "This joint is dead tonight. Want to see my place? It's really cool. I decorated it myself."

I'd like to hang around the bar a bit longer to see who else might wander in, but I say, "Okay." I wonder if Jason wants to show me something else besides his decor.

He parks on the side of the house, and we walk up an outside staircase to a second-floor balcony on the front of the house, where he has his own entrance. Inside, the one big room is almost an attic, with the side walls slanting into the ceiling. They're striped vertically in black-and-white wallpaper. In fact, the place is entirely black-and-white. Black-and-white hound's tooth bedspread with black-and-white polka dot pillows, black-and-white paisley curtains, a sofa upholstered in black velvet, a club chair in a black-and-white harlequin pattern, and a white desk with a black swivel chair. It dawns on me that the Avanti is black, and Jason's wearing all black. The black-and-white unframed photographs on the walls are probably his. Each one is a close-up of a group of stones or pebbles blown up to a fourteen-by-sixteen print.

While I'm looking around, Jason puts on an album.

"I guess you don't like much color."

"I abhor it!" Jason goes into the kitchen area, a wall by the entrance with all the appliances and a black square parson's table with two white chairs.

"Who's that singing? She has a haunting voice."

"Morgana King." He hands me a glass of white wine.

He shows me his photography portfolio. Yes, the close-ups on the walls are his, but what he's really interested in photographing are male nudes. I recognize a few of the models as other students at art school. The nudity is quite discreet, with the figures barely emerging from a black background. Sometimes the faces are obscured; always, the penis is hidden in darkness.

As Jason flips through the photographs, his hand or arm often touches mine. I probably shouldn't have come to his apartment. Maybe he thinks it automatically means we'll have sex.

He puts on a Billie Holiday album. He lights six black candles and turns off the light. He refills our wine glasses and then sits very close to me on the sofa. "I told you I like romance."

"But you don't want a boyfriend."

"That's not what I said. I said I'm not *looking* for a boyfriend. You never get a boyfriend when you look for one." He kisses my lips.

"Take off your shoes and stand up," he commands. "I want to see exactly how short you are."

Before I unlace my shoes, he's nude. His body is… average. There's no definition. The chest simply fades into the stomach, then the hips. No chest hair. No tan line. Just a long, thin, and erect penis.

I don't know how to say no.

He takes my hand and leads me to his bed. Black-and-white pinstriped sheets. He unbuttons my shirt, and I let him undress me. Pants. Socks. White t-shirt. He slowly lowers my white briefs and takes my flaccid penis in his hands. "Italian sausage."

He takes it in his mouth. I shut my eyes and think of Peter Brant. When I'm hard, he lies on his stomach, his flat white ass pointing up at me, but I can't stay erect. He flips over on his back, positions me on top of him so that I, too, face the ceiling. He masturbates my penis as if it were an extension of his own.

I'm about to say I'm sorry when Jason says, "Don't say anything. Just let me hold you and fall asleep."

"Just one question, please. Who lives downstairs?"

"My mom."

I CAN'T BELIEVE the President's been shot. I rush out of art class, hurrying to the television in my dorm. By the time I get there, Walter Cronkite announces, "President Kennedy died at 1:00 pm central standard time, 2:00 pm eastern standard time—some thirty-eight minutes ago."

Almost everyone in the room cries, including some of the jocks. I sit motionless, stunned. I find it so hard to believe that the man who gave America a fresh hope and the promise of a better future is gone. Murdered as his motorcade drove through Dallas, Texas. John Kennedy's vitality was contagious, and it made me, and so many others, want to do great things. Now, where I felt hope, there is a hole.

When the university, like the rest of the nation, shuts down, I replay my father's last words to me and know I can't go home. I call Mom, she's crying too, even though she voted for Nixon.

"Poor Jackie," she says. "Come home, Anthony. I'll handle your father."

"Thanks, Mom, but I'm going to stay in Ann Arbor. But don't worry, I won't be alone. Jason says I can stay with him and his mom."

Jason's mother's eyes are red from crying, but I can't find the words to comfort her. Jason sits next to her on the sofa in her living room, holding her hand. We are glued to the television. When it's announced that Lyndon Johnson has been sworn in, Jason's mom says, "We have the same name as the new President." She bawls.

We watch the casket emerge from Air Force One, the plane that flew it to Washington. The camera focuses on the passenger door at the top of the metal stairs. First Lady Jacqueline Kennedy emerges. She looks horror-stricken. I know her Chanel suit with a matching pillbox hat is pink, even though the television is black-and-white. When I notice the bloodstains on her skirt, I mentally see red, and I gasp. Jason and his mother hold each other. She convulses in a painful moan. Jason cries without a sound, wipes his tears and nose on his cuff.

Later, Mrs. Johnson makes macaroni and cheese. "We need comfort food." I eat only a few spoonfuls.

Nothing appears real. Everything seems to have wound down, as if I'm watching a movie in slow motion. My mind seems incapable of comprehending, of processing any more information. I sit zombie-like, listening as Lyndon Johnson briefly addresses the nation. But I cannot repeat, let alone recall, one word of what he's said. As Jason switches among the three networks, my mind is overwhelmed with all the conjecture about the alleged assassin, Lee Harvey Oswald.

"I can't watch anymore." Mrs. Johnson kisses us both good night. In a little while, Jason runs his hand across my shoulder as he walks behind my chair. He goes up to his room without a word. I watch until NBC ends its coverage for the night.

Neither Jason nor his mother said where I am to sleep: the guest room downstairs or with Jason in his attic. I brush my teeth in the guest bath. Then I climb the stairs. I don't want to be alone. I don't want Jason to be alone, but I hope he's asleep.

I undress in shafts of gray light penetrating the shutters. Jason is on his back, the covers up to his neck. I get into bed as quietly as possible.

"I don't know how we're going to get through this." He looks at the ceiling, not at me.

"I keep feeling as if I'm going to vomit."

Jason turns his back to me, slides closer. "Hold me."

I wrap my arms around him. "I feel everything has landed in the pit of my stomach—the horror, the evil, the sadness," I whisper, "and if I can just vomit, it will all disappear. I can flush it down the toilet, and it will never have happened."

Jason strokes my arm. "Of course, I know Lincoln and other presidents were assassinated. But I cannot believe this is happening in our time. That we are still so primitive, so animal. I feel a tremendous loss, not just that the world will never be the same, but that something good is gone forever. That hope has been murdered."

"Oswald killed our dreams."

Jason's body shakes with tears, and I hold him tighter. I kiss his neck. Eventually, he falls asleep. I wonder if I will. When I shut my eyes, I see Mrs. Kennedy's horrified face.

We watch television all day Saturday. Jason and his mom go for a long walk, but I stay inside. I can't pull myself away from the television. For dinner, Mrs. Johnson makes meatloaf and mashed potatoes.

On Sunday morning, she makes blueberry pancakes. I know she wants to console us with food, but I don't taste anything. Then, as if I'm not already in a universe I could never have imagined, everything shifts again with the totally unexpected and unforeseen.

"He's been shot! He's been shot!" a TV newsman shouts. "Lee Oswald has been shot!" I watch in shock as Jack Ruby guns down Oswald, who is being transferred to another jail. I want to scream for everything to stop. *Stop! Stop!*

Jason and his mother talk. Maybe to me. I don't know what they're saying. I am numb.

Later, mourners file past Kennedy's coffin in the Capitol rotunda. At eight o'clock, I watch *A Tribute to John F. Kennedy from the Arts*. Robert Frost reads a poem, Fredric March recites the *Gettysburg Address*, and Marian Anderson sings spirituals. I feel the whole world is as gray and white as the television.

Jason's mother doesn't cook the next day. There are leftovers, but I'm not hungry. We watch the slow, sad funeral procession to the Cathedral of St. Matthew. The television commentator is silent. There is only the mournful sound of horse hooves clopping on the crowd-packed streets. Then the announcer says today is John Kennedy Jr.'s third birthday. As the caisson slowly passes by John-John, he salutes his father. I think: *He'll never again feel his father's love.*

My body spasms, and my throat chokes. Jason pulls me to his chest. I cry and cry.

CLASSES RESUME. I watch Judy Garland at Jason's. Sometimes we sleep together. But we aren't boyfriends. Peter and I continue our shirtless workouts. I like being with him, the smell of our sweat mixing together in the air. But we aren't really friends.

There is an overcast of sadness everywhere.

The day before the holiday recess, I am lying on my bed, crying, when there's a knock on the door. I manage to get out the words, "Come in."

It's Peter. I blow my nose, hoping he'll think I'm having an allergy attack.

"Oh, you have been crying. Are you still upset about your president's assassination? It is a terrible thing." He sits down on the bed.

Peter rubs my shoulders. I can't tell him why I am really crying.

I'll never again feel my father's love.

Age nineteen

Pop Culture

"TURN ON THE radio right now." Jason's phone call wakes me up from a nap. He is excited about a new group, The Beatles, from Liverpool, England. Their song, "I Want to Hold Your Hand," is utterly infectious.

As soon as we see their photo, Jason and I let our hair grow over our ears and cover our foreheads. Most people think we look funny, but soon it seems half the younger generation has Beatles haircuts. A few students tell Jason he looks like George Harrison. I want to look like Paul McCartney, but nobody is *that* cute.

"Stick out your tongue," Jason says as we enter his mom's living room to watch The Beatles on *The Ed Sullivan Show*, their first American appearance.

"What is it?"

"Just something to make you happy." Jason puts a small circle of crystals, no larger than a dime, on my tongue, and it quickly dissolves.

Ed Sullivan is smart enough to put the Beatles on first.

"Probably none of the other acts would agree to appear before them," Jason says. "No one would pay any attention."

And there they are, singing "All My Loving" on the black-and-white screen, in their tight, four-button jackets with ties.

They may be dressed in men's clothes, but they're slender, almost delicate. Androgynous, with their long, thick hair and pointy, high-heeled boots.

"We don't want to see her," I say when the camera pans to a screaming teenager in the audience.

There's one boy in the mass of girls. He sits rigid, showing no reaction to the singers on stage or the wild frenzy in the audience around him.

"He probably has his hand in his pocket beating his meat," Jason says.

The camera flashes on a woman as excited as the girls. Jason's Mom says, "She must be forty if she's a day."

"Shh!" Jason says.

"Oh, you're allowed to talk, but I'm not."

"That's right," Jason and I say simultaneously. We all laugh, even Mrs. Johnson.

Next, The Beatles sing "Till There Was You."

"Ringo's cuter than he looks in photos," I say.

"You just like guys who sneer." Jason curls his lip.

While the camera zooms in for individual shots, the singers' names flash in white. Under John, it says: *Sorry, Girls. He's married.* They finish the set with "She Loves You." In the second part of the show The Beatles sing "I Want to Hold Your Hand," but my mind is not in the room. I see colors where there are none. The flat images on TV look three-dimensional. Jason seems outlined in white neon.

"What did you give me?" I whisper in his ear.

"LSD."

After the show, Jason takes me up to his bedroom and grabs things out of his closet. Of course, everything is black or white. He puts on a black coat that reaches to his ankles and wraps a long white silk scarf around his neck. He tosses me a black cape lined with white satin. He takes my hand, and we dash out of the attic, flying down the stairs and up the middle of South State Street with our arms out like wings, his scarf trailing us like a jet stream. We have so much energy, we run all the way to the center of campus without stopping. We stand on the steps of the library, holding hands and shouting, "I can't hide, I can't hide." Other students join us, and we sing all The Beatles' songs, clasping hands and jumping up and down. We're so happy inside.

This joyous quartet from England has taken us out of the sadness and despair that started with President Kennedy's assassination.

I AM ON my stomach, my shirt off, waiting for the next prick.

"Am I hurting you?" the intern asks.

"No. It sort of tickles."

"Let me know if it gets too much, and we'll take a break."

He's about twenty-five, has close-cropped hair, and his skin is as black as ink. He has a dimpled chin and a wide smile showing lots of teeth. He's so thin, I wonder if he earns enough money to eat three meals a day.

His long fingers insert tiny pins into my back. If the surrounding skin swells or turns red after the prick, it means I have an allergic reaction. There are 140 pins, each indicating a type of mold, spore, grass, plant, or food.

"There's even one for common household dust," the intern says.

"So plebian," I reply.

"That's an unusual word."

"Barbra Streisand sings it in 'Cry Me a River.' I love that the lyricist rhymes *plebian* with *me, and.*"

"Oh, yeah, I know that song." The next pin goes in. "It was a big hit for Julie London. She used to be married to Jack Webb."

"From *Dragnet?*" I flinch as another pin pierces my back.

"You're doing fine." He strokes my neck. "Tell me, what exactly does 'plebian' mean?"

"I asked my father that question when I got Barbra's album." Another prick. "He said he didn't know and seemed mad I'd asked."

"No father wants to look stupid in front of his son." Another prick. "So did you find out what it means?"

"Oh, sure. I looked it up. *Commonplace or vulgar.*"

Another pin. "So I take it you like Streisand?"

"Yeah, she's great. Did you see her on the cover of *Life* magazine? She looked so grown up." I brace myself for another pin, but there isn't one.

"I like *Life* magazine. So many interesting articles." The intern strokes my neck again. "Did you see the article this week on homosexuality?"

Sweat drips from under my arms. Of course I saw the article! I bought a copy at the newsstand and hid it in a drawer under my sweaters. The article was titled *Homosexuality in America*, and I've already read it three times. It starts off with a large black-and-white photograph taken inside the Tool Box, "a leather bar" in San Francisco.

Is the intern trying to find out if I'm homosexual? Maybe he's one. He hasn't stuck a pin for a while, just continues to massage. He's sweet and attentive, but I don't find him attractive. But why should that stop me? I don't find Jason attractive, but every couple of weeks, he either sucks me off or we masturbate together. I hope I'm not prejudiced because of the color of the intern's skin. I look over my shoulder and ask, "Are we finished?"

He pats my butt. "You take care of yourself, okay? The doctor will call you with the results in about a week."

It turns out I'm allergic to grass, mold, and household dust. So plebian.

I HAVE A job at the Art & Architecture Library, working at the front desk and shelving books. It's easy work, and I get to peruse all the beautiful books, but what I enjoy is watching the male undergrads. Most of the architecture students dress in corduroy slacks and narrow wool ties. The only colors they wear are shades of brown, navy blue, rust red, and, of course, black. I bet they wear their hair exactly as they did in high school: precisely parted and neatly trimmed above the ears. They're already men, already in competition with each other. I've never seen them laugh.

The guys in art school are always in jeans, ripped at the knees, and splattered with paint or clay. A few of them don't wash their long, wild hair or take a shower for a couple of days. They're always discussing their work, joking and playful with each other. Half the men in art school are queer, but we seem to pay more attention to the women students than the straight guys, who seem only interested in their art.

I don't think a single architecture student is homosexual, and I sense that they don't have much tolerance or respect for us art-school boys.

I get a second job. Four days a week, I'm an usher at the Michigan Theater, which is great, because besides providing a much-needed paycheck, I can see all the films for free. But I never get to watch an entire film unless I come back on my day off. When the movie starts, I'm still out front taking tickets from latecomers. During the film, I have to clean the toilets and change burned-out lights in the marquee. I never get to watch the end of a movie because I'm in the lobby opening all the doors so the people can stream out.

The puce uniform is too big and smells of other people who wear it on other days. The first movie I usher is *Mary Poppins*. The parts I see are fun the first and second times, but not on a Saturday with a theater full of screaming kids running in the aisles.

There's one movie I watch parts of over and over: *Night of the Iguana*, adapted from from Tennessee Williams's play. I even go in on my day off so I can see it uninterrupted. I memorize the poem Hannah's grandfather finishes before he dies. I don't understand why this film has such an effect on me. I'm only nineteen, with my life before me. Why do I identify with these lost souls?

I make Jason see the movie with me. He thinks, "Those people are pathetic, and the film is morbid. Why do you want to be sad, Anthony?"

Another question I cannot answer.

THE ART SCHOOL auditorium is packed for the Second Annual Ann Arbor Film Festival. The lights dim and several short films are screened. After a brief intermission, the film Jason and I have come to see is shown.

Scorpio Rising by Kenneth Anger has a reputation for being truly "underground," but I'm bored. For almost ten minutes, a James Dean-type works on his Harley motorcycle while pop songs play on the soundtrack. Ho-hum. Well, at least it's in color. As the camera pans up the legs of a man putting on tight jeans, my interest perks up. And it's funny, too, because the song is Bobby Vinton's "Blue Velvet." There's a quick shot of a guy lying shirtless on a bed. A flash of another shirtless man in white jodhpurs and a black leather jacket. Then, while The Crystals sing "He's a Rebel," a biker strutting in butch boots is juxtaposed with black-and-white scenes of Jesus leading his apostles out of the desert. I nearly howl.

Jason elbows me when there's a glimpse of a penis. A pink butt. The editing is incredible and funny. When the bikers initiate a man by pouring hot mustard on his groin, it looks as though Jesus, sitting at a table, is watching. The song is "Torture." I want to look at Jason to see if he's enjoying this as much as I am, but I don't want to miss anything by glancing away from the screen, so I squeeze his knee. He squeezes back.

During the song "Point of No Return," men race their cycles as Jesus rides a donkey on Palm Sunday. Then a leather-clad man cycles in the night as Little Peggy March sings "I Will Follow Him." And of course I love that. The film ends with "Wipeout" and sirens. We all loudly applaud, cheer, and hoot and stamp our feet.

I want to hang around and hear what everyone says, but Jason grabs my hand and pulls me up the marble stairs to the darkness of the second floor. He pushes me against a wall, unbuckles my belt, and kneels in front of me.

"I didn't think anything could top that film, but you did," I say when we skip down the empty stairs. Jason stops, kisses my lips. He smells like me.

Then he runs down the rest of the steps and out the door. By the time I'm outside, he's nowhere in sight. I know he's somewhere in the dark, that he's doing this on purpose. And then I hear what he screams.

"I wish you loved me."

BEFORE LAST TERM ended, I had thought of asking Peter Brant to be my roommate, but he pledged a fraternity, so I'm stuck with a meek English major. We talk about books and writing, but we never do anything together socially. He spends a lot of time with his girlfriend, and if I'm not at one of my jobs, I'm at Art School. I don't think there are any homosexuals in my dorm besides me, but that's okay, because I spend most of my free time with Jason.

Mom calls when Dad is at work and Bobby's at school. She does most of the talking. I never mention Dad, and she doesn't volunteer any information. She also doesn't ask questions. Maybe she's afraid of the answers.

This will be the second Christmas I haven't been at my parents' home.

"The holiday doesn't mean that much to me, Mom."

"Thanksgiving was awful without you at the table. I left like I was missing an arm." Her voice cracks, but she doesn't cry. "We should be together as a family."

"I'm going to have dinner with Jason and his mom."

"You know what I should do?"

"What?"

"Bring Bobby down there to see you and let your father sit here alone on Christmas. That would serve him right."

"You know you'll never do it."

"You're right, but it feels good to think about it."

"I'm going to work at the theater on Christmas. Most of the

staff will be away, so I'm going to do two shifts and make time-and-a-half."

I sneak Jason into the theater, and he watches *My Fair Lady* three times. That night, he enacts the final scene, since I haven't seen it. Then he plays all the main characters in the Ascot scene. He's very good as the overly refined Mrs. Higgins.

One weekend, there's a retrospective of early Alfred Hitchcock films at the local art theater. Jason sees all ten shows, but because of my work schedule, I only get to see four. We go to The Flame after the last show gets out at midnight.

"I'm glad I finally got to see *Rope*," I say. "It was a bit talky, but I liked it. Did you?"

"A bit talky! There was *no* action," Jason says. "You just liked it because you are obsessed with homosexuality."

"And you're not?"

"Not like you." Jason smiles. "But before you ask, yes, I think the two men were queer and, yes, James Stewart's character was a repressed homosexual who couldn't face the fact that he wanted to bed a male student. I also think that cute little Farley Granger is probably a faggot in real life."

"Why do you say that?"

"The way he moves his hands."

"Maybe that was the character he played."

"He had some of the same gestures in *Strangers on a Train*."

"Shall I get us another round?" The bar's not crowded, and I quickly return to our booth with two cold bottles of beer. "I don't know why we keep coming here. There's rarely anyone remotely appealing."

"See, Anthony, that's where we're fundamentally different. You come here to look at people, and I come here for people to look at me."

"Do you ever come here without me?"

"Sometimes."

"And do you ever leave here with someone?"

"Sometimes." Jason takes a long swig of beer. "But I can tell *you* aren't getting any lately. Certainly not from me—although I'm always available. But I know, you just don't *feel* that way about me. But, sweetie, if you wait around for *the one*, you'll be too old to get it up."

I'm not listening. I'm wondering how he knows I'm not "getting any." Do I come off desperate? Do I look too eager? Maybe that's why no one ever approaches me.

"It's easy to find a sex partner in Ann Arbor," I hear Jason say, and give him my full attention. "And I don't mean one of these losers." He waves his hand toward the guys slumped at the bar. "Here's what you do. Stroll around the Art and Architecture building just after two in the morning. Everyone knows that all the queer boys are in art school. Take your time. *Amble.* When a car slows, look directly at the driver. If he's interested, he'll circle the block, then pull up beside you. He'll say, 'Isn't it cold?' or 'Do you want a ride?' and if you're interested, you say, "Do you have a place to go?' because you certainly can't bring a man back to the dorm, and you cannot bring him back to my place. Unless I can participate. Or at least watch."

"Is that what you do?"

"I've had a *ménage* or two—or should I say three?—in my time, but I've never watched."

"No, I meant, do you *amble* around the A&A building?"

"How do you think I know about it?" Jason pats my hand. "Only *I* don't do the walking. My Avanti is a magnet. Unfortunately, most of the guys I'm attracted to just want a quick blowjob while they lean back and inhale the scent of leather. But I aim to please."

"Do you think it's safe to go to a stranger's apartment?"

"These guys are looking for sex, Anthony. They aren't serial killers. The only thing they're interested in shooting is their load. Just make sure you find out where a guy lives before you get in the car, because he'll probably fall asleep as soon as he comes, and you'll have to walk home."

I guess I look doubtful, because Jason adds, "I think cruising the streets is safer than giving blowjobs under the toilet stalls at the Union—where a security guard can walk in and bust you."

"Did that happen to you?"

"Once." Jason is never embarrassed. "Now you know all my secrets."

"I doubt that very much."

The next night, I walk too fast around the Art and Architecture building and never lift my eyes from my feet. And still, a car stops.

The driver lowers his window. "Need a ride?"

I do a quick scan: early thirties, thick blond hair. I get in without speaking.

"It's cold out there."

I nod.

"Do you have a place to go?"

Shit, that was supposed to be my question. "I live in a dorm."

"That's okay." He pulls away from the curb. "I have an apartment."

I hope it's not in Detroit. That would be quite a hike back.

"You have to be quiet when we go in," the man says. "My roommate's straight. My name's Philip."

"Where's your apartment?"

"Not too far. On Lincoln Avenue."

After he unlocks his apartment door, he puts a finger to his lips, signaling me to keep quiet. He removes his shoes; I do the same. He kisses me as soon as he shuts his bedroom door.

"Aren't you going to close the curtains?"

"I like moonlight." He steps out of chino slacks, removes his socks, and lifts a black turtleneck jersey over his head. He has a well-defined body with thick chest hair, which is always a plus to my eyes.

"Do you work out?"

"Yeah. Aren't you going to undress? Or do you want me to do it for you?"

I let him.

Then I put my hands on his hips and lower his white Jockey shorts.

"What do you like to do?" He caresses my chest.

"Not answer that question."

"Okay. Then we'll do what *I* want."

And we do. And I like it.

Afterwards, he collapses on his side, pulls my back to his chest, his arms locking me, his index finger idly making circles around my navel.

"Are you a student?"

"Yes."

"What year?"

"Sophomore."

"So, you're, what? Twenty?"

"Nineteen."

"Even better."

He kisses my neck.

"What are you studying?"

"Art."

"I teach sixth-grade geography."

He softly relates "the abridged version—just the highlights" of his life story. "Well, to make a long story short—"

"Too late." I can't see his face, but I sense he doesn't think that was funny.

We're quiet. Maybe I fall asleep for a bit.

He whispers in my ear. "I wonder if I can come a third time." We both do.

"You could be the one." He kisses my forehead, my nose, my eyes. "I think I could love you."

"Tell me that when I'm dressed." He doesn't smile. Is Jason the only person who appreciates my sense of humor? "We've been intimate, but you don't know anything about me." I nearly say, *I bet you don't even remember my name.*

"So, let's see each other again so I can get to know you better."

I get out of bed and pull on my jeans. "I want you to be honest with me. How many guys have you shared 'just the highlights' with?"

"A few."

"And how many guys have you thought were 'the one'?"

He doesn't answer. Doesn't look at me. I finish dressing. When I turn to go, he quickly gets up and leads me through the apartment. He's silent while I put on my shoes, but before letting me out, he says, "You're going to be a very lonely man."

"DO YOU WANT to go to a salon?" Jason asks me at Dominick's. "Sorry, Ruth, it's only for guys of a certain persuasion."

"Isn't it always?" Ruth cuts her pizza and eats it with a fork.

"Gee, with all the unisex salons opening, I'm surprised

someone's opened a beauty shop just for men." I take another pizza slice.

"Not that kind of salon, silly," says Jason. "This is a literary salon, like in eighteenth-century France."

"Oh, you mean like Gertrude Stein?"

"That was twentieth century, and hers was an art salon. This one's more about philosophical ideas."

"You never need an encyclopedia when you're with Jason," I tell Ruth. Then I turn to him. "Sure, I'll go. When is it?"

"Sunday evening."

"Who's the host of this soiree of enlightenment?" Ruth asks. "Please tell me it's not Gregory Russell."

"As a matter of fact, it is." Jason gives her a dismissive sneer, but he can't pass up gossip. "Why, what have you heard?"

"Only that he's a fraud, passing himself off as an intellectual, when all he really wants to do is bed impressionable pretty boys."

"Well, I'm not in the least impressionable, and I'm invited."

When Ruth opens her mouth, I'm afraid she's going to say, "You aren't pretty either," but she asks, "Did Gregory personally invite you?"

"Well, no. Terry Tyler invited me."

"And Terry Tyler is a very pretty, very naive boy." Ruth takes out her lipstick. "In fact, he's so naïve, he asked you to the salon when Gregory was probably expecting him to ask other innocents." She smears vermillion across her lips without using a mirror.

"Jason *is* innocent." I burst out laughing before I finish the sentence.

"'I am as pure as the driven slush,'" Jason says in a gravelly voice.

"'Only good girls keep diaries,'" I say in my own Tallulah Bankhead imitation, "'Bad girls don't have time.'"

"You guys are such clichés," Ruth says.

"Better a cliché than a—." Jason decides not to finish the sentence.

I tell them how Dad wouldn't let me watch the end of *Lifeboat* with Tallulah when his friends came over for dinner.

"YOU ARE NOT to ask personal questions, like you usually do," Jason warns as we walk to Gregory's bungalow south of campus. "You are not to make catty comments about the decor. And you are not to talk incessantly about films."

"Yes, Mother."

"And you are not to disappear into the bedroom with Terry Tyler. That's *my* job."

"You wouldn't dare." I look at Jason as we climb the steps. "Would you?"

Gregory Russell is probably forty. He's tall and very slender. Gray hair flecks his manicured haircut with an exact part. He looks like he's wearing the same clothes he did when he went to college: khaki pleated pants, pale blue button-down shirt, Topsiders. Terry Tyler presents us to our host, just as more guests enter, so the introductions are brief. There are about fifteen men, everyone except Gregory under thirty. Maybe under twenty-five.

Terry Tyler fits the mold: barely twenty, slender, almost blond.

"The redhead in the corner is still in high school." Jason points discreetly with his pinkie finger. I raise my eyebrows. "I did not ask. He volunteered."

"I feel out of place among these Adonises." I think all these young men could be models. I don't fit in.

"You? Did you see the look Gregory gave *me*? Like he wishes I would blend into the tacky wallpaper."

"I thought we weren't allowed to critique the decor."

"*You* aren't allowed to critique the decor." Jason leads me to a bar set up in the corner of the dining room. "He doesn't have anything alcoholic!"

"Maybe he doesn't want anyone getting drunk." I pour root beer into a glass.

The chairs are all occupied, so we sit on the floor by a basket filled with books and magazines. I thumb through a catalog from Hudson's Department Store.

"Oh my god!" I point to a young man modeling underwear. "I went to high school with this guy. His name's Ray Hutton."

Jason grabs the brochure from my hands. "He's cute. Is he one of us?"

"Sadly, no."

Jason hands me back the catalog. "Try not to get it sticky."

I wonder if I can sneak it into my coat before we leave. Three young men place several dishes of food on the dining table. Jason stands. "Let's get something to eat."

"I know you said not to comment," I whisper, "but this place looks like an old lady lives here." I put Swedish meatballs on my plate. "It reminds me of the house in *Psycho*."

"What did I say about movies?" Jason's plate is colorful with carrots, radishes, and pepper slices. Most of the guys save seats for each other, so Jason and I sit back on the floor.

When Gregory glides into the living room, Terry jumps up from a wingchair with a hideous blue-and-brown flame-stitch, and Gregory sits down in his place. Terry crumples at his feet. Gregory clears his throat and thanks us all for coming. Then he looks around the room.

"So, tell us, Jason, the first time you saw the adorably cute Anthony, what was your immediate reaction?"

I imagine Jason is even more surprised than I that Gregory not only remembers our names but also asks him a question in front of everyone. But Jason reacts quickly. "I wanted to jump his bones."

"Exactly," Gregory says when the laughter stops. "Even if we won't admit it as blatantly as Jason, that's always our first thought when we see a handsome man."

I feel everyone staring at me, deciding whether I'm handsome or cute or none of the above.

"This is the way gay men have always reacted, from the first time Cain saw Abel to—"

"You're saying Cain was homosexual?" Everyone turns toward the high school redhead crunching a celery stick.

"Why do you think he killed his brother?" Gregory smiles but looks displeased at the interruption. "But that's a topic for another time."

"That boy won't be asked back," Jason whispers.

"I know many gay men," Gregory continues, "who have been in long-term relationships. One of them for thirty years. But not one of these couples is monogamous. Oh, sure, they started out that way, but within a year, within a month, one of them was fooling around. Of course, there are those who don't have sex outside of the relationship, but that's only because they don't have any sex at all." Gregory looks around the room, daring anyone to contradict him. "Homosexuals—I'm talking about men, not lesbians—should never attempt to emulate heterosexual relationships. Why would we want to mirror their marriages when they've obviously been such failures at it? The divorce rate keeps rising every year. Man simply cannot be monogamous for any length of time. So why force it?"

Gregory doesn't speak in words or sentences. He speaks in paragraphs. He expounds for another seven minutes, then asks one of the men a question. This, I surmise, is our signal that we may discuss Today's Topic. It doesn't take long for small groups to break into separate conversations, and the room is alive with male voices. Drinks are refreshed, and two trays of desserts are brought out.

"It's funny you should mention *Psycho*," Jason says when he comes back from the bathroom. "There's a photo of Anthony Perkins above the toilet."

"I'm not surprised. Don't you think Gregory looks a bit like him?"

"Yeah, when he's dressed as Norman Bates' mother."

"You're just mad because he caught you off guard. But you recovered well. Something I'd like to do to that wingchair."

"At least I didn't blush, like you did when he called you 'adorable.' Which you are." He kisses my neck. "I saw Gregory put his hand on your ass when he thought no one was watching."

"You don't miss a thing."

"I'll get our coats." Jason heads toward the bedroom. "I think we can safely depart without seeming rude."

"I'm going to hang around a bit longer."

Jason puckers his lips and leaves without saying goodbye to our host. Not that Gregory Russell notices.

Everyone soon departs except Terry Tyler, who offers to help clean up. While he and Gregory are in the kitchen, I pick up a notebook lying in the basket in the living room. I flip the pages to a bookmark.

Why should we want to mirror their marriages—

So, Gregory wrote down everything he said tonight. He

probably rehearsed all afternoon. I put the notebook back in the basket, stuff the Hudson catalog in the arm of my jacket, and head for the kitchen to say goodnight. Gregory and Tyler aren't washing the dishes. They're kissing. I walk out the front door without making a sound.

ANN ARBOR IS filled with visitors excited about the "big game" against Michigan State. I'm not in the least bit interested, but Jason says he has special plans for us. Ruth's included.

Jason's small second-floor balcony faces South State Street, and a lot of people have to walk past the house to get to the football stadium. He moves two three-feet-high stereo speakers onto the balcony.

"I'm only going to do this if I get to be the lead," I tell Jason.

"Of course, you're the lead. I thought of this when I saw you lip-synching the other day."

Ruth refreshes her usual vermillion lipstick, but Jason and I aren't wearing any makeup. We don't have on costumes, just our regular jeans and bulky sweaters. No wigs. Not a sequin in sight. But we know who we are.

I take my position at the balcony rail, and Jason, after dropping the needle on a record, stands behind me next to Ruth.

Our hands shoot out like traffic cops.

We are The Supremes, and we want everyone to *Stop! In the Name of Love.*

I push my head forward on my neck, lift my shoulders toward my ears, just like Diana Ross and lip-sync. Jason looks at me and croons, "Haven't I been good to you?"

I crook my finger in admonishment, telling him to think it over. Then our hands again shoot forward like traffic cops. And people do stop. Maybe some of them are laughing at us, but a lot of them applaud. Even guys.

When the song finishes, Jason changes the record. I immediately stand rigid, my chin lifted, my eyes above the crowd.

I am aloof. I am Dionne Warwick. I demand everyone to "walk on by."

We pantomime every record we own about walking or running. It doesn't matter if the singers are male or female; we lip-sync them all. Jason takes the lead for Frankie Valli and the Four Seasons' "Walk Like a Man" and Ray Charles' "Hit the Road Jack." Ruth is out front for The Shangri-Las' "Remember (Walkin' in the Sand)" and Del Shannon's "Runaway." And, of course, I take back the lead for Little Peggy March's "I Will Follow Him" and an encore of "Stop! In the Name of Love" as stragglers head to the stadium.

JASON KNOWS I'M pissed that he is 45 minutes late, so he opens the Avanti's passenger door for me. "I couldn't decide what to wear."

"How hard could it be when everything you own is black and white?"

"But cotton or silk? Tight or bouffant? Laces or loafers? These subtle differences mean everything."

"To you."

He starts the engine. "Besides, it's not a sit-down dinner. We don't have to arrive on time. Don't you want to make an entrance?"

"I don't care what time we get there. I care that I was ready when you told me to be, and you kept me waiting. Again."

"I'm sorry." He blows kisses at me. "I bet you didn't just sit there pouting."

"I cut a woodblock."

"You're the most productive person I've ever met. What's the subject?"

"A variation of the trees I photographed in snow." I know he's showing an interest to make up for being late, but there's something else on my mind. "Jason, promise me you will only smoke pot tonight. That you won't take any other drugs."

"How do you know I haven't already?"

"Have you?" I cross my arms.

"Stop worrying. I did not take anything. Not even one hit." He stops at a red light and holds up his right hand like a Boy Scout. "And I promise not to ingest a single drug until we are safely inside Manuel's apartment."

"If you start tripping like you did last weekend, how are we supposed to get back home?"

"You can drive. I trust you with my baby." He pats the dashboard.

"I can't drive a stick shift."

"Well then, my precious, maybe we won't get home. Maybe we'll spend the night sleeping with strangers. It's Saturday, and we don't have any place we have to be tomorrow."

"I hate when you're like this."

"I love when we argue." He rubs my leg. "I can pretend we're an old married couple. After all, we haven't had sex in ages."

I'm not going there. "Manuel's the guy we met a couple of months ago who works in advertising at Hudson's, right?"

"Yeah, he's a stylist."

"Who else is going to be there?"

"The usual Woodward Avenue crowd. Plus Manuel's brother, who's visiting from Puerto Rico. He's the reason for the party." Jason turns onto I-94. "I wish *my* brother were queer."

"Your sister's a lesbian. Doesn't that count?"

"Oh yeah, we're real close. Is your brother queer?"

"Jason, he's eight."

"I knew I was queer when I was eight. I had a crush on Ricky Nelson."

"Did you like Bud Anderson on *Father Knows Best*?"

"I *loved* Bud Anderson. I used to fantasize about Billy Gray tying me up."

"I was bored whenever the stories weren't about Bud," I say. "Princess was okay, but I couldn't stand Kitten."

By the time we get to Detroit, I know every young male celebrity Jason ever lusted after. And he knows mine.

At Manuel's apartment, I'm amazed at an enormous collection of records stacked next to the turntable.

"They're for our game," Manuel says. "And now that almost everyone's here and you have your drinks, we can begin."

"I'm sorry we're so late," I say.

"It was my fault," Jason adds.

"No problem." Manuel stops the record that's spinning, grabbing everybody's attention. "Okay, the way this game works—" There's a knock on the door. "Juan, would you get that?"

We all look to see who is the last, very tardy guest.

Manuel points his arm like a magician's assistant. "Everyone, this is Ray Hutton. You may recognize him from his photographs—in underwear, no less—in the new ads in Hudson's catalog." Someone whistles. "Sorry, guys, but Ray's straight."

Ray waves and quickly heads for the bar in the corner. I jab Jason with my elbow. "That's the guy from my high school!"

"He looks like your father."

"He does not! And when have you ever seen my father?"

"You showed me pictures," Jason says. "For one thing, they both have the same color hair."

"They do not! Dad's is red, and Ray's is strawberry blond."

"Oh, big difference. What about their eyes?"

"All right, I'll give you that. They both have amber eyes. But they don't look *anything* alike."

"You keep telling yourself that as you drool."

Before I can protest further, Manuel taps loudly on a table. "Okay, everyone! The way this game works is that each person picks the one song that they would most like to dedicate to someone in this room. Give me the record, and when I have everyone's selections, I'll play them at random, and when your song comes on, you sing it to your special someone."

"Or maybe you choose a song to sing to an ex-boyfriend," Juan says.

"So during the next half hour, pick a song, have some food, refill your glasses, and somebody," Manuel pauses, "please pass me a joint!"

I'd never have guessed Manuel and Juan are brothers. Manuel's tall and beefy. Juan's short, wiry, and a lot cuter.

Jason takes a small plastic bag out of his pocket. "Are you sure you won't join me?"

I shake my head, but I'm curious. "What is it?"

"MDA. It's more potent than LSD. I have enough for both of us. It will be more fun if we take it together."

"I don't want to."

"Why not?"

"I like to be in control."

"But you're so cute when you're not."

I walk across the room and flop down on an oversized pillow on the floor. "Hi, Ray, do you remember me? Anthony Dimora."

"Sure, from high school."

Ray still has the most radiant hair I've ever seen. It shines like topaz. He wears it longer than in high school, combed straight back, and touching his shoulders. And there's that sexy smile.

"So, what have you been doing since high school," I ask, "besides modeling underwear?"

"I've only recently been modeling. You might remember that I've always been interested in cars, so I decided to make cars. I work on the line at the Ford Plant in Dearborn. I've been there for two years. Great pay."

Someone passes him a joint, and he inhales. He offers it to me, but I shake my head.

"How did you hook up with Hudson's?"

"A guy in payroll at Ford knows Manuel. You know he's Hudson's main stylist for men's clothes, right?" I nod. "He told me he had a full roster of models, but if I was willing to pose in underwear, he could use me. I think he just wanted to intimidate me."

"Or get you out of your clothes."

"Probably, but there was no 'casting couch' or anything." Ray's eyes roam the room. I wonder who he's looking for, or maybe he's uncomfortable with me sitting next to him. I notice he hasn't asked me anything. Is he too self-centered or simply uninterested?

"I'm studying art at U of M," I volunteer. "It's only a half hour from Dearborn. You should come for a visit one weekend."

"I couldn't do that, Anthony."

"Why not?"

"You're dangerous."

I'm about to ask him how I could possibly be dangerous, when Manuel claps his hands, announcing the game is about to begin.

He puts a record on the turntable. An older man croons "Dedicated to the One I Love" to another man about his age. They've probably been together for decades. During "My Boy Lollipop," a young skinny guy sits on a chubby guy's lap and licks his face.

Manuel puts on the next record.

Jason rises with the first notes and, singing along with The Supremes, tells me that whenever he's near, he hears a symphony. When Diana sings about lips touching, Jason kisses me, putting his tongue in my mouth, while the guys hoot and holler. It isn't until he's singing again that I realize he's slipped a tiny pill in my mouth—and I've swallowed it.

Guys sing "Baby I Need Your Loving," "Our Day Will Come," and one man smokes a joint to "Puff (the Magic Dragon)." Then my song comes on. I'm already sitting next to Ray, so I just look into his eyes as I lip-sync "Anyone Who Had a Heart."

Ray smiles but looks embarrassed. When the song's over, he says, "I told you: You're dangerous."

Someone performs "Sixteen Reasons Why I Love You." I'm bored by reason four.

"The Shoop Shoop Song" starts, and Ray jumps up. Every time he mouths, "It's in his kiss," he offers his cheek to another man—but not to me.

More songs until our host does the last tune. "It's My Party (and I'll cry if I want to)."

When I tell Ray that Jason slipped me a pill and I feel nauseated, he brings me a Verner's ginger ale. "I thought he was your boyfriend."

"No. He'd like to be, but—"

Jason drops down on the other side of Ray. "I'm his best friend. So, what about you? Do you have a boyfriend?"

"I've been living with an airline stewardess." Ray's smile looks huge. Is that the drug causing distortion? "She's blond and has big tits."

"She sounds like a cliché."

"Yeah, I like them that way."

I want to say something, but the room is starting to spin off its axis.

"Why didn't you bring her to the party?" Jason asks.

"She's on layover in Hawaii. Besides, Manuel made it clear the party was men-only."

"So why did you come to the party, Ray?"

Ray turns to me instead of answering. "Anthony, are you okay?"

Jason reaches across Ray and takes the ginger ale out of my hand before I spill it. "He's fine."

I'm not, but I can't seem to open my mouth to tell them. I wave my arms in front of me as if I'm peddling a bike with my hands. Jason's talking, but I don't understand what he's saying. I don't think I even hear him. I look around and can clearly discern conversations on the other side of the room, but I can't hear a word Jason says.

"This is really weird." I finally speak. "The whole room looks like a Cubist painting. Everything is divided into cubes. Ray's face is broken into cubes, and all the pieces keep coming toward me like a moving train. The cube of Ray's right eye moves forward, and the cube of my left eye moves toward him. All our various cubes are moving toward each other at different speeds, but we never connect."

"It's just the drug, Anthony." Jason sounds annoyed, or maybe it's condescension. "Sometimes the drug gives you insight into your deepest thoughts. You're just projecting your relationship with your father."

"I think he's really sick," Ray says, as if I'm not right there next to him.

"I have to use the bathroom." I get up. In the middle of the room, I turn around and look at Jason and Ray sitting on the pillows on the floor.

And I'm sitting there too.

The me on the floor looks at the me standing up. We stare back and forth at each other, and one of us screams, "I don't know which one I am."

I crash to the floor.

"I don't know which one I am. I don't know which one I am."

I WON'T LET Jason take me to the hospital. "It's a weird sensation, but I know it will get better on its own. I know I'm physically sitting here next to you in the Avanti, but I feel I'm suspended from my body, that my soul or essence, or whatever you want to call it, is in the backseat watching my body in the front seat. It was frightening before, at Manuel's, because I didn't know which one I was, but now I do, and it's sort of interesting."

"You are really freaking me out." Jason looks in the rearview mirror. "Your voice even sounds like it's coming from the backseat."

"I'm going to be all right. I just panicked for a moment back there."

Jason drives through the darkness. "I'm sorry."

"For what?"

"For giving you the MDA."

"I forgive you for giving me the drug. Forgive for giving."

"Is it going to be like this all night?"

"I think it's going to be like this *for days*."

And it is. Each day, my presence behind me moves a little closer to my body in front. By the third day, I'm right up against myself. I can see every follicle of my hair as if it were under a microscope. Jason doesn't want his mother to know what's going on, so he tells her I'm sick. He feeds me homemade chicken soup and reads to me in the bathtub. I can't concentrate on the words, but his voice soothes me. In bed, he pulls my back to his chest, his erection pressed against my ass. He touches me, feels my softness. He kisses my neck and lets me sleep.

"I'm back!" It's the fourth day. "Colors are still very intense, and my hearing is still amplified, as if I can hear the air moving. But I'm back." I go into the bathroom and come out with the book Jason has been reading while I slept. *The Collector* by John Fowles. "Is this how you saw me, as a butterfly, a specimen behind glass?"

"It's just a book." Jason strips the sheets from his bed.

"You kept me naked the whole time."

"Come on, Anthony. I took care of you."

"You kept me locked up like one of your possessions."

"I think maybe you're not *entirely* back. You're still a bit paranoid."

"What day is it?" I see my clothes on the sofa and get dressed.

"Wednesday."

"I have to go to work."

"I called your boss at the theater and told him you had the flu. I also told Gloria at the library, so everything's covered."

"And you could have me all to yourself."

"I didn't molest you, Anthony. You know that, don't you?"

"Yes." He looks so sad. I hug him.

"It's okay, Jason. I'll call you tomorrow."

"Wait," Jason says. "I'll drive you back to your dorm."

"No thanks. I need the fresh air."

As I walk back to the dorm, I find a small piece of paper in my shirt pocket. I unfold it. It's from Ray. Four little words: *I have a heart.*

Age twenty

Naked

RAY ASKS ME to meet him at a new restaurant in Dearborn. When I say I don't have a car, he picks me up in a silver Corvette Sting Ray. As we concentrate on our menus, I wonder if we're going to run out of things to talk about before we finish dinner— or at least subjects that might hold my attention.

"So, how's your girlfriend?"

"Cindy and I broke up." Ray shrugs as if it's no big deal. "But I'm still living at her apartment. She's always flying off somewhere, so she's not there very often. But I've got to find my own place soon."

"My first two years at college," I say as our salads arrive, "I lived in a dorm, but this term I moved into Jason's mother's house." The waiter brings warm rolls dripping with garlic butter. They smell wonderful, but I don't want garlic breath. Ray digs right in. "Mrs. Johnson has a nice house near campus, and I rent one of the bedrooms. Jason has a big attic room upstairs. We're always together, so I thought it would work out, but I'm starting to think it's not such a good idea. Jason can get a bit possessive. I'd love to have my own place, but I can't afford it. I'd have to find a roommate."

Ray's eyes narrow, and I wonder if I'm talking too much.

He says he's looking forward to *Thunderball*, the new James

Bond 007 film that comes out in December, and spends the entire time we're eating our entrees talking about *Goldfinger*.

"Do you like Shirley Bassey?"

Ray looks puzzled. "Who's she?"

"She sang the Goldfinger theme song." I softly sing the title word, stretching it the way Shirley does.

"Oh, yeah." Ray glances around, as though he's afraid someone might have heard me. "Great song."

He doesn't want dessert and insists on picking up the check. In the parking lot, he says, "I don't mind driving you back to Ann Arbor, but I'm feeling really tired and afraid I might fall asleep at the wheel coming back home. I don't want to risk damaging the 'Vette."

I wonder if I have enough cash to take a taxi thirty miles.

Ray offers another solution. "Do you mind if we just crash at my place? Cindy's off somewhere. The apartment's only a few miles from here. I'll drive you back in the morning."

When we get there, Ray doesn't seem so sleepy. He pops open a beer and flops on the sofa. I use the bathroom. And peek at the bedroom. An unmade double bed. I jump when he puts a hand on my shoulder.

"Here." He hands me a toothbrush wrapped in plastic. "Cindy has tons of these. She gets them from first class on overseas flights."

While I brush my teeth, I wonder if he's getting out sheets for me to sleep on the sofa, but when I step back into the hall, the living room is dark. A red-and-orange lava lamp pulsates in the bedroom, casting a fake glow of sunset. Ray tosses his boxer shorts on the floor.

"My turn." He smiles as he struts naked toward the bathroom.

I stack my clothes on a chair and get under the sheet.

"Hey!" He smells of peppermint. "You're on my side of the bed." I scoot over. "Oh, nice and warm."

We lie on our backs. He is so near, so naked. My body is painfully aware of him. I feel I'm a scrap of metal, and he's a magnet. If I stretch my leg so it grazes his, will he pull away? Why set myself up to be rejected? I should just say "goodnight," roll on my side away from him, and hope sleep comes before morning.

"Anthony?" Ray's face is a silhouette, but his hair looks on fire in the lava light. He whispers, "I want you to fuck me."

RAY'S NOT IN bed when I wake up. He's not in the apartment. Was he so ashamed about what happened last night that he couldn't face me? Or himself? I dress, wondering if I'm going to have to take a taxi to Ann Arbor after all. Then Ray walks in.

"I bought bagels." We sit at the kitchen counter. "I was thinking about what you said last night." He scoops a mound of cream cheese. "I'm going to have to double my routine at the gym to work this off. Anyway, you said you need a roommate, and I need to move out, so maybe we could get a place together."

I nearly spit my bagel across the room. Then my practical side takes over. "I don't have a car, and I have classes five days a week and two jobs. I have to live in Ann Arbor."

"It's only thirty miles between Ann Arbor and Dearborn. I can commute. Besides, I work the second shift, so I'm never in traffic."

"Well, if you don't mind the drive, I think it's a great idea."

"Good. I don't have to see the place. Whatever you choose will be fine. But the sooner the better. Cindy wants me out of here."

Back in Ann Arbor, I have second, third, and fourth thoughts about living with Ray. I barely know him. We share few interests. Am I going to be bored with our conversations? Will he be bored with me?

I guess all that matters is that when I see him, I melt.

Of course, Jason thinks I'm making a *colossal* mistake.

I found a one-bedroom furnished apartment just south of Art School. Ray doesn't have many possessions, and mine are mainly books and art supplies, so we easily move in an afternoon. We order pizza and spend the evening hooking up stereos—Ray's in the living room because it's better quality, mine in the bedroom, which has twin beds separated by a three-foot area rug. At ten-thirty, Ray plugs in his lava lamp. Then he pushes the beds together.

In the morning, he pushes them apart.

SOME STUDENTS ARE excited about figure drawing class: nude models!

Excitement dwindles each week as we see the models. Most are chubby older women. Once the model is about twenty, but she's so thin we can draw her bones. Maybe that's the point. Another time, a bald man about fifty poses; he's so fat his penis is hidden in rolls of flesh. Then, one afternoon, the model is attractive: a blond man about forty, with no hair to obscure his well-defined chest and muscular calves.

Mr. Boyd, our teacher, starts the class as usual with three-minute active poses with the model's arms outstretched or his body twisted. We are to capture the essence in ink. We move on to fifteen-minute poses, with the model sitting. We're instructed to draw the entire figure in charcoal or pastel.

As usual, after a break, there is one long pose, with the model lying on his back on a red sheet. This time, the drawing medium is up to the student. I select a pencil. I like to make a definitive study, with precise shading, very detailed, with no abstractions. In the past, when we had a 45-minute pose, and I drew in pencil, I never had time to finish. I'd sketch a general outline of the body and shade the torso or the legs, but the rest of the anatomy would be unfinished. The teacher praised my work, but I found the incompleteness unsatisfying. I wanted a finished drawing.

So this time, with a handsome man before me, I decide not to do the entire figure but instead concentrate on one area. I choose the penis. I select a light gray paper for the background. With explicit shading, I capture the flow of the long vein and the rise of the glans. I add highlights with a white pencil. A few broad black strokes suggest the pubic bush, then I sharpen my pencil and draw individual curling hairs.

Mr. Boyd looks over my shoulder. "Well done, Anthony, but obsessive."

RAY LIVES FOR Saturday nights. He works from three in the afternoon until eleven at night on the Ford assembly line, so come the weekend, he wants his beer and pizza. I have a glass of wine. We cuddle on the sofa, watching *The Man from U.N.C.L.E.*

One Friday, he says, "I have a confession to make." He looks into my eyes. He suddenly seems frightened. He closes his eyes, doesn't say anything. Then he looks at me again, and it all rushes out. "I used you as an experiment. I wanted to see what it was like to have sex with a man, so I used you. The problem is I fell in love with you."

I'm about to ask why that's a problem, but Ray puts his index finger on my lips to silence me.

"I'm not a homosexual, Anthony. I don't desire other men. Just you." He caresses my cheek. "But one day I want to get married—to a woman—and have children."

He's silent, and I realize he's expecting me to say something.

"Why do you push the beds apart every morning? Who are you afraid will see—and judge you?"

Ray gets up from the sofa and walks into the bathroom. I follow him.

"I don't think the way you do," he says. "I don't analyze everything or try to figure out the psychology behind it. I just go with my feelings." He puts toothpaste on his brush and hands me the tube.

"Are you telling me all this now because you've met someone—*a woman* you might want to marry?"

He shakes his head, then spits out toothpaste and rinses his mouth. "That's not it at all. It's just—I don't know, Anthony! I just felt I had to tell you."

"Well, I'm glad you did, although I'm not certain how I feel about being an 'experiment.' But, okay. One day, you'll meet someone and get married. But for now, can we keep the beds together?"

RAY OCCASIONALLY MODELS clothes for Hudson's. One night, when he shows me the latest catalog with four photographs of him in underwear, I ask if he'll pose for me. Nude.

He immediately strips off his clothes. "How do you want me to pose?"

Almost every night, I do a different drawing of Ray. Sometimes

I sketch his whole body. Other evenings, I draw just his face or a close-up of his lips so meticulously detailed it could be a medical drawing. I draw his hands. His feet. His torso. His penis.

He makes me promise not to show the penis drawings to anyone, not even my teachers. I ask if we can move on to photography.

"I don't want photographs of me nude in existence."

"Why not? Are you planning to run for president one day?" Ray smirks.

"What if I do just details, like my drawings, so that you won't be able to be identified?"

For several nights, I photograph Ray's penis from various angles, from flaccid to erect.

Then I move on to vegetables. I lay a sheet of white paper on the dining room table and position Ray so his penis lies flat on the paper. Next, I arrange mushrooms so that the head of his penis looks like just one more morel.

I photograph Ray's penis with a gourd. With a cluster of red grapes covering his pubic hair. Another time, I sit him on a chair, his testicles obscured by mounds of walnuts.

"Why," Ray wants to know, "are you so obsessed with cock?"

"I'm not. Just *your* cock."

Ray smiles. He doesn't know I lied. The pictures are black and white, so I can develop the film in a dark room at Art School, but when I'm aiming my camera so close to Ray's crotch, I can't help but notice that his pubic hair is as bright red as my Dad's and that the head of his cock is the same pale pink.

ONE EVENING, WHILE Ray is working, Ruth and I see *The Glass Bottom Boat*, a movie Ray predicts will be awful. He's right.

Ruth's been dating a married man from Detroit, but doesn't want to talk about it, so we talk about me. "I don't know that many homosexuals," Ruth says, "just the ones at art school, but I think you're the most well-adjusted homosexual I've met."

"That's because I didn't have to adjust. It seemed perfectly normal to me to be interested in boys."

"You went to Catholic school. Weren't you told that sex with other boys was wrong?"

"No. All the priests ever talked about was masturbation, or 'self-abuse,' as they called it. None of them said a word about homosexuality. It was only after I read about it that I learned that other people considered it abnormal."

"But didn't you realize you were different from the other boys?"

"I knew I was different because I didn't like sports and was called a sissy. But I didn't connect being a sissy with liking boys. I thought boys were stupid for wanting to chase a ball."

"When you watched movies," Ruth says, "you know, fluffy love stories with Doris Day—like the stupid one we just saw— didn't you notice that they were all about a man and woman? Didn't you feel different then?"

"You know how children think they're the cause of their parents' arguments when they had nothing to do with it? And how they think every family is just like theirs? We all imagine the world revolves around us, so when I watched movies, I didn't think I was watching them any differently than everyone else. I never paid much attention to love stories. Whether Doris Day and Rock Hudson ended up together was the least interesting aspect to me. I was more interested in the decor and costumes. And I liked the sidekicks—Thelma Ritter and Tony Randall. Doris Day annoyed me. The only Alfred Hitchcock movie I dislike is *The Man Who Knew Too Much*. I hate that stupid song that Doris sings."

Ruth sings, "*Que sera, sera.*"

"One more *sera* and I'll throw my drink in your face. Anyway, the only Doris Day movie I like is *Midnight Lace.*"

When I get back to the apartment, Ray is on the sofa staring at the television. Only the set isn't turned on. He's holding a crumpled piece of paper.

"What's wrong, Ray?" I sit next to him "Did something happen?"

"I've been drafted."

"IT SEEMS I only call you when something traumatic happens," I say when I telephone Tony Tomasso.

"I'm always pleased when you call," he replies, "and I'm always here for you. So tell me what happened. Is Ray still at boot camp?"

"Yes. He hates it, and I miss him, but it's not that." I take a deep breath and exhale. "Have you seen *Who's Afraid of Virginia Woolf?*"

"Just last night. Powerful film."

"I've seen just about every one of Elizabeth Taylor's movies. I'm so glad this wasn't one of the awful ones, like *The Sandpiper*, or even worse, *The V.I.P.s.* And the way she looked! She practically had a double chin. But she was great, wasn't she?"

I can tell by the way Tony says "yes" that he wants me to get to the point. He gets paid as a psychologist, and I'm asking him to help me for nothing.

"Anyway, Ruth and I went last week, and I loved the movie and was mesmerized by the dialogue—the brutal honesty. Then, when Martha started talking about their child, I thought, *I know this boy*. And at the end, when Martha whispers she's afraid, I cried. The usher tapped my shoulder and said, "Sir, you have to leave now." I looked around, and the theater had completely emptied out. Ruth walked me home, and I cried the entire way." I take another deep breath, so I won't cry now. "The next day, I saw the movie again with Ray. And again, I bawled when Martha said she was afraid. I saw it again yesterday, and the same thing happened."

"So, you want to know why you cried," Tony says. "You want to know what frightens you. This is very hard to do over the phone, Anthony. But, earlier in the movie, did any of the characters say something that you felt applied to you?"

"Yeah. George called their son a beanbag, and I thought, *That's how my parents used me, tossing me back and forth between them*. Like when Mom would make me go get Dad when he was gambling at Gernano's. And as I said, when Martha talked about their son, I felt she was talking about me."

"You know the son wasn't real, don't you?"

"Of course. Just one of their games to survive."

"When you were a little boy, did you ever feel that your mom treated you as if you weren't there?"

"No."

"What about your dad? Did you ever feel that maybe he wished you weren't there?"

Tony's silence while I cry is like an arm around me, telling me it's okay to let it out. I blow my nose. "I'm back."

"Why do you think," Tony asks, "Martha was so upset when George killed their child if he wasn't real?"

"Because he got her through a life she found unbearable."

"And what do you find unbearable in your life?"

I cry again, but manage to get out two words. "Lake Erie."

"Yes, Lake Erie. I remember when you told me. I'm sorry I can't be there with you, Anthony. I'm sorry you have to go through this alone."

I take more deep breaths. I want to tell Tony the truth, but I know if I do, the tears will never stop.

Age twenty-one

Empty

I DON'T UNDERSTAND Barbra's song. How can people who need people be the luckiest people in the world? I don't want to need people. I want to be a rock. I want to be an island. All the people I need have left. *How lucky can you get?*

Ray gets sent to Vietnam. The one letter I received from him is almost illegible. And then his mother phones. I only hear two words. *"Friendly fire."* Ray is killed by someone in his own unit during a battle with the Viet Cong.

After he graduates, Jason moves to New York. In the first week, he gets a job at an art gallery. For a while, he sends newsy *Letters from Manhattan* with witty drawings in the margins. But he rarely writes anymore. Maybe his life in the Big City is all he needs.

Ruth gets pregnant but won't tell me who the father is. She quits art school and moves to San Francisco to have the baby and put it up for adoption.

I moved into Jason's room at his mother's house. I stand on his balcony, wishing I had my backup group with me.

Age twenty-three

Maneuvers

AFTER I GET my art degree, I enroll in graduate school to become a teacher. I don't want to teach, but I'm hoping to keep my student deferment. But no one is fooled, and my military status changes to 1-A. It won't be long before I receive "Greetings" from the United States Army.

"You should enlist," a classmate tells me as we walk through yellow and brown leaves littering the campus. "You'll get better treatment."

"Don't you have to sign up for three years? If I'm drafted, it's only two."

"Yeah, that's usually the case, but I heard you can enlist for two."

"Why are they doing that?"

"The Army's desperate. Most guys will die in Vietnam before their stint is up."

Like Ray. I run away from my classmate, tears blurring my vision. I race across campus, wanting to just run, run, run, not thinking where I'm going. When I finally stop, I find myself in front of the apartment building where Ray and I used to live. Where Ray pushed our beds together. Ray.

*

"WITH YOUR COLLEGE education," the recruiting officer says as he looks at my paperwork, "you qualify for officer's training. You could have your pick of assignments. And at OCS—Officer Candidate School—you could train for any career you want."

"What about filmmaking?" I ask.

"Why not?" He has a big smile.

"I like remote places. Do you think I could be stationed in Greenland or Alaska?"

"I don't see why not!" He must have half a dozen extra teeth.

I enlist for two years.

THERE ARE HUNDREDS of young men at the induction center. The place reeks of nervous sweat. We're divided into groups of thirty, led into classrooms, handed a questionnaire, and a number two pencil.

"Answer ALL the questions," says a sergeant not much older than us. "*Each and every* question." He says it very slowly, as if he knows he's still going to have to send guys back to their seats when they turn in the questionnaire with blank spaces. "When you have answered *each and every* question—and only then, put down your pencil and sit there. IN SILENCE!" He shouts. "Answer *each and every* question." He looks around the room, probably trying to guess who's going to skip a question. "One more thing. Be honest. Because the Army will find out anyway." He glares at someone who giggles. "Okay. Begin. *Each and every* question."

After filling in my name and other vital information, I began checking off *YES* or *NO* boxes. *Have you ever had measles? Have you ever had mumps? Have you ever had chicken pox? Have you ever had gonorrhea? Have you ever had syphilis?*

And then, there it is.

The question.

Have you ever had homosexual tendencies?

I've had homosexual *experiences*. Just last night.

Be honest. Because the Army will find out anyway.

I still face the physical exam. Maybe my poor eyesight will disqualify me. Or my allergies will send me home. Maybe I'll get an erection when I'm surrounded by three hundred men walking around in their underwear. That would certainly answer the question.

But I check *NO*. Not because I'm ashamed or deny who I am. I check *NO* because I want to go to film school. To Greenland. Or Alaska.

I don't want a way out of the Army. Because if I go back to Ann Arbor, my worst fear will come true: I'll end up an art teacher.

ABOUT FIFTY OF us are bused to an induction center at Fort Knox, Kentucky. We arrive at night. A shouting sergeant leads us to a supply store where we're given bedding and assigned to a barracks and a bunk.

In the morning, another sergeant shouts that since it's a holiday weekend—Monday is Veterans Day—there's no one on base to take care of a bunch of dumb-assed pansy recruits with long hair and bad attitudes. We're confined to the area between our barracks and the mess hall. Most of the guys sit on their bunks smoking and exchanging tales of what I am sure are exaggerated sexual adventures. I'm not about to join *that* conversation.

By Tuesday, I'll have read both books I've brought.

We're shorn and dressed in Army green. Mostly, we're shouted at. No one talks to us. Sergeants get right in a soldier's face and scream orders. I can tell they hope someone will lip off or forget to say "Sir" so they can yell louder and act tough.

Before dinner, all the new soldiers from four barracks are assembled outside in the cold November air. A sergeant shouts, "AT EASE." Then the fattest, tallest, loudest sergeant steps forward.

"TOMORROW YOU ARE GOING TO BOOT CAMP! Sergeants twice as mean as me—and I'm meaner than a pimp who's been stiffed by his whore." Snickering. "SILENCE! No one makes ANOTHER SOUND, or you will all drop and GIVE ME TWENTY! Tomorrow, sergeants twice as mean as me will KICK YOUR ASS until you become a REAL MAN and not the HIPPIE! SISSY! FAGGOTS! you are. You will be in boot camp for SIX WEEKS. And if you think it's cold now, you just wait until you're CRAWLING THROUGH SNOW AND MUD AND ICE. Do you hear me?" Silence. "DO YOU HEAR ME?"

"YES, SIR!"

"After six weeks, you will be a PROUD SOLDIER in the ARMY of the UNITED STATES OF AMERICA! The proudest nation in the world. You will have had EVERY LAST MOTHER-FUCKING SMIRK WIPED OFF YOUR FACE."

He puts his face up to a soldier whose skin is dark brown.

"Do you hear me, soldier?"

"Sir! Yes, Sir!"

The sergeant turns around, keeping his back to us for a moment. When he swings around, his face is blood red.

"You will at last be real men." Now he speaks quietly but intensely. "And then you will be sent to Vietnam." His eyes move along the rows of men standing before him. "AND NOTHING ANY HOMETOWN RECRUITING OFFICER HAS SAID AMOUNTS TO A FUCKING HILL OF BEANS!"

SNORING RICOCHETS THROUGH the barracks. I quietly get out of my bunk and look out a window into the darkness. What a sucker I am. There's no Officer Candidate School for me. No filmmaking classes. No Greenland. No Alaska.

No future.

I DECIDE TO slit my wrists. I take a new razorblade out of my kit and hide it on the iron rail that holds my mattress to the bunk bed.

I want to bleed. I do not want to die. Not here. And certainly not in Viet Nam. I just want to get the Army's attention. Surely the Army doesn't want someone who is suicidal. Not that I am. I just want to get out of here. As soon as possible.

I don't sleep well. I worry I won't wake up in time and will miss my opportunity. I wonder how deep to make the cuts. I have to have enough blood to cause a reaction, but not so much that I endanger myself or get sent to the hospital for an extensive stay.

When the blackness at the window fades to blue, I know it's time. Just before the sky shows its first streak of yellow, I take the razor blade and make a shallow cut across my left wrist. I assume the blood will dribble out, but it spurts up like water from a broken pipe. Before I have time to panic, to think this is a crazy idea, I quickly slit my right wrist. This time, the blood trails down my arm. I just stare at it, transfixed as it paints a road map to my elbow. The blood is darker than I expected. It seems eager to abandon my body, as if it's tasting freedom after being confined inside for all these years.

I thought I'd have to act scared and disoriented, but I don't have to perform. This is all too real. For a moment, I think I'm going to pass out, but the barracks door slams against a wall, startling me out of my trance.

Rattling bunks, Sergeant Casey shouts for us to ROLL OUT. Guys moan; others dash to the latrine. Chris, the thin man in the bed above me, jumps down, sees the blood, and says, "Sergeant, I think you better come over here."

"Holy shit," the sergeant says when he sees the red blood dyeing the white sheet. It is the only time I haven't heard him shout.

He takes a handkerchief from his back pocket and ties it tight around my left wrist.

"You got a hanky?" He asks Chris. He wraps my other wrist. He pulls back the sheet and sees I'm naked. "Which locker is his?"

"This one." Chris points.

I've left it unlocked.

"Get his pants." Sergeant Casey looks at the other soldiers surrounding my bunk. "The rest of you, this ain't your business. I expect all of you to be dressed and ready for formation in fifteen minutes. Move it! NOW!" He points to a big, muscular man looking down at me. "You, get dressed on the double and come back here."

The hankies are red and dripping. "Get more hankies," the sergeant instructs Chris. Then he spins my legs over the side of the bed and puts my feet into the pants. "Do you think you can stand?"

I nod, and he helps me up. I look down at this tough man pulling up my pants, tucking in my penis, and buttoning me up. Tears suddenly pour from my eyes. His help overwhelms me.

"Sit down." Sergeant Casey grabs my boots from the locker and puts them on my feet without socks. He tucks the laces inside.

The big man with muscles is back, standing awkwardly by the bunk.

"Do you think you can walk?" Sergeant Casey asks me. When I nod, he turns to Muscles. "Do you know where the Infirmary is?"

"No, Sir."

"It's two barracks past the Mess Hall. You can't miss it. There's a big red cross on the door."

"Yes, Sir."

"As soon as you drop him off, report back here."

Muscles salutes.

When we're outside, Muscles says, "You walk on your own. I don't want no blood on my uniform."

We walk up a slight slope to the Mess Hall and beyond. I see the red cross. So does Muscles. "Youse on your own, from here. Youse crazy." He turns and heads back down the hill.

I don't say anything when I see the young attendant look up from a book he's reading by a small gooseneck lamp. He eyes the red hankies, doesn't say anything either. He motions for me to lie on a nearby bed. He unwraps my wrists and wipes the clotting blood away with a strip of gauze. He dips a Q-tip into a brown jar and runs the swab across the cut on my left hand. It stings. He does the same to my right hand. It stings just as bad, even though I'm prepared.

"You don't need stitches," he says. He piles on gauze and wraps it tightly with white tape.

The door slams open, and we both look up. Sergeant Casey.

The doctor—nurse?—approaches the sergeant and whispers. The only word I can make out is "superficial."

Sergeant Casey asks me questions, all starting with "why," but I won't answer. All I say is, "I want to see the chaplain."

I'm taken to an empty barracks and told to wait. I sit on the edge of a bunk for more than an hour. I'm cold. I still have on only my baggy pants and boots. No underwear, no shirt, no socks. A private brings me a thin pillow, a gray blanket, and sheets smelling of bleach. He doesn't say anything, just tosses everything at me and leaves.

I look at the metal bunk beds. I don't want to be next to a wall, too close to the latrine, or too close to the door. I play it safe and pick one halfway down the room. I make up the bottom bed with the sheets, wrap the scratchy wool blanket around my torso, and lie down, my knees up near my chest, my boots hanging over the edge. I lift a corner of my bandages. There's only a small patch of dried blood on the gauze of my left wrist. The only pain I feel is from the bandages being wrapped so tightly.

I wonder how long I'm going to be left here. My unit must have finished breakfast, packed their gear, and headed off to basic training by now. I hate the uncertainty, wondering when I'll get to see the chaplain. *If* I get to see the chaplain.

When the door opens, I jump up. Before I salute, I see it's the private. He looks at me without acknowledgement. As I walk toward him, he drops a duffel bag on the floor and leaves just as quickly as he did before. No time for me to ask any questions.

It's my bag, all the stuff from my locker jumbled inside.

I don't know what to do. Should I put my things in a locker? Am I going to be here for a while? I dump everything on the bed and go through it to make sure nothing's missing. That doesn't take long. I still can't decide whether to use a locker, so I take off my pants, slip on underwear and socks, button up a shirt, and put my pants back on. Just as I'm finishing lacing up my boots, I hear someone shout.

"SUICIDE, get me some coffee!"

It takes me a moment to realize he's talking to me.

I step out of the barracks. A sergeant sits on a folding chair facing the door, his feet propped up on the second step. A cigarette burns in his left hand. A comic book lies across his lap.

"You heard me. Go to the Mess Hall and get me a cup of black coffee, SUICIDE."

That's what he calls me. All capital letters.

"SUICIDE, run over to Barracks 24 and ask Sergeant Cross what time we're playing pool tonight."

"SUICIDE, go to the Mess Hall and ask Myron what's for chow tonight."

I obey every order but don't speak except to ask again to see the chaplain. "Yeah, we know," the sergeant says.

I try to reread one of my books, but can't concentrate.

Precisely at five o'clock, the sergeant shouts, "SUICIDE! Get out here!"

I stand on the narrow, two-step porch.

"Take this chair and follow me."

I fold the chair, and I hope the weight won't make my wrists start bleeding. We walk past six barracks, then the sergeant holds open a door for me. It's a classroom.

"Put the chair over there." He points his chin to a stack of similar chairs. "You have any chow today?"

"No, Sir." It occurs to me that I haven't eaten since last night. I've been too anxious to even think about food.

"Go to the Mess Hall and get something. Then go back to the barracks."

"Am I going to sleep there tonight, Sir?"

"Unless you want to sleep under the stars." He walks across the room and leaves through a door on the far wall.

I get in line at the Mess Hall, suddenly very hungry. I keep my head down and hold out my tray for the privates on KP to pile on pepper steak, mashed potatoes, and creamed corn.

"You look like y'all could use an extra helpin' of my special bread pudding."

I look up at a blond soldier with a broad smile. His nametag says *Cramden*.

It's the first smile I've seen all day. "Thank you."

"You bet." Cramden winks.

I try to keep my sleeves covering the bandages, but I can tell some of the soldiers notice them. No one sits at my table.

Back at the barracks, I turn the light on in the latrine. Hundreds of cockroaches scatter. I don't know how I'd keep the bandages dry, so I decide not to take a shower.

I open every locker, hoping someone has left a book behind. I'd like a good mystery, something to distract me. Just as I'm ready to give up, I feel a paperback on the top shelf of one of the last lockers. Truman Capote's *In Cold Blood*. I read until I hear Taps. Lights out.

Looking out a window, I watch the base close for the night. I wish I could keep a light on, especially in the latrine, to keep the cockroaches away. But I figure I'm in enough trouble already without having some sergeant come bursting in, screaming at me to turn off the light.

Lying on the bunk with my boots on, I begin to panic. I know the medic told the sergeant my cuts were superficial. Maybe the Army has figured out I cut my wrists just to get sent home. Maybe they know I wasn't seriously thinking of killing myself, which is why I've been left alone in this empty barracks. No suicide watch needed for me. Maybe in the morning, I'm going to be sent to boot camp after all. I know I won't be able to endure two years of being called "Suicide," of being bullied by beer-bellied yelling sergeants.

I pace up and down the dark barracks. I tell myself everything's worse at night; tomorrow, in the light, it will be better, but I can't get my mind to calm down. Up and down. Back and forth. Over and over. I finally exhaust myself and look at my watch. Three o'clock. I fall on my bunk without taking off my clothes.

"YOU WANTED TO see me," a white-haired chaplain says the next day. There is no compassion in his voice. He's Army first, chaplain second.

I guess an attempted suicide doesn't matter to the Army. Especially one with "superficial" cuts. But I know what does matter. I look directly into the chaplain's cold gray eyes. "If one more man drops his pants in front of me, I think I'm going to lose my mind."

"Are you telling me you're homosexual?"

Clever man. He asks me a few more questions. "Well, without revealing the confidentiality of our conversation, I will speak to your commanding officer." He waves me away with a pudgy hand.

I return to the empty barracks and wait. Twenty minutes later, a private with red hair leads me to another barracks that has been converted into offices.

I stand facing my commanding officer. This is the first time I've seen him. I didn't know I had a commanding officer. And he certainly is commanding. Taller than six feet. Very blond. Very chiseled features. Practically Nordic. Totally gorgeous. Apollo on Earth.

"Without revealing the confidentiality of your conversation," he says, "the chaplain let me know that you are a homosexual."

I wonder how the chaplain told him without breaking confidentiality. Did he flick his wrist? Cock a pinkie? Prance on tiptoe?

"This is not a simple matter," Major Apollo goes on. "If you stick to your story, there will be an investigation by the CID. Criminal Investigation Division. Do you understand that, soldier? *Criminal.*"

"Yes, Sir."

"You will have to supply the CID with names of men you've had sex with, and CID special agents will contact them and ask them to corroborate your story. Do you want your friends to be contacted like this?"

"Yes, Sir."

"If, however, you say that you made a mistake," Major Apollo continues, "that you were under undue tension, the entire matter could be forgotten. There is still time to rejoin your unit at boot camp."

"I can supply the agents with a list of names."

Major Apollo looks crushed, as if he's not used to someone not obeying his every whim. "SERGEANT!"

The young redhead rushes in.

"Take him away."

The redhead drives me in a Jeep to a one-story wood building. The outside looks like a barracks, but inside it's divided into rooms with a center hall. I sit in a tiny room with two uncomfortable chairs. I wait for three hours, without a thing to read, before a soldier leads me down the hall to a door with a glass pane stamped with gold letters: CID. He opens the door and announces, "Private Dimora."

The two men from CID look FBI: dark suits, white shirts, plain narrow ties. One of them sits at a gray metal desk. He's dark, skinny, unattractive. Smokes.

"Sit down, Dimora," he says.

The other one—fat, pasty, and chewing gum—stands too close to me. Sometimes he's behind me, sometimes to the side. But always too close.

Skinny says, probably by rote, "Everything that's said in this room is confidential. Only those with a need to know will have access to the information." Then he repeats almost word-for-word what my handsome commanding officer told me. "If you recant, you can hook up with your unit in boot camp. No questions asked."

"I understand," I respond. What I understand is that the Army has a policy against homosexuals in the military, but isn't eager to get rid of me. One more soldier to fight in Vietnam. "I wish to proceed."

Skinny puts out his cigarette in a crowded ashtray and picks up a pen. He moves a pad of paper to the center of his ash-sprinkled desk. "We need the names and contact information of three homosexuals you've been with. We'll contact these men and ask them to tell us, on tape, exactly what you two did together."

"And he doesn't mean sat and had tea with." Fatty stands in front of me, his toes right up against mine, his crotch in my face. "He means faggots who fucked your ass, because I'm sure no one's going to let a pussy like you stick your puny dick anywhere."

I look around him to Skinny. "May I borrow your pen?" I write down *Jason Johnson*. I know he will love talking to a CID agent. He'll probably wear his white fur coat, bend toward the microphone, and whisper ala Marilyn Monroe. I hope he tells them about us making out on the stairs of the Art School.

One down, two to go. Even if Ray were alive, I wouldn't give them his name. He would have been mortified.

I can't put down Tony's name. I simply can't do that to him. I'm sure he'd know how to handle it, since he's a psychologist, but what if one of his patients found out? His career could be ruined. Especially in such a small town, in such a closed Italian community.

Who else is there? The few others I've been with were strangers.

I don't really want to do it, but I have no choice: I write down Tony Tomasso. I hope he won't be upset. I hope he'll understand. I hope, for his sake, not mine, that no one in Castleton finds out.

One more name. I write down Ruth Roman and hand the pad back.

"Ruth Roman?" Skinny sneers. "We need the names of *men*."

"I don't know the names of all the other guys I've been with." I hope that sounds like I've been with a lot of men. "They picked me up on the street." Does that sound sordid enough? "Or in a park. Or a toilet." Good. *Toilet* sounds dirtier than *restroom*. Not that anyone's picked me up in a toilet. Or restroom. "Ruth Roman knows I'm queer. She asked me almost as soon as we met."

"You only gave us this Jason Johnson's address. We need the other two."

"I don't know their addresses by heart. My address book is in my duffle bag."

"Okay. When my aide drives you back, you give him the info. Then pack your stuff, and he'll take you to your new barracks, with the other transients."

Are they through with me? He hasn't said, "Dismissed." Maybe since he's in civilian clothes, he won't. When I start to get up from the chair, Fatty stands behind me and pushes me down. He keeps his stubby hands on my shoulders, breathing hard and smelling of stale Tutti-Frutti gum.

"We can't predict how long the investigation will take." Skinny closes a folder. "Sometimes it takes a month. But with Thanksgiving and the holidays coming up, your case might take longer."

Fatty hits my head, as if he saw a fly. I force myself not to react. Skinny jerks his head slightly to the right. Fatty moves away to lean against one wall.

"If everything pans out, you'll receive a general discharge under honorable conditions." Skinny takes his time lighting a cigarette. Camels. Unfiltered. "If you're caught having sex with a man while you're in the Army, you'll get a *dishonorable* discharge."

Fatty grabs his crotch and pushes it toward me. No one could be that desperate.

Skinny empties the ashtray in a tin trashcan. It's a matte olive green color, like everything else in the Army. "If you're caught having sex with a woman, the whole case will be dropped. You'll be sent to boot camp, and all the time that's been wasted will be added to your tour of duty. And you'll have to pay back any expenses the Army incurred during the investigation." He blows smoke in my face. "Get outta here."

The redhead is standing by his Jeep. "I'll take you to your new barracks. You'll stay there during the investigation. Your stuff is in the back."

As soon as I walk into the new barracks, a very thin man, wearing white boxers, a dirty t-shirt, and untied combat boots, grabs my duffel bag.

"Lemme show ya yar bunk'n'locker." He stumbles down the center aisle, almost to the opposite end. "We're so glad yar here. Jimmy got 'is freedom last week, and we're feelin' outnumbered. Us fairies gotta stick together."

Men idling on their beds glance at me. So much for confidentiality.

"This here's you." He puts my bag on the bottom bed, second from the end. He sticks out a bony hand. "Oh, by the way, I'm Freddie."

"Ooh wee, sugar! You sure are sweet!" A young man with round brown cheeks, lying on an upper bunk with his head propped on his elbow, smiles at me. "My name is George. But you can call me 'Miss Georgia.'" He extends his hand palm down as if he expects me to kiss it. His nails are painted lavender. So are his toenails.

Freddie unzips my duffel. "Ya wan' me ta unpack fir ya?"

"That's all right, I'll do it."

He sits on my bunk, crossing his ankles. "So, where y'all from?"

"Ann Arbor, Michigan." I open the tall, slender locker next to the head of my bed and wipe the shelf with a handkerchief.

"Uh-huh." George pretends to flip the pages of the magazine in front of him, but I know he's watching me. "College boy."

"Wan' me ta 'splain about this here barracks?" Freddie looks sixteen.

"Sure." I arrange my few possessions in the locker.

"Weese all transits." Freddie waves his arms, encompassing the floor. "Down here are the Limbo Men. Most of them are waitin' fir some medical reason." He points across the aisle to a young man reading a comic book in an upper bunk. "Long John's gotta have a hernia op. He's one of the nice ones. A couple of the guys down here ain't so nice. But most of 'em just ignore us. Us pansies, I mean." He counts off on his fingers. "There's Miss Georgia and me and Sal—don't ever call 'im 'Sally,' 'cause he'll punch ya so hard it'll hurt fir weeks." Freddie gently rubs his upper arm as if he's still in pain. "And now there's you!"

He opens the locker next to mine and takes out a bottle of Pepsi. "Ya wan' one?" I shake my head. He uncaps it with an opener attached to a long red ribbon hanging from a hook. The entire bottom of the locker is stacked with bottles of Pepsi. He takes a long swallow. "I know, I know. But I don't like it cold. I like it room temp."

"Where's your bunk?" I'm afraid it's under George and across from me. I'm right. "Who's in the bunk above me?"

"Sal. He's on furnace patrol right now." Freddie looks at his watch and sits on his bed. "Ya met 'im soon. That used ta be my bunk, but I didn' like being opposite Miss Georgia. For such a femme fatal, she sure likes ta show her dick! I'd rather be down here so I don't have to see that thing wavin' like a flag."

"Maybe he wanted you to salute," I say.

"Ooh! You and I are going to get along just fine." George is barely wearing a black kimono, too shiny to be silk. He massages one of his nipples. It's very pink against his dark skin.

"Anyhoo," Freddie says, "upstairs are the uniforms—guys who've served their tours but re-upped and are waiting fir their orders."

"Lifers," George mutters.

Freddie chugs down the last of his Pepsi. "Oh me, how can I be so silly! I forgot ta tell ya about Myron! He's the Reception

Station cook. He has that room by the door." He points down the hall. "Myron's married and has two kids—little girls, I think—but he's real friendly with us fairies."

"I know you wish he were a lot more friendly with you," George says.

Freddie lies back and kicks George's mattress with his boot.

Above us, it sounds as if an Irish stomp has begun. Then the wall next to George and Freddie's bunk shakes as heavy-booted soldiers run down the stairs, along the center aisle and out the door.

"Time to get dressed, girls." George tosses his magazine down to Freddie.

"Where are they rushing to?" I ask.

"Chow." Freddie laces his boots.

I look at my watch. "Dinner's not for another half hour."

"They like to fight over who's first in line." George slithers down from his bunk. "And who's second in line. And who's third. Men!" He hangs his kimono in his locker. He's wearing lavender panties.

A short, dark man comes in from outside and flops down on Freddie's bed. "I am whooped!"

"Sal!" Freddie screams like a dying soprano. "Git yar sooty ass off my bed!" Sal ignores him and unties his boots. "Yar the rudest man ever! Didn't ya notice we got someone new? This here's Tony."

"Anthony."

"Hey." Sal looks up at me. "You Italian, Anthony?"

"Yes. Both sides."

"Me, too. Sal Santoro. I'd offer my hand, but I got soot all over." He stands up, stripping off his clothes and dropping them on the floor. "I got to hit the showers."

Sal has a firm, compact body. Not much hair for an Italian. He opens his locker and takes out a bar of soap. He grabs a towel hanging from the foot rail of his bunk and heads to the latrine. Across the aisle, the soldier reading a comic book jumps down from his bunk and tosses off his clothes. I see now why they call him Long John. He takes his towel and follows Sal.

George says, "Steam's gonna be rising."

EVEN THOUGH WE haven't been in touch lately, I called Jason to let him know about the upcoming CID investigation. He laughs and promises to send me a letter with all the details as soon as they contact him. Then I phoned Tony. I'm relieved that he's not upset and says he's happy to help and not to worry. Ruth says the whole thing is weird, but of course, she will tell the agents about my "proclivities."

Because of my art background, I'm assigned to Major Hale at Headquarters. Most of the time, I print names of towns and land elevations on hand-drawn topographic maps. One day, I paint STOP in gigantic letters on the asphalt at an intersection. Another day, I design decorations for a Canasta party given by the major's wife; I make huge face cards in psychedelic colors. Wonder what the ladies will think of that.

We Limbo Men alternate furnace patrol. During a twenty-four-hour shift, two soldiers make sure coal fires are kept burning at the twelve buildings of the Reception Station. If an NCO finds his office cold when he arrives in the morning, the guys on furnace patrol have to scrub latrines all day as well as keep the fires stoked.

It all becomes routine as weeks pass and there's no word on the CID investigation. Then Sal gets his papers.

"I'm gonna miss ya," Freddie says as Sal packs.

"How long did your investigation take?" I ask.

"Three months and four days." Sal zips his duffel.

Freddie, his eyes wet with tears, hugs Sal.

"Good luck, you guys." And Sal's gone.

"How long have you been waiting?" I ask Freddie.

"Two months, one week, and three days."

I look up at George. "Two and a half months," he says.

EVERY SATURDAY AFTERNOON, George sits on his bunk in ruffled panties—he has pink, baby blue, lavender, and "melted butter"—and manicures his finger- and toenails. Then he caresses a honey-smelling lotion into his skin. One day, I hand him a bottle of nail polish I bought at the PX. *Stolen Sunset.* With a name like that, I couldn't resist, and I think the slight orange cast will flatter his coloring. When George finishes with his Saturday beauty treatment, he always asks the same question.

"Where you boys taking me tonight?"

Usually, we're "girls," but when he wants someone else to pay, we're male.

We walk across the base to the Army movie theater. Only fifty cents a film. We've already seen *Yellow Submarine* four times. If we get off-base passes, George calls up a lesbian WAC, and we go to a dance bar. I like dancing with the WACs because they lead.

One night, after watching *Barbarella* for the third time, I come back to the barracks and fiund one of the lifers from upstairs sprawled across my bed.

"What are you doing on my bunk?"

"Waiting for you." He's about twenty-five. His hair is buzzed, but I can tell he's a redhead. He has freckles.

"What do you want?"

"Some fun." He rubs his crotch and smiles. The Army has a term for such a grin. *Shit-eating.*

I'm not surprised one of the lifers is coming on to me. One of the gay career soldiers I met at the dance bar told me it's not the queers in the Army who make advances. It's the married men. What surprises me is this soldier making the suggestion in the middle of a crowded barracks.

"No one will care," Redhead says. "They're all busy doing their own thing."

I give him a *you-got-to-be-out-of-your-mind* look and head back out the door. Maybe he's a CID plant to catch me so they can dishonorable discharge me.

I don't think I'm attractive, especially since the Army sheared off my long hair. I wonder if Redhead finds me appealing or merely assumes all homosexuals are automatically available. Even though they're not attracted to every woman they meet, it seems most straight men think queers find all males sexy.

Except as friends, none of the other gay men and very few of the straights in the Army interest me. I don't think the other homosexuals in my barracks are having sex with each other or the lifers upstairs. Except maybe George. He's effeminate, but I see a lot of the lifers eyeing him.

Sometimes in the middle of the night, I hear a solitary man take matters into his own hand.

ALL THE SOLDIERS on my floor sleep in their underwear except Long John and me. We sleep nude. Our bunks are directly across from each other, and every dawn I watch for Long John's morning display. When reveille sounds, he buoyantly jumps down from his bunk, his stiff, long penis saluting the flag being raised outside. He has a short, slender body with hard, tight muscles—and the most acne-scarred face I have ever seen.

"I heard you were waiting for a hernia operation," I say one night when we're on furnace patrol together.

"That's right." He lifts a shovelful of coal into the large black furnace.

"What's the hold-up? You've been here a while."

"Oh, there's some medical complication. I don't understand it." He takes off his gloves and wipes the sweat on his forehead with a hanky while I bank the fire. It's cold outside, but hot in the furnace room. "It's fine with me. I'd rather be here than in 'Nam, and that's where I'm going as soon as I recover from the operation."

"Are you married?"

"Yeah, three years."

"Any children?"

"Not yet."

"How old are you?"

"Twenty-two."

I shut the furnace door, and we walk to the next barracks.

"So, did I pass?"

"Pass what?" I look over at him. I'm always surprised when guys aren't taller than I am.

"All these questions. Is this some kind of test?"

"Sorry. Just making conversation." Our eyes meet. "Just curious."

"Yeah, I'm curious about you, too."

On Mondays, the furnace patrol roster for the week is pinned to a bulletin board in the barracks. Assignments are rotated, and if there are enough Limbo Men, any two soldiers usually have duty together only twice a month.

"This is the second time in a row I'm on duty with John," I tell George.

"You *was* on duty with me. Long John gave me a carton of cigarettes to switch places with him."

"You don't smoke."

"Girl, I can trade those cigs for something fine."

"Why do you think John wants to be on duty with me?"

George opens his mouth and traces a finger around his lips, then he sucks on his index finger.

That night, I figured it was best to be direct with John. As we're shoveling coal into a massive furnace, I ask, "Why'd you switch patrol with George?"

"I thought maybe you and me could have some fun." He grins.

I've seen the smile before, on a redhead lying on my bunk.

"I don't think so, John."

"Come on. I see you watching me every morning. I know you want it."

"Not tonight." I wonder how many times his wife has said those same two words.

DINNER'S SERVED AT five-thirty. The barracks are usually empty by five-fifteen. I think it's stupid to wait in line, especially for meatloaf and mashed potatoes.

One late afternoon, John lies in his bunk reading a Spider-Man comic as the other soldiers rush to the Mess Hall. I'm reading *Death in Venice.* When we are alone, John jumps down and, looking directly at me as I peer over the top of my paperback, he slowly strips off his uniform. His erect penis juts through his fly, and he strokes it a few times before stepping out of his boxers. He tosses a towel over his shoulder and saunters to the shower.

Oh, God. He certainly has a beautiful body. And that long, long dick. It seems forever since I've been with anyone. A hot shower might be just what I need.

All four faucets are on hot, creating such dense steam I can't even see John when I enter the latrine. We'll be safe behind the mist.

By the time we get to the Mess Hall, they've run out of meatloaf.

THE RECEPTION STATION cook, Myron Cramden, is young, blond, and cute, with a wide, eager smile. He's from the Appalachian Mountains of West Virginia. He always smiles at me when I go through the dinner line if he's out front and not back in the kitchen. And he always seems to be out front when I'm in line.

"He's one of us," I tell George and Freddie.

"He's not!" Freddie insists. "He's married with kids."

"A ring doesn't mean a thing," I say.

George is good at spotting "girls like us," but even he thinks Myron is as straight as his rolling pin. But I've seen the way he holds that cooking utensil when he's chasing someone out of his kitchen. But the real reason I know is that when all the other soldiers are watching *Ironside* in the Rec Room barracks, Myron and I are in his room enjoying *That Girl*.

Twice, Myron has asked me to join him for "a night on the town" in Louisville. I've declined. Then, early one afternoon after reading *TV Guide*, I head for the Mess Hall.

"If you still want me to go to Louisville with you, I will," I tell him, "but it has to be on December ninth. And you have to get a room with a color TV."

He smiles, showing off his dimples. "Okay, but what's on?"

"Diana Ross and the Supremes. They're doing a special with The Temptations called *TCB*. Takin' Care of Business."

"I know what *TCB* stands for!" Myron's indigent. "Just cause I'm from the mountains don't mean I'm dumb. What night of the week is that?"

"Monday."

"Shit, Anthony. I gotta get up early to make breakfast the next day. Can't we just watch the show in my room?"

"You know if George finds out we're watching Miss Ross, he'll invite himself." I stick a finger in a vat of chocolate cake mix and lick it. "And if George's is there, Freddie will be right behind. He'll talk through all the songs."

"You're right about that." He scratches his forehead. "Maybe I can get one of my assistants to make breakfast that day. But listen, we can't be seen leaving here together. In fact, we'd better take separate buses to Louisville."

"Okay, I'll check the bus schedule."

Monday, I wait inside the Louisville depot for Myron's bus. It's late, and I want to go directly to the hotel, but Myron insists on stopping to buy a bottle of rum and a six-pack of Coca-Cola.

I adjust the television and the bed pillows while Myron mixes drinks. I kick off my boots and fall on the bed as the NBC peacock spreads its colorful wings. Myron lands next to me. Just as Diana makes her entrance, he rolls on top of me and kisses my lips.

"Surprised?" he asks with his dimpled smile.

"Not at all." I push him off me. "But I want to watch Diana. This show is only an hour long, and we have all night."

*

THE CID INVESTIGATION into my sex life doesn't even begin until after the new year is a week old. I figure once they've spoken with my contacts, things will move along quickly, but nothing happens for a couple of months. I work on more maps and make more decorations for officers' wives. Myron and I continue to watch TV together in his room. George is released. Freddie gets out, too. My case seems stalled. Finally, in late March, word comes down that I am to be discharged.

Then General Dwight D. Eisenhower dies. The Army revered Eisenhower. As Supreme Commander of the Allied Expeditionary Forces, he called the shots on D-Day. After World War II, he commanded NATO. Then the five-star general was elected—for two terms—President of the United States. When he dies, Janis Joplin is bumped from the cover of *Newsweek*, and my discharge papers are not filed.

The Army intends to fully honor its hero. The memorial service, to be held in Washington, D.C., will be broadcast to all Army bases in the United States. Every soldier *will* attend. No excuse will be accepted.

"We can't completely cut ourselves off," Major Hale informs me. "Ft. Knox is a vital base. So Headquarters has decided one soldier will man the phones. And that soldier's going to be you, Pvt. Dimora. After all, you were supposed to be out of the Army by this time."

The day of Eisenhower's funeral, I walk to Headquarters with my dress shoes polished so bright I can't look at them in the sun. All around me, soldiers, from the lowest recruit to the highest commanding officer, get on buses, climb in Jeeps, or are chauffeured to the various auditoriums to listen to the memorial service.

"Sit over here, Pvt. Dimora." Major Hale points to a large

wooden desk cleared of paperwork. All that's on it are a white notepad, a ballpoint pen, and three telephones. "This white one's for inter-base calls. It won't ring today. The black one's an outside line. If it rings, take a message, but it probably won't. And this one, the red one, is a direct line to the Pentagon." He rests his hand on the earpiece. "Don't fool around with it. If you pick it up, you will reach the Pentagon. No dialing. No ringing. If it rings here, it means trouble. Big trouble."

Major Hale holds a small piece of paper in front of my eyes. "Memorize this. It's the combination to the safe." I look to my left at a large gray vault. Then I study the paper, reciting the numbers over and over in my head. "Got it?"

"Yes, Sir."

He tears the paper into ever smaller pieces. "It's changed daily."

"If I may ask, Sir, what's inside the safe?"

"The locations of the intercontinental strategic missile silos."

So the Army is discharging me because I'm homosexual, fearful that queers can be blackmailed to reveal government secrets, but today it gives me the combination to a safe with top-secret information the Russians would love to know.

THE ENVELOPE HAS my parents' return address, but when I take out the letter, I'm surprised it's from my dad, not my mom. There's no salutation, no *Dear Anthony*. It just begins in my father's scratchy handwriting:

Your mother said you are getting out of the Army soon. I don't know what your plans are, but I want to make it clear that you can't live with us. You can come see your mother one afternoon if you want. She'd like that. Dad.

I wasn't planning on living with my parents, so that's fine with me. I plan to get my own place in Ann Arbor.

MY LAST DAY in the Army is Good Friday. How funny is that? Major Hale throws a party for me. The Lieutenant Commander of the Reception Station poses for a photograph as he presents me with a gold-sealed Certificate of Achievement. It states, in part, *PVT Dimora's performance of duty was truly outstanding and vastly superior to that normally expected of an individual of his grade and experience. His cooperative attitude and selfless devotion to duty are in keeping with the highest traditions of the military.*

There's chocolate cake and vanilla ice cream, and a lot of soldiers come by to shake my hand. A few of them say that they can't believe I'm queer and want me to admit it was just a hoax to get out of the Army.

"No, I'm really homosexual. It's Good Friday, and that's my cross to bear." And I give them a big smile.

I receive, in typical Army fashion, reams of official papers. One of them states that I am being separated from the Army "for Homosexuality under AR-63S-89." I think it's a nice touch to capitalize the *H.*

Age twenty-four

Underwater

IT'S SUPPOSED TO be a party for me," Mom says on the phone, "but who ever heard of celebrating your forty-third birthday? It's really for you, Anthony. Everyone wants to see you."

"Exactly who do you mean by *everyone*? Bobby probably doesn't even remember me, and Dad—"

Before I can say more, Mom interrupts. "You won't believe how tall Bobby's gotten. As soon as he turned twelve, he shot up. He's as tall as me."

"Bobby and I don't know each other. I went to college when he was *six*."

"So, this is a perfect opportunity to find out about each other."

"And what about Dad?" I ask. "He's made it quite clear, he doesn't want me there."

"It was your father's idea to invite you."

I hear the lie in her voice.

"Yeah, right, Mom."

She tries a different tactic. "I've invited Nick and his family, and he's really looking forward to seeing you."

"Well, I'd like to see Uncle Nick. Unfortunately, he comes with Aunt Lily, Nick Junior, and Rose."

"They're harmless." Mom uses her final ploy: a loud sigh. "Come on, Anthony. Do it for me."

I don't know why I am being so difficult. I can't refuse her.

MOM WAS BORN on Friday the 13th, and this year her birthday falls on a Friday again. She considers it lucky. "Both my boys are here."

I barely get in the front door before she smothers me with kisses. "Are you hungry?" She walks into the kitchen. "The refrigerator's full of your favorites." She opens the door, displaying shelves overflowing with food.

"I'll have some grapes." I pinch off a bunch.

Mom's hair is flecked with gray. I'm glad she's not dying it. She obviously went to the beauty parlor yesterday. Her coif is as round as a football helmet. And probably as hard.

Dad comes down the stairs and into the kitchen. "Is that your car in the driveway? You parked it right in the middle, blocking both garage doors. I won't be able to get out."

"Hello, Dad. I can move the car. Which side do you want me to park on?"

"I'm not going anywhere right now. I'm just saying, if I wanted to get out, I couldn't. What kind of car is it?"

"It's a Plymouth Valiant. Not attractive, I know, but it's what I could afford. I got it used. I'll move it in a minute."

Dad shrugs. His hair is turning gray, too, but it's not the rich silver of Mom's. It's a dirty yellow-gray, like Mama Luisa's.

Mom yells out the kitchen window. "Bobby, your brother's here!"

I hear the lawnmower shut off, and Bobby comes in through the dining room sliding glass doors. He's skinny. We face each other, awkwardly, then, at the same time, reach out and hug. Dad's probably about to drop to his knees in prayer, because his homosexual son is holding in his arms the twelve-year-old boy who used to stand in Dad's palm, and the boy doesn't have on a shirt.

I look at my hands, wet with sweat.

"Sorry," Bobby says. "I was cutting the grass."

"No problem." I wipe my hands on my jeans. "Great tan."

Bobby smiles.

"Put your shirt on," Dad tells Bobby.

"I'm going to finish up outside before I take a shower," Bobby says to me, ignoring Dad. He asks Mom, "What time are we eating?"

She looks at the oven clock. "Nick and his family are coming over in about an hour and a half." She turns to me. "I know you just arrived, but I forgot something at the supermarket. Would you mind going with me?"

"Of course not."

Dad goes into the family room and turns on the television.

As soon as we're in my car, Mom says, "I have everything I need from the grocery, but I wanted to talk to you in private. Just drive around the neighborhood."

I turn off the radio. "Is something the matter?"

Mom clears her throat. "It's your father. Oh, there's nothing wrong physically, but he's been very depressed. He thinks he's a failure as a father. I don't know if you noticed, but Bobby didn't even speak to him."

"I did notice. Why is that?"

"Just after he turned twelve, Bobby said he didn't want to go to Mass anymore. He and your father got into a big argument, and Rusty slapped Bobby across the face. Bobby's barely said a word to him since."

"Did Bobby say why he doesn't want to go to Mass?"

"He says the Church is hypocritical, that it has all this wealth and 'gold trappings' but doesn't help the poor." Mom twists her hands. "Bobby's very smart. He keeps up with all the news, and he's very aware of what's going on. He was very upset when Martin Luther King was killed."

"Why didn't you tell me any of this when we talked on the phone?"

"I wanted to keep our conversations happy. I didn't want to cry, and I knew I would if I started talking about it." She turns to the side window for a minute. When she looks back, her voice is angry. "And frankly, Anthony, I didn't think you'd be interested."

"Why wouldn't I be interested? He's my brother."

"You rarely ask about him."

"You always tell me every little detail when I call. If you get a ding in the car door at the supermarket, I hear about it. If one of the neighbors, whom I don't even remember, breaks her arm, I hear about it. I figured if anything interesting was happening with Bobby, you'd let me know."

Mom sits with her arms crossed. When she doesn't say anything for a while, I say, "So Dad thought he was a failure because Bobby stopped going to Mass."

"Yes, because both of you have left the Catholic Church." She fusses with her purse. "And because you're—that way."

"*That way!* Can't you say it, Mom? Your son is a homosexual."

"Why do you always have to throw it in my face?"

"Because you ignore it." She doesn't say anything. "You're just as bad as Dad is. Maybe worse."

"How can you say that?" She takes a tissue out of her purse but doesn't use it. "I would never tell you not to come back home."

"I know that, but dealing with Dad kicking me out wasn't so awful. It was a clean break. I could move on. I could forget about him. Most of the time. But with you, it's a constant reminder."

"A reminder of what?"

"That you deny who I am. What I am." I take my eyes off the road to glance at her.

"I don't know what to say."

"You could ask me."

"Ask you what?"

"If I liked girls, the first question you'd ask is, 'Are you dating anyone?'"

We go for miles in silence. I slow down when we come to my high school. I think of the first time I saw Ray Hutton and his beautiful topaz hair.

Just as I'm completely lost in my memories, Mom asks, "Are you dating anyone?

"No. Thanks for asking." I pat her hand. "That wasn't so hard, was it?"

"Harder than you think."

"Should I turn back now?"

"No, keep driving. I haven't told you what I really want to say. I told you, it's about your father, not Bobby. Or you."

I drive.

"Your father was so upset he went to therapy."

"That's great."

"I didn't think so." She looks straight ahead. "I didn't want him telling all our secrets."

"You must know everything a therapist hears is confidential, just like a lawyer or a priest."

"Yes, and I didn't see why Rusty couldn't go to a priest. I even suggested he should go to one in another diocese if he doesn't feel comfortable with the ones in our parish."

"Priests aren't trained like therapists."

"That's exactly what Rusty said."

Just what I want to hear: That I sound like my father. "What were you afraid would happen if Dad went to a therapist?"

She makes a dismissive gesture with her hand.

"You must have been afraid of something."

"A therapist would judge me!" She spits it out. "A priest would forgive." I hold her hand while she cries. She blows her nose, releases my hand. "Keep both your hands on the steering wheel."

I grip the wheel and sigh. I want to ask if she thinks a therapist would judge her because that's what she does: judges.

"Anyway," she continues, "Rusty said he had to go, that his depression was starting to interfere with his concentration at work." She looks out the side window, speaks more softly, even though I'm sure she wants me to hear. "It certainly interfered with our love life." She fusses with her skirt.

I can sense, rather than see through her dark glasses, that she's looking for my reaction. I don't give her one. I go back to what interests me. "So, Dad said he felt he was a failure as a father because his sons left the Church and because I'm queer. What did you say?"

She turns toward me. "I said I wasn't going to have him pay fifty dollars an hour for a therapist to blame me, to say I mothered you too much." She lashes out as if I'm the one who caused all her distress. "I said I didn't need to hear it, and that I didn't buy it. I said I refused to believe that it's my fault!"

"What was Dad's response?"

"He said, 'Of course it's our fault. We're parents. Everything's our fault.'" She sits back. Calm again. Resigned.

"When Dad said he felt he failed me, did he mention Lake Erie?"

"No. What's Lake Erie got to do with anything?"

"Nothing. Go on."

"I said if he felt he failed you, he should tell you he was sorry. You know what he said?"

I shake my head.

"Sorry would never be enough for Anthony."

"Maybe it wouldn't have been enough," I say, "but it would have been nice to hear."

"He did say something that might surprise you. He said he admired you because you don't give a damn what anyone thinks."

"Thank you for telling me. So did you let him go to therapy?"

"I never 'let' your father do anything." Her anger stresses the word. "He always does exactly what he wants."

I don't contradict her. I don't want the argument. "So he went to therapy."

"Yes, and of course, she wouldn't let him discuss any of it with me."

"She? Dad had a *female* therapist? How did he find her?"

"Our regular doctor recommended her. Her name was Anna Delaney."

"Did you meet her?"

"No."

"But you were angry because she wouldn't let Dad talk about his sessions with you."

"Oh, I found out." She says it proudly, as if she solved a crime. "The first few weeks, he'd come home from seeing her feeling worse off than before. He went on Saturdays. He gave up golf to see her! That tells you how much pain he was in." She sniffles, wipes her nose. "Once he came home, pulled down the blinds in our room, and stayed in bed all afternoon. I felt helpless. I didn't know what to do."

"So, you cooked."

"I'm a wife and mother. That's what we do. You want to be a smarty-pants, or do you want to hear this?"

"Sorry. Go on."

"Well, one day he comes home all excited, and even though he's not supposed to discuss it, he can't hold it in. Dr. Delaney wanted to know if he remembered the first thing he had told her when she asked him to tell her a bit about himself during their first session. He couldn't remember, and she said he hadn't mentioned being married, having two children, or anything about his job. The first thing he told her was that when he was thirteen months old, his mother died. She said that wasn't an accident."

I whisper Freud's statement: "*There are no accidents.*"

"That's what *she* said—that the first thing out of his mouth was the most important thing in his life."

"You didn't believe her?"

Mom waits until a truck noisily passes us. "Dr. Delaney said a baby knows who's holding him, that studies show that within days a baby recognizes his mother's smell, and within a few weeks he recognizes her voice. So when Rusty's mother died when he was thirteen months old, he knew she was no longer there. She said his body remembered his mother's touch, her smell, her voice. And when she died, Rusty felt abandoned. Dr. Delaney said this feeling stayed with Rusty his whole life, that it was like a wave, sometimes almost overwhelming and sometimes just an undercurrent. But it was always there. And it affected everything in his life."

"She sounds very good."

"Yeah, well, wait a while." Mom takes a roll of Lifesavers out of her purse. She twists off a bit of the foil paper and offers me the tube. It's the variety pack. I take the top candy. Pineapple. She sucks her Lifesaver for a while. Cherry, I think. "So, your father was in a good mood for a couple of weeks. It was great to see him smiling again. And I thought, *Maybe this therapy isn't so bad after all.* But then she ruined everything."

She stares out the window as if the unchanging landscape suddenly fascinates her. She's quiet for so long, I say, "So is this where Loretta Young says, 'And now a word from our sponsor'?"

"I don't remember you being so flip."

"Maybe you weren't paying attention."

"I've devoted my life to you boys!"

I want to say, *And you've used that devotion to make us feel guilty. Maybe if you hadn't been so "devoted," you wouldn't be so angry.* But, of course, I don't say any of it. "So how did Dr. Delany ruin everything?"

"One afternoon, Rusty didn't come home from his session. He didn't come back until it was dark. As soon as he walked in, he said, 'I don't want to talk about it. Let's just eat. What's for dinner?'"

"It was veal and peppers, one of his favorites, but he hardly touched it. We lay in bed half the night, not sleeping, until he finally sat up and turned on the light. He said, 'I told Dr. Delaney how upset I was when you told me to take a sweater when I went to play golf last Sunday.' I didn't even remember saying that, but I *knew* she would blame everything on me. She asked him how he felt when I said that, and he said he felt like a little boy. Then the doctor asked who would tell a little boy to bring his sweater, and Rusty said 'his mother.' And Dr. Delaney asked if Mama Luisa ever told him to take a sweater when he went outside, and he said Mama Luisa didn't care what he wore as long as it was clean. And then Dr. Delany said, 'You didn't have a mother, did you?' Rusty said he started to cry. But tears weren't enough for the almighty doctor." Mom twists her body to face me. "No, she had to go in for the kill. She said, 'You never had a real mother. *So, you married one.*'" Mom acts as if I'm the therapist, as if I'm the one who's made her so angry. "And she still wasn't done. 'You married a woman who would take the place of the mother you never had. But when she does mother you, you feel emasculated.'" She sits back, exhausted.

It makes incredible sense to me, but I don't say so.

"I have to use the bathroom," Mom says. "Let's go back."

I make a U-turn. "So, what happened in therapy after that?"

"Dad never went back." Shocked, I glance at her. "Don't look at me that way! Keep your eyes on the road." She fiddles with her roll of Lifesavers but doesn't select another one. "Your father and I talked about it, and he decided that Dr. Delaney was wrong. He decided—*on his own*—not to go back."

I SET THE table, then go upstairs to see Bobby. As Mom said, at age twelve, he's already taller than her. Anyone would know we're brothers; we have the same wide nose, the same dark skin tone and hair, the same thick lips. The only difference is Bobby has light eyes, amber like Dad's.

My old bedroom smells different from how I remember. I guess it's Bobby's smell. Pre-teenage boy smell. The walls are now sky blue, not sun yellow. There are no posters on the walls, no paintings or drawings, not even a photograph. Instead, the walls have a frieze of sheet music about four feet above the floor. I look at the title: *Rachmaninov, Piano Concerto No.3.*

"Do you play that?"

"It's the most difficult piano concerto ever written," Bobby answers. "I *aspire* to play it."

I sit at his messy desk—papers, more sheet music, magazines, and candy wrappers litter the top; not neat like when it was mine. I put a cap on a pen.

Bobby puts a small piece of paper to mark his place in the book he's reading: *Setting Free the Bears* by John Irving.

"Is that any good?" I ask.

"It's interesting, but rambles. What are you reading?"

"I just finished *Myra Breckinridge* by Gore Vidal. It was awful."

I ask how he's doing in school. All *A*s. I ask about his interest in music. He's taking private piano lessons. He asks about my job. We could ask each other lots of other questions, but there's really only one thing I want to know. I lead up to it with other questions that interest me.

"Do you like Dad? I know you always love your parents, or least most kids do, but do you like him?"

"He's okay. I don't understand how he could be so, so—how he could let the Catholic Church dictate what he should do. I thought he was smarter than that."

"What about Mom?"

"We get along okay."

"But do you *like* her?"

Bobby leans forward. "You know, I don't think she likes me. I know she loves me, would do anything for me, but I don't think she *likes* me."

"Do you remember when Dad held you up in the palm of his hand?"

"I've seen pictures, but I don't remember it."

"I was never the son Dad wanted me to be." I wonder if Bobby knows I'm "that way," as Mom put it. Probably not. Mom and Dad would never have told him. "I tried to please Dad, but I felt I always did everything wrong. Then, the moment he held you up in his palm, I knew I'd lost him, that you were going to be his special son. I think Mom knew she had lost you, too."

"I'm sorry."

"It had nothing to do with you. You were an innocent baby who could smile on cue when his father held him up in the air."

Bobby smiles on cue.

I ask, "Did he tell you to stop calling him 'Daddy'?"

"I stopped on my own when I was nine. I wanted to be grown-up."

"Did he tell you to stop kissing him?"

"I stopped that when I was nine, too. Did he tell you to stop calling him 'Daddy' and to stop kissing him?"

"He had Mom tell me. Right after you were born." I quickly add, "But it wasn't your fault."

He lies on his back, staring at the ceiling.

Then I ask *the* question. "Did you ever play submarine with Dad?"

"No. What's that?"

"Just a game. I ask too many questions."

UNCLE NICK'S HAIR, even on his arms, is turning white. Otherwise, he's still in great shape. Aunt Lily has dyed her hair a brassy shade of red, but with deep wrinkles on her face, she looks older than her husband. I'm mean, I know, but I'm pleased that Nick Junior has gained at least thirty pounds. Finally, I'm in better shape than he is. He arrives with an equally overweight woman named Maria. Nick Junior's only twenty-six, and he's already on wife number two. His sister Rose married last year and moved to Los Angeles with her husband, so she's not here.

"We were in L.A. last month," Aunt Lily says when we sit down to dinner.

"So did you see any movie stars?" I ask just to be polite.

"We saw Rita Hayworth at a restaurant," Uncle Nick says. "Still as gorgeous as she was in *Gilda*."

"She uses too much color on her hair," says Aunt Lily. "It looks fake."

"You should talk." Nick spears a meatball.

"What do you mean? This is my natural color."

"Right," he says. "You and Lucille Ball."

Aunt Lily ignores him. "What was the name of that actor we saw? He's in all those Westerns."

I don't like Westerns, but there's one big star. "John Wayne?"

"Yeah, like someone's going to forget John Wayne's name." Dad directs his comment to Nick.

"These westerns have a funny name," says Aunt Lily.

"Revisionist?" I suggest.

"What's that?" Maria wants to know.

"Where the Indians win instead of the cowboys," I respond.

"Your spaghetti sauce is really good, Mrs. Dimora," Nick Junior says. "Better than my mom's."

"Spaghetti!" shouts Aunt Lily. "They're called *spaghetti Westerns*."

"Clint Eastwood," I say. "*A Fistful of Dollars. For a Few Dollars More.*"

"That's right." Uncle Nick nods. "We saw him in a shop in Beverly Hills."

I look at Mom, Dad, and Nick Junior. "*The Good, the Bad and the Ugly.*"

"I can still whoop your ass," Nick Junior says.

"Only problem is, he'd like it." Dad grins as if he's won the game.

But I've just started playing. And this one's for the championship.

BOBBY AND I clear the table, and Aunt Lily cautiously carries in a cake with forty-three flaming candles. It takes Mom three tries to blow them all out.

"Did you make a wish, honey?" Dad puckers his lips like a fish.

"It already came true." Mom looks at me.

Dad plants a noisy kiss on Mom's cheek.

"How did you two meet?" Maria asks Dad.

"Not that story again," Uncle Nick says. "Wait, I'll get my violin."

Dad turns to Maria. "I met my lovely wife the day I enlisted in the Coast Guard." Dad talks as if he's on stage. "This was right after America entered World War II. My pals Rags Gernano and Dave Calvi signed up with me, and we—"

"And Tony Tomasso, too," I interject.

He goes on as if I hadn't spoken. "We were all keyed up and looking for someplace to celebrate—and meet girls. Rags suggested the local bowling alley, and just before we go in, I say, 'Listen, fellas, we shouldn't get interested in any particular girl right now because we're going to war, and something could happen to us. So, let's just have fun—nothing serious or anything.'"

Nick Junior yawns. Dad frowns.

"Anyway, we go in the bowling alley, and I look over at the first lane and see the most beautiful girl I had ever seen." He looks down, and when he goes on, his eyes are wet. "It still chokes me up. I guess I'm just a sentimental old fool."

"You got that right," Uncle Nick says, "but don't let me interrupt."

Dad talks to Maria as if she's the only person in the room. "So, I see this beautiful girl going down the lane with a ball, and I blurt out, 'Wow!' She looks up and drops the ball. It goes into the gutter. And she says to me—" He points a finger at Mom.

She knows her cue. "*You made me drop the ball!*"

"And I just stare at her. And she stared right back. I walked her home that night, and a year later, we got married when I was on leave."

"And Tony Tomasso was your best man." I nearly add, "And mine too."

"If no one wants more ice cream," Aunt Lily says, "I'll put it in the refrigerator before it melts.

Bobby, who's been practically silent through the entire meal, says, "Anthony, did you know that Uncle Nick built a swimming pool in his backyard? Why don't we all go over there and play water volleyball? Sons against fathers."

"You shouldn't go in the water so soon after eating," Mom says.

"Anthony, Nick Junior, and Bobby against me and Rusty," Uncle Nick says. "That's three against two."

"He can count," Nick Junior says.

"If you play the way you used to, it will be more than fair. You always cheat. Bobby, do you have an extra swimsuit I can borrow?"

"Nick and I get the shallow end since you have the advantage of youth," Dad tells Nick Junior.

I follow Bobby upstairs. "Swimsuits are in the bottom drawer," he says, pointing to a chest.

There's quite an array. Board shorts, trunk, briefs. Red, black, blue. Floral, stripes, solids. And: I shut my eyes and take deep breaths. Then I reach into the drawer and take it out. It's just a small piece of white cloth. Printed with black shells and starfish.

"That's Dad's old swimsuit," Bobby says. "I don't know why I have it. I've never worn it."

I undress and put on the swimsuit. It fits perfectly.

Bobby changes into a red Speedo.

"Go on ahead," I tell him. "I want to use the bathroom."

I look out his window, and when he's across the street, I grab my clothes and put them in my car.

Mom, Aunt Lily, and Maria sit in lawn chairs at the edge of the pool and watch the game. I have a firm body from working out, but I'm still uncoordinated, still the worst player on the team. A couple of times, lunging for the ball, I completely miss it, sink into the deep, and come up spitting water.

"Still plays like a girl," Dad says. When I mess up again, he adds, "I always wanted a daughter."

It doesn't matter that I'm so bad, because Nick Junior, even with his extra weight, is a great player. Bobby's nimble, his skill almost as good as his enthusiasm. The sons beat their fathers by ten points.

Uncle Nick lifts himself out of the pool. "I need a cigar."

I swim under the net, jump onto Dad's back, and push him underwater.

I can tell everyone thinks I'm merely horsing around, the victor celebrating his win by defeating his opponent one more time, but as Dad struggles and I hold him down, it dawns on them that I'm serious.

"What are you doing?" Bobby's eyes are wide. He hangs on to the pool ladder.

I'm doing what I planned from the minute I knew we'd be in the pool. Maybe from the very first time Dad called me a girl. Maybe what I've wanted to do since I was eight years old.

"Stay away!" I shout when Nick Junior swims toward me. He obeys.

This is my moment. This is my time. My revenge.

Uncle Nick turns back, a smirk on his face. I wonder if Dad ever told him. Ever confessed.

Dad's arms flail, trying to grab me, but I wrap my legs around his torso and keep his head submerged.

Mom runs to the rim of the pool, her hands on her cheeks like the famous Munch painting. "Anthony! He'll drown."

I wave to her, just like I did when I was eight, and she was on the shore.

"If we're lucky," I mutter.

Dad twists and jerks. I push harder to hold him down. I wonder what he's feeling. I wonder if he's remembering.

I am.

And I'm waiting, waiting until he's out of air. Waiting for the bubbles to rise. Then, only then, I release my grip.

Dad bursts up, gasping for air.

"So," I say, "did your life pass in front of your eyes—or just Lake Erie?"

I get out of the pool before he stops coughing.

"I love you, Mom." I kiss her cheek and dash across the street. I don't bother to change out of Dad's wet swimsuit. I get in my Plymouth Valiant and head back to Ann Arbor.

I feel exalted, but I know there's more to do.

Age twenty-five

The Longing

I WANT TO start therapy," I tell Tony Tomasso over the phone. "I feel I have to do this before I can begin a new life."

"Okay," he replies. "I'll check with some of my colleagues and find out if they recommend anyone in Ann Arbor."

"I want *you* to be my therapist."

"What? We live 250 miles apart."

"Can't you shrink the difference?" I grin, but I sense Tony doesn't think it's remotely funny. "Seriously, I have two weeks vacation coming, and I thought I could spend them in Castleton."

"Surely you know that it doesn't work like that," Tony says. "Therapy can take years."

"You already know a lot about me, so that should save a bunch of time." I rush on before he can reject what I'm suggesting. "I want to work on one particular issue. Maybe it will take years, but can't we just meet for two weeks and see how far we get?"

Tony is silent for more than a minute. Finally, he says, "We can't socialize at all. We can only see each other during our sessions."

"Fine."

"You have to tell me *everything*. No holding back. Virtually stream of conscious. Do you think you can do that?"

"Absolutely."

"Sessions will be two hours every day, including Saturday and Sunday. And you have to pay me my regular fee: fifty dollars an hour."

I quickly do the math. "That won't be a problem. I've saved money for my vacation. I was going to San Francisco. But Castleton's just as exciting."

"Yeah, a real paradise. Listen, Anthony. Therapy can be frustrating and painful. It's up and down, back and forth, following trails until finally you find the truth."

"I'm ready to face it."

"I hope so." Tony's voice becomes more casual. "So, how is it going at the advertising studio?"

"Great. I drew a cockroach lying on its back and holding a lily for Dow Chemical, but my most interesting assignment was for Dow Pharmaceuticals. I did an illustration of a fish for Quide, a new drug for schizophrenia."

"You did that? I saw the ad in one of the medical journals I get."

"Did you think the fish looked like it was drawn by a mental patient?"

"I didn't really think about it, because I'm a therapist and not a psychiatrist. I can't dispense drugs, so I wasn't interested in Quide. But I remember it was a clever ad, with the goldfish in the corner."

"That was the whole idea: to show something wild and bizarre, like a ferocious tiger, then have a pussy cat in the corner. The ad campaign also has a predatory bird and a parakeet, and a rabid dog and a puppy. You'll see those in future issues. Before they ran the campaign, the ad agency gave the drawings to a psychiatrist to make sure they looked as if they'd been done by mental patients; he wasn't told that professional artists had drawn them. So, in front of the clients and all the important people at the agency and everyone I work with, the doctor held up my fish and said, 'This person is probably not violent, but he does have severe mental problems, probably brought on by latent homosexuality.' I was sitting in the back of the room and shouted out, 'There's nothing latent about me.'"

Tony laughs. "So, I take it you don't want to go into therapy because of your homosexuality."

"Oh, God, no. I'm glad I'm gay."

"So why *do* you want to be in therapy?"

I don't answer, and three weeks later, when I arrive in Castleton and have my first session, Tony repeats the question. Again, I don't answer.

I've taken a few psychology courses at the university and know that in therapy, every action, every word, has a meaning. When I walk into Tony's office, he points to a sofa upholstered in a nubby brown tweed. I wonder why he chose a fabric that looks like it scratches. Maybe he doesn't want his clients to get too comfortable. He sinks into a leather club chair separated from the sofa by a coffee table with a marble top that has such intricate veins it could be used for Rorschach tests.

I realize that my decision to sit or lie down on the sofa will say something to Tony. I think if I lie down, it leaves me vulnerable, makes me submissive. I'm not ready for that. If I sit at either end of the sofa, Tony will think I'm distancing myself from him and therapy. I sit smack in the middle.

"I know I'm the one who's supposed to do most of the talking," I say, "but before we begin, there's something I have to ask. Do you think my dad had homosexual tendencies and that's why he was so upset when he found out I'm gay?"

"It doesn't matter if your father had homosexual feelings. What matters is that you wonder if he did. What matters is that you are homosexual."

"But I told you on the phone that homosexuality isn't my problem."

Tony doesn't say anything.

The room fills with silence. Finally, I say, "I love cocksucking."

And Tony says, "That doesn't mean you love the cocksucker."

AFTER MY SESSION, I drive to our old house on top of the hill. It's rundown, in need of paint. I know things appear bigger to a child, but when I walk to the backyard and look down the hill, it still seems mighty steep. I remember how my tricycle fell over the edge.

But I'm not really interested in our house. When I knock on the front door of the house next door, a stranger opens it.

"Hello. I used to live next door when I was a kid, and I wonder if you know what happened to the people who lived in this house. The Salvatores. They had a daughter named Noreen."

"We bought this house from them," the old man says. "But I don't rightly remember them. We only met them one time."

"There was a young man living with them. It's him I'm trying to find. His name was Frank Salvatore."

The man turns his head into the house. "Molly! Come here a sec. A kid wants to know what happened to Frank Salvatore, and I don't remember."

A chubby, elderly woman comes to the door, wiping her hands on a dishtowel. "Frank Salvatore. We never met him, but he's the reason we got this house. After he passed, his family decided to move. Outta state, I believe."

"Do you know how he died?"

"There was some confusion. He was driving an old car—Lou, what do they call those cars the kids fix up?"

"Vintage?"

"Yeah, that's right. He was driving his vintage car out in farm country, and he crashed into a tree." She twists the dish towel. "I'm sorry to tell you this, sonny, if you knew him."

"I remember now," the man says. "There was speculation. No one knew whether he had done it deliberately."

The woman slaps his arm. "You don't blurt something out like that to someone who knew him."

"It's alright, Ma'am," I say. "I want to know. He was always very nice to me." My eyes fill with tears.

She reaches into a pocket of her apron and hands me a tissue. "It's clean."

AT MY NEXT session, I tell Tony, "When I was eight years old, Frank gave me a ride in his 1939 Buick Roadmaster. He took off our shirts. I remember how thrilled I was. Years later, in college, when I told someone about it, she called Frank a pedophile. But I didn't think of Frank that way. He never even hinted at anything sexual. He was very kind to me."

"How old was Frank when you knew him?"

"Eighteen. When my parents fought, I'd sneak out the back door and go stand by Frank while he worked on his car. I felt so calm next to him. But excited too. Serenity and frenzy—both at the same time. I think I've been hoping to repeat that same sensation ever since."

*

"NORMALLY, I LET you talk about whatever you want, but we don't have that luxury, not with our time constraint. So, I must lead you." Tony sits very straight, both feet on the floor, hands curled over the end of the armrests. "You must talk about your father. Tell me your earliest memory of him."

"When I was about two years old, I would jump into my parents' bed after Mom had gotten up and say, 'Airplane, Daddy. Airplane!' That's what we called our little game. Airplane." I face Tony, but I see myself as a child in blue pajamas with soft cotton feet. "My father would lie on his back and hoist me onto his feet, then lift his legs toward the ceiling. I would stretch out my arms and pretend to fly. Then he'd dip his legs, and I'd swoop into a dive onto his chest. I loved it."

"Don't stop. Keep going."

"I liked landing in his thick chest hair. I liked the way he smelled."

"Go on."

I take a deep breath. "Sometimes the fly of his white boxer shorts would separate, and I could see a sliver of his penis peeking through. I wanted to touch it."

"Did your father ever get an erection while you were playing Airplane?"

"I don't think so." I look at the marble table. "Not then."

"When?"

I look around the room, hoping to find something other than the marble tabletop to distract me. There's not much here: the sofa, Tony's chair, and the side table. A box of tissues. A nearly invisible wire wastebasket. A discreet gold clock on the side table.

"When?"

There are no paintings. No knick-knacks. The room has no personality.

"When?"

I scowl at Tony. "When I was about six, my mom told me to bring Dad the sports page. He was on the toilet, and when I opened the door, I could see his penis. It looked enormous. With a big pink head. I'm sure it was erect because it wasn't hanging into the bowl but pointing straight ahead."

"At you."

"Yes. At me."

"Did your mother see the sports page and tell you to bring it to him?"

"No, Dad called from the bathroom asking for it."

"And he specifically asked for you to bring it?"

"I think so."

"Can you recall your reaction to seeing his penis?"

"Shock. Awe. Fascination. I wondered if mine would grow like that."

"Did you want to touch it?"

"I don't think so. I wanted to get closer to it so I could stare at it."

"Did your father touch himself?"

"No. But he saw where I was staring."

"Did he say anything?"

"He told me to hand him the paper. I did, and then I left. End of story."

"Not quite." Tony looks directly at me. "Anthony, you do know, don't you, that there was nothing wrong with imagining touching your father's penis when you were playing Airplane? These thoughts and feelings are just part of childhood."

"But I don't think I outgrew them." I run my hand through

my hair, massaging my scalp. "Even as a teenager, I had sexual thoughts about my dad. Sometimes I would masturbate thinking about him."

"Did you fantasize about particular sex acts with your father?"

I shake my head. "Most of the time, I'd shut my eyes and picture him with his shirt off. I'd think about lying my head on his hairy chest, and I'd come."

"Landing on his chest just like you did when you played Airplane."

"Yes."

"Maybe what you longed for was the feeling of being loved. All you wanted was your father to love you. But you could never say that—not to him and not to yourself." Tony's eyes look as sorrowful as I feel. "What we find too difficult to express— emotions, needs, longing—are often expressed in a sexual manner. In your case, I think it is much easier for you to say you thought of your father sexually than to say you wanted him to love you."

I rub my thumb back and forth across my ring finger, as if I were twisting a ring. I stop when I notice Tony watching my hands.

"In your fantasies while you masturbated," he says, "did your father do anything? Did he touch you in your fantasy?"

"He'd run his fingers through my hair."

"Like you did just a minute ago."

"I USED TO wish I could become the son my dad wanted," I tell Tony at another therapy session.

"I don't think anyone could be the son Rusty wanted," Tony says.

"Ray, my boyfriend in college, could have been. He liked sports and didn't care about art or any of the things that might be considered 'faggy,' like musicals or fashion. Isn't that funny? I couldn't be the son my father wanted, so I fell in love with a boy who was."

"If you had to choose who judges you the hardest, you or your father, whom would you pick?"

"My mother."

"She wasn't even one of the choices!"

"But she's the one who's the hardest judge." I pick at a nub in the sofa fabric with my fingernail. "She thinks everyone is judging her, so she judges everyone first."

"Do you think you take after her?"

My eyes narrow as I stare at Tony. "Are you saying I'm judgmental?"

"I usually say exactly what I mean. I think you should consider whether you judge yourself too harshly." Tony crosses his leg. "You just said you used to want to be the son your father wanted. What made you stop wanting to be that boy?"

"That boy was boring. I'm much more interesting than the son my father wanted."

"You certainly are. It's a shame he doesn't appreciate you."

"Once I tried to talk to my father about things that interested me, and I asked him semi-philosophical things such as, "If you had to give up one of your five senses, which one would you choose?" And you know what he said? 'You think too much.'"

"How did that make you feel?"

"Furious. He doesn't think enough."

"The way I see it, Anthony," Tony says, "your father didn't know how to handle his feelings toward other men. He didn't understand you could love a man without it being sexual.

Probably when he first thought you might be homosexual, it terrified him. He wanted to protect you from what he thought would be a lonely, dangerous life. But maybe you didn't want that kind of protection from your father. Maybe you wanted something else. Maybe you wanted him to love you unconditionally, and that probably frightened Rusty even more."

"Once I asked my mother if Dad loved he. I knew I disappointed him, and that was my biggest fear: That he didn't love me."

"What would it mean to you if he didn't love you?"

I twist the fabric nub between my nails.

"That I am unlovable."

"Don't beat yourself up, Anthony."

"The first day I came here, you said I didn't love myself."

Tony leans toward me. "No one showed you how to love yourself. In fact, most people think that it's selfish to love yourself. But that's the opposite of the truth." Tony points a finger at me. "You didn't have any role models. Neither did your father. He didn't love himself either. It's a pattern that goes way back and continues forward until someone breaks it."

"So what you're saying is Grandpa Dimora didn't love himself, so he didn't teach Dad how to love himself, so he didn't teach me, so I don't love myself."

"You make it sound simplistic, but yes, that's basically it."

"So how do I learn to love myself?"

"You're doing it by going to therapy. But you're holding back." Tony looks into my eyes. "I think it's time you told me the truth, Anthony."

Sweat suddenly rolls down my side.

"I have told you the truth."

"Not all of it."

How does he know?

"I don't know what you're hiding, but you are hiding something."

"WE'VE BEEN MEETING for more than a week, Anthony," Tony says, "and you still have not answered my initial question. Do you remember the question?"

"*Why do I want to be in therapy?*"

Tony raises his eyebrows. "So?"

"I think my fascination, my fixation, with my father has been unhealthy. It's what's keeping me from fully committing to another man."

"That's probably true."

"I also think I'm obsessed with cock," I say. "Not in the sense that I want to have sex with lots of men, but I seem fascinated by the penis. In Life Drawing class in college, when everyone else was drawing the entire figure, I made incredibly detailed drawings of just the penis. I drew and photographed Ray's penis in all kinds of poses and situations. Beautiful photographs with fruit and vegetables. Sometimes when I walk down the street, I notice that my eyes are looking at the crotches of passing men. I don't want to have sex with them, I just want to know what their penises look like. So one of the reasons I'm here is I want to understand why I'm so obsessed."

"These are recent events. Can you think of something that happened when you were a teenager? *There!* You had a reaction. Tell me the first thing that popped into your mind. No censoring."

"When I was fourteen, I used to go to the locker room after Dad played basketball, and I would hand out towels to the guys after they showered. I liked looking at their cocks, at the variety."

"Okay. But something happened. I saw it in your face earlier. Tell me."

"They didn't have individual stalls, but a big, tiled room with four or five showerheads on each wall. One time, Nick was the last person to shower, and I was standing outside the shower entrance. He called my name, and when I looked at him, he turned around and had an erection."

"What was your reaction?"

"Shock. Excitement. Fear."

"Not quite the same reaction as when you saw your father's erection. What was the fear? Why were you afraid?"

"I thought Nick would see that I was excited and punish me."

"Did you have an erection?"

"Oh no. But I was mentally excited."

"And what did Nick do?"

"He winked. Then he grabbed a towel and dried off."

"What did you do?"

"I went to one of the toilet stalls so he wouldn't see me, because I was afraid I was going to cry. I didn't. I took some deep breaths, and when I came out, and he was dressed, we didn't talk about it."

"See if you can go back farther, to an earlier time when seeing a penis excited you in some way. Don't think about it, just the first thing that pops into your mind."

"When I was about eleven, a few of the boys in school would chase a kid who was a real sissy. They'd grab him in the back of the school where they'd be hidden from the nuns by some trees, and they'd take down his pants and underwear and make fun of him because he didn't have any pubic hair."

"Did it excite you when you saw his penis?"

"Not in the least. It was a tiny mushroom."

"What did excite you about the incident?"

"I wanted them to do it to me, to pull down my pants and expose my cock."

"Did you have pubic hair?"

"No."

"But you wanted them to look at your penis." Tony rests his chin on his folded hands. "Go back further. Go back before you saw your dad's erection when you brought him the newspaper. Go back as far as you can."

I'm amazed at how clearly something springs to mind.

"When I was three, Mommy and Daddy were going out, and she gave me a bath, then, because she was busy putting on her makeup, she handed me a towel to dry myself. And I got an erection. Mommy told me to run into the bedroom and show Daddy. He was furious. He stormed into the bathroom, dragging me behind him, and he slapped Mommy across the face."

I'm suddenly exhausted. Tony says, "There isn't anything earlier, is there?"

"No."

"There wouldn't be." Tony seems pleased. "As an adult, you think, you hope, that if you make detailed drawings and beautiful photographs of a penis, that it will make up for—that it will erase—your father slapping your mother. You thought it was your fault, that he did it because you had an erection, even if at the time you didn't understand what that was. Your fascination with the penis originates from that incident."

"DO YOU CONSIDER masturbation sex?" Tony asks at our penultimate session.

"Sure. Did you read John Rechy's *Numbers*?"

"No. The only book I read by him was *City of Night*."

"Well, in *Numbers*, the narrator keeps track of how many men he's had sex with. He gives them each a number. It's more than a hundred. I wanted to count how many men I had sex with and decided I had to first establish the criteria. What act would count as having sex? I decided that someone had to climax, either through fucking, sucking, or masturbation."

"Are you still counting?"

"Yes."

"And?"

"Twenty-four."

"When do you think you'll stop counting?"

"Well, if I ever have another relationship, I'd stop counting because I'd be monogamous, like I was with Ray."

Tony sits silent, waiting for me to say more.

"I suppose," I say, "it's silly to count, but it's hard to stop once you've started. I told one man what number he was, and he was furious. I can understand his anger, but I also thought it was funny—and honest—to tell him. I mean, sometimes you pick a person just for sex. That's all you want, and you know it's never going to go beyond that. But there are some guys who think every occasion might be 'the one.' I think that's unrealistic."

"For you, Anthony, but not for a lot of people. I don't think you realize it, but you think differently than most people. I'm certainly not agreeing with your father when he said, 'you think too much,' but you do think about things that most people don't think about, in fact, avoid thinking about."

"Why don't they want to think about these things?"

"They're afraid of what might come up. They don't want to face it."

"Do you think 24 is a lot?"

"I'm not your mother. I'm not going to judge."

"But you must have had a reaction when you heard the number."

"My first reaction was to do the math. I estimated that 24 broke down to three a year. Some people have a lot more than that. Others have less, and some don't have any—for years." He leans forward. "What do *you* think? Is 24 a lot to you?"

"No. Sometimes I wish it were a lot more."

Tony rests his elbows on the chair arms and his chin on his crossed hands. "Eight years ago, in this very house, you told me that I was the first person you had sex with."

"You were. I didn't have sex until I was seventeen. No playing doctor. No 'I'll-show-you-mine-if-you-show-me-yours.' I wish I had 'explored' with my cousins, but nothing. Zero. Zilch. Zip."

Tony repeats, "And I was your first?"

"Yes!"

Tony is quiet for a long time. Finally, he says, "And masturbation is one of your criteria for what constitutes sex with another person?"

"Yes."

Again, the silence. Tony stares straight ahead, and I can see in his eyes his mind thinking, seeking order. He uncrosses his hands. His arms are loosely at his side; his feet are apart. He looks as though he is ready to accept whatever someone—*me!*—might throw at him. He says, "What about your father? Why don't you count him as the first?"

Now I'm the one who's silent. Sweat immediately starts dripping from my armpits. And I have to breathe through my mouth.

"That day, right over there in my bedroom," Tony whispers, "after we had been together and before your father came bursting in, you told me that when you were eight years old, you played Submarine in Lake Erie with Rusty. You told me he took your hand and made you masturbate him."

I cross my arms over my chest.

"Why don't you count your father, Anthony?"

I stick my forefinger in my mouth and bite it.

"Why don't you count your father as number one?"

I cover my eyes. My body trembles. I cry.

In the softest voice I have ever heard, softer than a mother comforting her child, Tony says, "Anthony, what really happened at Lake Erie?"

Age eight

Lake Erie

DADDY SPREADS HIS legs.

"I'm a bridge," he says, "and you're a submarine."

I squeeze my nose, raise one arm, and sink into the murky water of Lake Erie. As I glide between his hairy legs, my hand grazes the bulge in Daddy's swimsuit.

When I surface, he looks embarrassed. "I think that's enough for today."

I crinkle my nose. "Just one more time. I forgot to put up my periscope."

Even though Daddy tells me not to open my eyes underwater because it's polluted, I do, swimming toward his trim white trunks decorated with black shells and starfish.

I lift my arm above my head. I rub my hand along Daddy's bulge.

Surfacing, I shiver even though the sun blazes in a clear sky. I look toward Mommy, reading on a blanket in the sand. She waves.

I make another dive. I swim toward Daddy. This time, I slide my hand up his leg, reach inside his suit, and touch him. There.

Daddy jerks my hand away, then he grasps my head, pushing me deeper underwater. I try to wiggle free. I press my feet against the mud in the lake. Daddy pushes down harder. I try to bend back his fingers, but he holds firm.

I've done a horrible thing, and now Daddy's punishing me.

I am running out of air.

Daddy's going to drown me because of what I did.

Bubbles rise to the surface.

He hates me. Daddy hates me.

I stop struggling.

Daddy. Daddy!

Daddy lets go.

I burst out of the water, gasping for air. Mommy stands up.

Daddy looks furious, like he wishes he hadn't stopped, wishes I had drowned.

Then suddenly he sweeps me to his chest and says softly, "My boy's just fine, isn't he?"

Age twenty-five

Release

IT NEVER HAPPENED," I tell Tony. "Daddy didn't take my hand and masturbate his penis."

"Do you know why you said that it did happen?" Tony asks.

"Because I wanted it to. Because I wanted to touch my father."

"But you felt that would be considered a horrible thing."

"Yes."

"Do you know why you want this horrible thing to happen?"

"I didn't think it was horrible. I thought Daddy was beautiful. I thought he would love me."

"Maybe he did love you. As much as he was able. But a horrible thing did happen, didn't it, Anthony? And in order to bury that horrible thing, you made up some other horrible thing and told yourself it was beautiful and loving."

I wipe my eyes. Part of me feels a tremendous sense of relief. I have told my terrible secret. And I am still here. The world did not collapse. Tony did not denounce me and say I am an awful, irredeemable person.

I reach for the box of tissues. Tony lets me cry.

After a while, I say, "I understand now why I couldn't stop crying at the end of *Who's Afraid of Virginia Woolf?*"

"Tell me. Get it all out, Anthony."

"Martha had made up a son to get her through a life she found unbearable. So when George killed him, Martha was afraid because now she'd have to live with the truth."

"Yes."

"My fantasy about my father in Lake Erie got me through a life I would have found unbearable. I thought that if I admitted he tried to drown me, I wouldn't want to live." I toss the tissue in the wastebasket. "But it isn't frightening."

"No, it isn't. It's a relief, a release."

"I feel calm and peaceful, as if my life were starting over."

"It is."

INSTEAD OF DRIVING directly to Ann Arbor, I take a detour. To Lake Erie.

I compulsively push the radio buttons, searching for a good song. Then I recognize a calming voice. Perry Como. The singer who used to soothe me when my parents screamed at each other about Dad's gambling; the singer who appeared so tranquil on television, I wanted him for my father. He hasn't had a hit record in quite a while, but he's back on the charts with "It's Impossible." I remember sitting between Daddy's legs in our big maroon velvet chair while we watched Perry Como on television. I remember tilting my head back and Daddy kissing my lips.

I pull to the side of the road. I can't see through my tears.

Back on the road, I know I'll never find the exact spot where my family had a picnic. Even if I could, sixteen years have passed; the land may have been built up, probably converted to a subdivision of mirror-image houses.

I stop at a small public beach. Since it's winter, the parking lot is empty.

A part of me wants to revert. I don't want to give it up. I want to keep the fantasy alive. But I have to let it go if I'm going to move forward. I have to accept the truth.

I lean against a tree and shut my eyes. I picture childhood events, fresh in my mind from reliving them with Tony over the past two weeks.

My body convulses. I cry so deeply I lose my breath. I bend over, clutching my stomach. How I loved this man! My Daddy. *Daddy!*

This man, who didn't know what to do with my love. This father who tried to drown his son's love. And still, I love him. And still, I long for his love.

I wipe my cheeks with my sleeve, take a tissue from my back pocket, and blow my nose. I'm ready now. I walk on the gray-brown sand and pebbles of the shore. There it is. Lake Erie.

No longer frightening.

I reach into my coat pocket and pull out the white cloth printed with black shells and starfish. Daddy's swimsuit.

I pick up a stone and wrap the trunks around it. With all the force that my father wanted me to display on a baseball field, I toss his swimsuit into the water.

The stone sinks.

Daddy's swimsuit floats in the current.

Away from me.

Afterthoughts

EVERYONE I KNOW who has read *What Happened in Lake Erie* asks me the same question. "Did that really happen?"

My reply is always, "It's a novel."

No one is ever satisfied. They want to know.

Personally, I have other questions: *Why do you think you have the right to know? What are you going to do with the information?*

A novel, a movie, a television series, even a joke about a spouse raises the question: *Is this a true story?*

The only time this requires an answer is in historical fiction. The scandalous miniseries *Mary & George* depicts George Villiers seducing King James I. True, George was with the king when he died, but did he poison James, as shown in the series? Benjamin Woolley, author of *The King's Assassin: The Fatal Affair of George Villiers and James I,* suggests he did.

History has not revealed the facts.

Even though Bob Dylan reviewed the script and has an executive producer credit on the biopic *A Complete Unknown,* not everything is irrefutably accurate. It's a movie, not a documentary.

What's that Mark Twain cliché? *Write what you know.*

That advice can go only so far. If writers wrote only what they know, *Game of Thrones* would have no dragons. *Interview with the Vampire* would have no dialogue.

But there would be a hunchback in a cathedral. At the time Victor Hugo wrote *The Hunchback of Notre Dame*, a "humpbacked" stonemason worked on the early 19th-century restoration of the Notre-Dame de Paris. But Quasimodo loved Esmeralda only in the author's imagination.

The mistress of one of author Leo Tolstoy's friends committed suicide by throwing herself under a train. And so did the title character in *Anna Karenina*. A novel.

It's called Inspiration. Death under the rails or a hunchback in a church is a single incident. It is not the whole story. It's at most a paragraph. The novel is created by the author.

Let me repeat: "It's a novel."

AT AGE SEVEN, I played Submarine with my father in Lake Erie. I raised my hand—my periscope—when I swam through his legs and touched his swimsuit. In *What Happened in Lake Erie*, Anthony, who was in the water with his father at age eight, continued the narrative.

Besides the age difference, here's another divergence: Dad's swimsuit had a motif of shells, starfish, and coral. In reality, the objects were green on a white background. In the novel, they are black. Black is more ominous than green. That's what an author does—adds drama.

Dad's trunks were inexpensive, probably purchased at J. C. Penny's. The pattern did not smoothly line up at the crotch seam. Had it been done so, more fabric would have been used, and that would have raised the price so high the swimsuit would have been sold at Troutman's, a local department store beyond my mother's budget. She, like most wives of the time, picked out my dad's clothes, including underwear and a swimsuit.

Most children did not play Submarine with their fathers, but many young boys and girls played Airplane with their dads, held aloft on his feet or knees and coming in for a landing on his chest. But how many boys relished the tickling sensation of the chest hair or the "Daddy smell"? Anthony did. Me, too.

I WROTE ANOTHER novel, *Inside*, about life at a sleek interior design magazine. Because I was the art director of *Architectural Digest*, a sleek interior design magazine, all my friends who read it asked the same question. "Did that really happen?"

And once again, my reply was, "It's a novel."

The editor-in-chief of *Architectural Digest* was Paige Rense. I worked at the magazine for just short of ten years. Paige and I had eight fun and creative years working together—followed by a two-year nightmare.

While I was still at the magazine, I decided to write *Inside*. I sat in meetings with Paige and wrote down what she was saying. Word for word. I wanted to capture her cadence and how she emphasized certain words. I wondered at the time why she never asked me what I was writing.

Much of what I wrote about the magazine *Inside* happened at *Architectural Digest*, and I have the memos and my diary to back me up. A lot of the sex happened, too. It always amazed me what people told me. But Anthony's romance? My imagination. One advantage of writing a novel is that you can fulfill your fantasies. You get the love affair you wanted. You get the ending you wished had happened.

When friends said their favorite character from *Inside*

was Cole, a sexually active gay teenager, I smiled and told them the truth—or at least most of it. Cole is a complete fabrication. I saw a photograph of a young male model in a Calvin Klein underwear ad and thought, *That's Cole*, and I fashioned a boy to fit the image. I created everything about him, except the size of his penis. That was based on someone I knew. Biblically.

A sad note about *Inside* is that many of the gay male interior designers who would likely have enjoyed the book had died of AIDS-related complications before it was published. I knew—and still miss—many of them.

People want to be told exactly what is true and what is fiction, but they seldom observe.

In Edward Albee's incredible play *The Goat, or Who Is Sylvia*, a wife is horrified when her husband admits he's in love with a goat. And a neighbor is scandalized when the husband passionately kisses his son.

When I met Albee, I said I loved the play and that I had read every review and article I could find about it. "What amazed me," I added, "is not one critic mentioned the son's name is Billy."

Albee smiled. "Yes, that was clever of me, wasn't it?"

I devised similar diversions with *Inside*—but no one noticed. Anthony is the main character in both my novels. His heritage is Italian. His surname is Dimora. In Italian, *dimora* means "home", an imaginative choice for a novel centered on an interior design magazine. Anthony *Dimora*. *AD*. *Architecture Digest*. Now, isn't that more fun than trying to figure out what fact or fiction is?

There are more of these diversions in both novels. Unlike a certain British queen, I am amused.

*

PEOPLE ASK WHAT really happened, but they never ask what—or who— is omitted.

In both novels, I never write about my sister, Barbara, who is eighteen months older than I am. She's read both books. "They're novels," she said when I apologized for excluding her. "I understand."

Had Barbara written a novel about our parents, it would not have been as forgiving as mine.

I also have two brothers, Greg and Tom. Only one of them appears in *What Happened in Lake Erie*. None of my siblings has a role in *Inside*.

I had been going to therapy for a while in Los Angeles. My therapist said something life-changing happened to me when I was about ten, but we could not unearth an incident. One day, talking on the phone to Tom, I mentioned that my therapist was stumped. Without a pause, Tom said, "I know what happened when you were ten. Greg was born."

Tom was right. When Greg was born, my relationship with my father completely changed. Dad turned all his attention on Greg, hoping that this son would be the sports star he always wanted. This information not only helped me in therapy, but it is also crucial to *What Happened in Lake Erie*.

Greg, who prefers to be called Doc, read the novel. He never mentioned the child modeled after him. Tom, who was born when I was twelve, as far as I know, has not read my novels.

Mom died before *What Happened in Lake Erie* was published, so, of course, she did not read it. But she didn't read *Inside* either.

Dad never read the novels either. I still wonder if I should have sent him a copy of *What Happened in Lake Erie?*

*

I WAS BORN in New Castle, Pennsylvania, fifty miles north of Pittsburgh, while Anthony was raised in Castleton, a fictitious town across the state border from Youngstown, Ohio, where my dad went to college on the GI Bill. I grew up in an Italian neighborhood, or neighborhoods, since my family lived in six homes by the time I was seven, and we moved to Ohio.

I lived in 12 homes—an even dozen—before I went to college. My Los Angeles therapist said moving that often was extremely difficult for a child since new friends had to be found— and then left behind—with each move. As an adult, I asked my mother why I never had any birthday parties when I was growing up. She replied, "You never had any friends to invite."

Once I asked that therapist if I was manic depressive, a term since replaced with *bipolar*. "No," she answered. "You never have any highs."

Writers can't make up these pithy comments.

Even though my last name is Ross, I'm Italian on both sides of my family. My paternal great-grandfather's name was Rossi. My mother said the "i" was dropped at Ellis Island, New York, where, at the time, most immigrants entered the United States. But I wonder if the name was legally changed, because my baptism certificate names me Charles Rossi.

Pennsylvania was home to the second-largest population of Italian immigrants, with New York being the first. *The New Castle News* estimated more than 100,000 Italians settled in western Pennsylvania between 1890 and 1921. Seeking *pano e lavoro*, "bread and work," most of these migrants did not choose to settle in the two major Pennsylvania cities, Pittsburgh and Philadelphia, but instead selected smaller industrial towns.

As with many of these locations, New Castle offered opportunities in nearby coal mines, limestone quarries, tin mills, and on the railroads, such as the Baltimore and Ohio, the oldest railroad in the nation, where my paternal grandfather worked. But New Castle claimed a uniquely explosive asset. It was the fireworks capital of America, home to two major pyrotechnics companies founded by Italians Leopold Fazzoni and Constantino Vitale.

Funny thing: I don't remember ever watching fireworks in New Castle. As a teenager in Dayton, Ohio, I was annoyed by observers *ooh*ing and *aah*ing. I thought they were calling attention to themselves rather than the fireworks.

A brief intermission about my family tree. My father had two older brothers whom I saw maybe once, and a much younger half-brother whom I thought was cute.

In *What Happened in Lake Erie*, Anthony not only wishes his dad's brother, Nick, were his father, but he is also physically attracted to Nick. Growing up, I wouldn't have known my dad's brothers unless I was introduced to them. But I knew his best friend, Nick Cagnetti. He was kind and emotionally generous, the father I wanted. Growing up, my ideal father was either Nick Cagnetti or Perry Como. But that's impossible.

Dad's sister, Madelaine, with her brazen red hair, was more memorable than her brothers. I'm sure the color was natural, at least when she was younger, and not died like Lucille Ball's flames. Dad's hair was copper-red before it aged gray.

Perhaps we visited Madelaine three times at her house. She never came to any of our homes. After Grandpa Ross remarried, when Dad was seven or eight, he stayed with his grandmother instead of moving to the new house with his stepmother. Just like in my novel.

Dad's mother died when he was only fourteen months old, and he was raised by his grandmother. She was a colorful character, a midwife and a numbers runner, but I didn't really care for her because she smelled "funny"—probably wearing some "old-lady" powder. Even at an early age, I had discriminating taste, finding the dead-yellow streaks in her white hair unappealing. Later, her piousness annoyed me when she made sure we knew she was praying the rosary as she walked through her home.

We occasionally saw Grandpa Ross, and I am sure he was the reason I later was attracted to men with mustaches. See "The Sons of Italy" chapter.

After we moved from Pennsylvania to Ohio, we drove to New Castle at least once a year, praying the rosary along the highway. We stayed at Mom's parents' house on Hawthorne Street, which dead-ended halfway up steep N. Croton Avenue. The sturdy house, with a view of downtown, was known as "The Fortress." Grandma Padula claimed she helped lay its rusty red bricks, and maybe she did. She was a fortress in her own way.

Her father was still alive when we lived in New Castle. He was quite old and the first person I saw dead in a coffin.

Grandma's husband had been injured in an explosion where he worked. Nearly blind, he stayed at home, his only activity making a potent red wine in the cellar of The Fortress.

Here's an odd coincidence—or are all coincidences odd? Both my dad and mom's fathers were named Charles, as was my father, and, of course, me. The third.

Grandma had been a maid for Grace Phillips Johnson in a mansion way up the hill. Made of rough-hewn stone, the house had twelve bedrooms and five-and-a-half bathrooms. Mrs. Johnson's father was an oil tycoon and a Congressman. Her husband, Charles, was the son of the founder of Johnson Bronze, one of the main industries in New Castle.

Also founded in New Castle was Shenango Pottery, which manufactured china for hotels and restaurants. In 1968, President Lyndon Johnson commissioned Shenango to produce a new service designed by Tiffany & Company for the White House. My Aunt Lena hand-painted ceramics at Shenango.

Grandma and Grandpa had eight children. The youngest, George, died before he was a teen. He had eaten a handful of apples off the backyard trees and complained of a stomachache. Not realizing it was appendicitis, Grandma gave him castor oil instead of rushing him to a hospital.

The remaining children were Nick, Lena, Angie, Lucy, Bob, Carrie, and the second youngest, my mom, Ann. Her father wanted another son, so when Mom was born on St. Anthony's feast day, she was baptized Antonette. It was supposed to be *Antoinette*, but they forgot the "i."

Nick and his family never came to Grandma's for family dinners or birthday parties—and there were a lot of birthdays. I asked Mom why not. "His wife is afraid the mafia will shoot them."

Lena had one son, a wild boy my sister thought was attractive. Angie married late and had no offspring. Lucy had five boys. Even at a young age, I was attracted to Donny and Bobby. Bob and his wife Nancy, who was from the beautifully named Mahoningtown, had five girls. Carrie had four children. She had been a nurse and thought she knew more than anyone else. She was also a terrible cook, and although she and my mom were close, I disliked her and her pompous husband. A lot.

I had a complicated relationship with Mom. She was supportive and protective, letting me play with paper dolls before my dad came home. But she also betrayed me, not just by reading my diary but by telling Dad I was attracted to boys. At various stages in my life, she used my accomplishments to make him feel inferior to me.

What sort of mother would tell her other children that I was her favorite? Did she not know how hurtful that was?

FROM NEW CASTLE, it took my father just over an hour and a half to drive north to Lake Erie. Mom sat "up front" in our black 1949 Ford, while my sister Barbara and I played silly games in the back, such as who spotted the most station wagons.

The question friends should ask me is not "Did that really happen?" Instead, they should inquire, "Did you really swim in Lake Erie?"

The answer is *no*.

Looking at a photograph of Mom sitting on a rock on the shore, I wondered why I could see land across the water. Lake Erie is more than fifty miles wide. No one standing on the south shore could see the north shore.

In this age of internet maps, I discovered that the portion of Erie, Pennsylvania, where my family swam was not Lake Erie but rather Presque Isle Bay. Starting at the west end of the city, a narrow strip of land—little more than a road wide—stretches into the lake as it widens into a peninsula forming Presque Isle State Park.

Swimming on the south shore of Presque Isle Bay, one can easily make out the peninsula. Lake Erie is nowhere in sight.

Still, my parents never said, "Let's drive up to Presque Bay and swim." It was always Lake Erie.

And that's where I played Submarine, raising my periscope hand and swimming through my Daddy's legs.

About the Author

IN ADDITION TO *What Happened in Lake Erie*, Charles L. Ross is the author of *Inside*, a novel about a sleek interior design magazine. He was the art director of *Architectural Digest* from 1978 to 1985. In 1987, he was the founding art director of *Veranda*, an interior design magazine that grew in status to compete with *Architectural Digest*. Besides designing *Veranda*, he also edited the text and had his own column until he retired in 2004. His writing has been published in *GQ*, *Christopher Street*, and *The Advocate*. Ross has completed a non-fiction book and is editing his diaries. You can find him on Facebook as CharlesLRossInside.

www.ingramcontent.com/pod-product-compliance
Lightning Source LLC
Chambersburg PA
CBHW031337020726
47499CB00005B/1309